Praise for
Somewhere in the Night

A new twist on chiller stand-bys, and an intriguing perspective on the complexities of gay life. Devilish energy and macabre wit glitter throughout. —*Publishers Weekly*

The stories in *Somewhere in the Night* are wonderful. Jeffrey N. McMahan's treatment of the supernatural is, by turns, witty and horrifying, often erotic, and even, sometimes moving.
—Michael Nava, author of *Goldenboy*

Reminiscent of Rod Serling's "Twilight Zone," and each story is, by itself, worthy of Mr. Serling's stamp of approval. McMahan's little book is a midnight gem. He writes with a droll cynicism that envelopes many of his characters in an aura of bemused self-depreciation. For those who share an addiction for horror, a book like *Somewhere in the Night* is a champagne fix. —*Lambda Book Report*

Chock full of horror and fantasy. *Somewhere in the Night* reveals a very special talent at work. McMahan can twist a plot, give the reader the creeps and spray blood with the best of them. More important, he can write. —*Bay Area Reporter*

McMahan's first book shows a mature talent that invites comparison to established practitioners in the horror field. We can already judge him more literate than Stephen King, subtler than Clive Barker, and — like John Farris — able to use humor while maintaining an atmosphere of horror. —*Guide Magazine*

Jeffrey N. McMahan proves to be a master of his craft with this collection of gay horror tales. *Somewhere in the Night* should be read by everyone who loves a good thriller. Two of the tales follow the adventures of a gay vampire named Andrew with a flair that should give Anne Rice something to worry about. And that's no small feat.
—The Miami *Weekly News*

VAMPIRES ANONYMOUS
a novel by
JEFFREY N. McMAHAN

Boston • Alyson Publications, Inc.

This is a paperback original from Alyson Publications, Inc.,
40 Plympton St., Boston, Mass. 02118.
Distributed in England by GMP Publishers,
P.O. Box 247, London N17 9QR England.

First edition, first printing: April 1991
                second printing: January 1992

5 4 3 2

ISBN 1-55583-183-4

CONTENTS

Special thanks ... once again and always to Third Street Writers Group for your ceaseless dedication to quality. Without you, Andrew and cohorts might have spent eternity locked in their coffins. Montserrat Fontes, who, more than two years ago, saw Andrew's potential and suggested I keep the bat on the wing; Katherine V. Forrest, my special mentor, who won't settle for less than best; Gerry Citrin (you built that set, use it!), Janet Gregory (every flying sequence is for you), Karen Sandler (who else would let me spend that much money in that little time?), and Jessie Lattimore (what more can I say that I haven't already?) — each of whom add their own special talents and insights to everything I write; our newest member, Vicky McConnell, who didn't work on this book but who fills our meetings with life and laughter (Oh, Baby, If You Stop, I'll Kill You!) — and one last time to Naomi Sloan, who contributed to the first half of this novel before she left us ... my gratitude and love to all of you.

Also to two very special women, Gillis and Sheila, for their encouragement and input when this was still a very thick manuscript. Love you both.

To Gary Sandler for the loan of the Kaypro and all the advice about getting a computer to call my own.

Again to Paulino Fontes, Tony Fly, and the staff of El Carmen Cafe ... who else would put up with us? You're the best...

To Richard Labonté and Mark Thompson for their generous support of *Somewhere in the Night*.

To Michael Nava, for driving me around town when I was without transportation, and for just being you and my friend.

And to Sasha Alyson, for publishing *Somewhere in the Night* and for having faith that the manuscript for this book which I originally sent him could become *Vampires Anonymous*.

Jeffrey N. McMahan
November 1990
Los Angeles, California

This One Is For...

The Zink Family Midgets:
"Mother" Connie
and
"Send-in-the-Sheep" Wayne
(both of whom have put up with more
than any friends should have to)

"Il Moroso"
William Morosi
(once you pass thirty...)

"Mom and Dad"
Sonnet and Fred Cohen
(your eldest thinks of you
even if he never calls)

and

"Oh, Marce ... "
Marcia Joan Kasmarcik
(thanks for sharing...
Love ya!)

I

ON A CLIFF DARKLY

Steven Verruckt swerves his Jeep into the Village traffic. In the passenger seat, Eddie Cramer grapples with his seatbelt and mumbles a halfhearted prayer that he will survive Steven's wild driving tactics. Jabbering curses, Steven, recently released from the state asylum — or did he escape? — cuts off car after car in pursuit of his prey — the Sleepy Hollow Killer.

At Eddie's feet a dirty rag of newspaper proclaims the latest in an endless, never-varying cycle of headlines:

SLEEPY HOLLOW KILLER CONTINUES
TO BAFFLE POLICE

Steven swears on his bartender's manual that the Sleepy Hollow Killer — Andrew Lyall — is behind the wheel of the Le Baron Turbo 5M convertible that he and Eddie are pursuing.

Steven's blue eyes flick between the newspaper, the Le Baron, and Eddie. "Will be quite the catch for Eddie old boy," Steven says, his voice crackling.

"Indeed it will," Eddie replies. He needs this arrest to save his floundering career as a policeman. Last year police harassment of gay establishments incited a riot in the Village. That night Eddie fought alongside the men and women of off-limits bars against his fellow officers. As a result, and because of his refusal to participate in continuing legal bashings, his position on the force has become precarious. Every day that he puts on his blue uniform, he sets himself up as a target for an accidental shooting. Or so the anonymous phone threats warn him.

If Steven and he are trailing the Sleepy Hollow Killer, Eddie can prove his worth by collaring the mutilator who has haunted this college town for the past seven years.

But at what price? Steven insists that the Sleepy Hollow Killer is the same man who prompted Eddie to battle the police force's prejudice.

Eyes glowing in the light from streetlamps, Steven whips the Jeep around a corner. He hounds the Le Baron's winking tail-lights.

"There! There!" Steven shouts. One hand on the steering wheel, he hangs out the driver's window and points skyward. The Jeep veers from one side of the road to the other.

Eddie peers through the streaked windshield at a skyful of stars — no, something else. Blotting out the stars, a large black shape wings toward the cliffs above the bay.

"What the hell—"

"Hell on wings," Steven mutters.

Hell on wings? Eddie cranes for another glimpse, but the shape has disappeared.

"Lost them," Steven states, gripping the steering wheel.

Eddie peers at the dark winding road ahead. The Le Baron has outdistanced them. "We'll never find them now," Eddie says, "not up here."

Steven chuckles quietly. "I know where," he mutters. "I know the spot well." He revs the Jeep up the road.

Eddie studies his companion. Steven was once just another good-looking blond college graduate bartending in yet another Village bar. The day after the riots, Steven was found wandering on a beach road, mumbling brokenly about men who change into bats. He led a squad of policemen, Eddie among them, to a bluff above the ocean. No man-bat awaited them, only a body — a body with a mismatched head — to lend any credence to Steven's story.

Another patchwork body and head were discovered in the apartment of Kevin Barker, a protégé of Andrew Lyall. But in Kevin's hours of chatter, Andrew's name never surfaced. Steven Verruckt was the villain of Kevin's tale. Steven had abducted the teenager and hung him bound and gagged in a tree at that cliff. When questioned about his escape, Kevin was struck dumb.

With such prime evidence, the prosecutor maintained that Steven Verruckt was the Sleepy Hollow Killer. Steven, obviously insane, made no protests of innocence. After a perfunctory investigation, he was confined to a padded cell. To some, the case of the Sleepy Hollow Killer was solved, best forgotten.

But Eddie suspected that a kernel of truth lay in Steven's disjointed words. Eddie's intuition proved reliable when the next — and the next — body was found. The Sleepy Hollow Killer was still at large. Nonetheless, Steven was kept indoors, away from sharp objects.

"This is the place!" Steven slams on the breaks, whips the car to the side of the road.

Leaving the Jeep hidden behind trees, Eddie and Steven hike up the road toward the cliffs. Gusting wind buffets Eddie. He fumbles with his police jacket zipper. Wild night for the cop and crazy on a wild bat chase, his mind taunts.

"Coming or jerking off?" Steven, his face and blond hair white in the moonlight, whispers.

Christ, what has he gotten himself into? Why in the hell did he even think twice about accusations made by a lunatic? Eddie does not believe for a moment that Andrew Lyall — tall, slender, round brown eyes, and long, swept-back dark brown hair — possesses the strength, much less the dementia, to be the Sleepy Hollow Killer. Andrew Lyall is just another pretty young man in a college town full of pretty young men.

That's not true. Andrew Lyall forced Eddie to re-evaluate the unjust conduct of the Village police force. Andrew Lyall helped Eddie realize that his life mattered more than his career. The career comes off with the badge and uniform; life must fit comfortably, like bulky sweaters and tight, worn-out jeans.

Eddie cannot — will not — believe that Andrew Lyall is the maniac decapitating college boys and abandoning their bloodless bodies in these hills. Eddie will not believe that his emancipator from a closeted existence could be such a creature.

But, Eddie did see the huge bat against the night sky. Then there was the Le Baron with the two men inside. The driver knew the twisting roads well enough to have traveled them nightly.

Nightly, of course — Steven says they only come out at night.

They reach a grove of scattered trees along the cliffside that block the view of the bay, and of whatever lies ahead. Steven reconnoiters the area. After interminable minutes, his face slashed with that mad smile, he bursts out of the trees. His feet slip in the mud. He tumbles down the hill, knocking Eddie down. They roll toward the cliffs. Eddie fumbles for purchase, anything to stop them. They crash against a tree.

"Found 'em!" Steven breathes. He squirms on top of Eddie; major areas of his anatomy press full-mast. "They're just past those trees! Got 'em."

"No doubt," Eddie replies. Steven's wiggling works unexpected magic. Temptation rises to forget the hunt, with its unpredictable consequences, and enjoy the moonlight.

Steven leaps to his feet. Eddie stares at him, perturbed, then unexpectedly reflective. Sex with a madman might prove too uninhibiting, anyway.

Mumbling and tittering, Steven digs through his duffel bag of tricks. Reluctantly, Eddie accepts the requisite weapons, then unhooks his gun holster and totes his service revolver — just in case. They forge through the trees.

Defeat often comes with victory; Eddie wishes they had lost.

At the edge of the high precipice, the trio writhes on the ground: a tall, blue-eyed Latino, a short, muscular Swede, and the dark-haired Andrew. The Swede's tan is milk chocolate against the pale skin of the vampires.

Vampires, Eddie's brain repeats, they *are* vampires.

The dagger fangs drip saliva, leave glistening trails on the Swede's sun-darkened skin. The blue-eyed Latino and Andrew poise their teeth to either side of their victim's throat.

Steven bounds into the clearing; Eddie cowers in the shadows. "Stop! Wait! Stop!" Steven shouts, flashing his crucifix at the trio of naked men.

They freeze; three sets of eyes turn. One set is dull, confused; the other two burn with shock and rage.

Andrew, hair swirling around his angular face, reaches for his clothes. From his jacket, he extracts a switchblade.

"Sleepy Hollow Killer exposed!" Chuckling, Steven prances a tight circle. "Got him! Won't get away this time!"

The switchblade snaps open. Andrew advances. "I have always been too kindhearted," he says. "I always say that: 'Andrew is too kindhearted.' Don't I always say that, Pablo?"

At the cliff's edge, Pablo, the blue-eyed Latino, still kneels tight between the Swede's legs. "More times than I care to remember," Pablo affirms.

Andrew tosses a look over his shoulder. Flipping the switchblade from hand to hand, he continues toward Steven. "I should have finished with you last year, Steven-Old-Boy. I should have let you fall from this cliff and been done with you."

"Didn't then, Andrew old boy!" Steven stops his dancing, hoists the crucifix. "Won't now."

Lips curled, Andrew halts. His flaming eyes shift between the view of the bay and the crucifix. "Don't count your stakes before you pound them."

"Eddie! Eddie!" Steven laughs. "I'm not alone this time, Andrew old boy! Brought the cops. Eddie, we're ready."

"All right." Struggling through the clinging branches, Eddie joins Steven on the cliff. Andrew recognizes him; is that disappointment in the brown eyes? Uncomfortable under Andrew's gaze, he swallows and sputters: "Sorry, Andrew, but—"

"I had hoped for better from you, too, boy-in-cop's-clothing." Andrew backs away. "Pablo."

Letting the Swede fall to the ground, Pablo sorts through the pile of clothes.

"Not now, Pablo," Andrew says. "Hit the sky." He scans Eddie and Steven. The switchblade jabs toward the blond bartender. "He'll take you down a thorny path, Eddie." The blade tips a salute. "Until happier nights."

The two naked human shapes transmute to monstrous bats with wide wingspans. They soar over the bay.

"Oh, Jesus," Eddie whispers, sinking to the ground. Nausea swells, clogs his throat. How could the man who brought him into the light be a creature of darkness? "Jesus, Jesus..."

II

VAMPIRES ANONYMOUS

1

"Hello, my name is Pablo, and I'm a vampire."

"Hello, Pablo!"

The cacophony of response nearly sends me flying to the ceiling. I, Andrew Lyall, am ever composed and merely shift on this uncomfortable metal chair. At the podium, Pablo, long-fingered hands straining, drags in a breath. His nervousness is apparent, especially to me. After all, day after day, I sleep in the coffin next to his.

"I've been a vampire for over two years now," Pablo continues, his blue eyes more interested in the stained ceiling than in the fifty other vampires gathered in this cramped room.

I note a conspicuous lack of females. Is VA strictly stag? I suspect that vampire women of my enlightenment are too bright to associate with this no-blood-for-lunch bunch.

"I don't place the blame of my position on anyone..."

This is exceedingly good news; I brought him to the night. On a beach it was, in a college town. The memory is cool and

-15-

refreshing, like an ocean swim in September. Provided I could still swim in the ocean. All that running water and those shifting tides would leave Andrew scarred, or deformed, or worse.

"I won't say where we — I am from," he continues. "We — I left rather a mess behind. A human has it out for me..."

Pablo would take responsibility for my accomplishments; he is always trying to protect me. I have done what I have done. My switchblade — eight inches of customized double-edged steel — is quite comfortable in my jacket pocket. That human — demented bartender that he is — has pursued us this last year with a vengeance. I glance around the room, half-expecting to see Steven-Old-Boy in attendance. He has an unnerving habit of popping up at the wrong time.

"My condition has taken me pretty low," Pablo says, straightening to his full height. This statement is news to me; I crane for contact with those crystal blue peepers; he is still intent on the ceiling. "Details are — painfully disgusting."

The men around me murmur agreement. They are a fascinating lot, to be kind. And I am always kind in my assessment of any race, human or vampire. Pasty bunch of buggerers is what we have here, to be bloody truthful. The undead on a self-imposed fast, hardly Andrew's style. I examine my hand, the skin thin but of a healthy hue. I cannot see myself sitting here nightly when the possibilities out in the darkness can be so rewarding.

"...midnight trysts in secluded places," Pablo says. "I've taken on six in one night. I sought more than their blood." He pushes at his long, black hair. "Sometimes, just the chase, the seduction lure me. Sometimes, the thrill of holding one man's life — his death — in my hands is my nourishment."

The boy has it bad and that ain't good. I did not teach Pablo such tactics. Andrew knows restraint. Andrew knows when to strike and when to enjoy the ride. During my two-year Relationship with Pablo, the switchblade has remained in my pocket as many times as it has ventured out into the night.

"I want to stop the killing," Pablo states. He looks right at me; the blue peepers display his torment. This confession startles me. I knew he had been restless of late. Who doesn't get restless with that loony bartender and that hunk of a cop tailing you from town to town? Still, I had no idea that Pablo wanted a way out, an escape from the existence I forced on him.

I flinch at the thought. Men around me turn to look. They whisper; they have figured us out. Let the sunrise take them. Each of them has no doubt brought one or two into the club.

"We all want the killing to stop, Pablo," a deep voice says from the back of the room. "Thank you for sharing."

I must be the only curious one in this group. They all stare toward the podium while I twist in my seat to view the owner of that baritone. He stands just inside the door, a tall, well-built silhouette with a halo of gray hair. His eyes gleam out of his square-jawed face.

A hand grabs my sleeve. I spin on my chair, ready for a tussle. No one handles Andrew's clothes. Hovering next to me, Pablo shakes his head, then sits down. What's the deal here? Is this clown a leper or something — a sunshine victim with a burn-scarred face? Curious as a bat, I try for another peek. Pablo's hand digs into my leg, pretty high on the thigh.

Sweating at the near damage of prized possessions, I focus on the podium and the next unhappy night traveler. Wonder what sob story he's gonna have?

I was so desperate I even put the drain on a laced-up kitten in spiked heels.

That sob story would be too frightening for Andrew. I'd probably have daymares for a month!

O

After our first Vampires Anonymous meeting, Pablo and I flit out of the desecrated church. Whoever runs this organization certainly knows how to pick a meeting place. In the alleyway, I scan the edifice. The walls — stones chipped, mortar cracked — drip green slime. Fallen tiles from the gabled roof litter the alley. From on high, scarred stone gargoyles glare down at me.

As the ranks of the undead file out of the side door, I tug at Pablo's sleeve. I want to split this outing. The blue peepers toss me an annoyed look. Excuse me, but I have had my share of these corpses for one night. I allow Pablo to mingle with the moaners mourning lost, sunlit days.

Our host does not emerge. The door is shut and bolted from inside. I am disappointed. I wanted a keen look at this charmer who's gotten all these boys off their diets.

What seems like sunrises later, Pablo bids his farewells. Head low, he ambles to where I, with a grand façade of patience, am waiting. His hand slips into mine.

"We could go for a drink," I suggest, nudging his shoulder.

"Andrew, the idea of this meeting is to stop all of that," he says testily.

"I mean a drink like in a bar, Pablo. Margaritas — strawberry, our favorites. How about it?"

Shaking his head, he stares down the alley to the dense flock of bats rising into the sky. For a moment, the smog-blurred stars are blotted out, then the mass explodes to separate entities that fan out over the city. I wonder where they all go? I wonder how many hearts stopped at the sight of them?

"Where shall we go?" I ask. Better to give Pablo the lead. I know these moods. If anyone ever thought Andrew was a killer when crossed, he hasn't stepped on the wrong side of Pablo Saldana. He can crush vertebrae between two fingers.

"Home," he breathes, his voice nearly snatched by the wind.

Home sounds boring, but I agree. I sure hope he snaps out of this red funk soon. I feel the need to feed.

O

I bolt the apartment door, slip the crossbar into place. All around I hear the cockroaches scratching for crumbs. A baby's squall, a blaring television, and the rattle of rock 'n' roll reverberate through walls and floor. Be it ever so humble...

From the kitchen, the blender whines to life. At least Pablo isn't too far gone; maybe a stiff batch of maggies will cheer him up. I hang up my jacket, shut the closet door, then turn to the kitchen. Lights are out. The whir of the blender blades, the clatter of crushed ice overwhelm the apartment.

"Pablo? What are you—" On the kitchen threshold, I halt. I see the red lights of the Oster, but no Pablo. Crossing the room, I flick off the blender. "This is no time for games." I head for the bedroom. "Pablo? Did you already hit the satin?"

Between the heavily draped windows, the two coffins rest on matching stands — Pablo's idea, not mine. Both coffins are shut. I knock on Pablo's lid.

"You in there, kiddo?"

The apartment's stillness is beginning to wear on Andrew's nerves. I knock again, Pablo's a heavy sleeper.

"Yo, Pablo!"

My senses tell me he's not in, but I lift the lid anyway. Sure enough, there's only pale blue satin — matches the blue peepers — and a thin layer of sand. The lid slips from my hand, clunks shut. Andrew is getting nervous.

What if—

"Steven-Old-Boy, are you here?"

My favorite psycho, so adept at head-napping and body-snatching for a bartender, is clever enough to break in, take Pablo out — even while I'm here — and leave me to clean up the mess. Steven-Old-Boy's dementia knows no bounds.

Back in the living room, I turn on the lights — not that I need lights. The yellow glow gives its own comfort — memories of past life and nightmare nights where the glow of a light was one's only friend.

"Come on, Pablo," I say; my voice holds out at a whisper. "Andrew is not laughing."

I return to the kitchen, flick on more lights. The blender of margaritas melts on the countertop. I take down a glass, lug the pitcher out of the blender, and settle at the table. I gulp the first glass of chilled sweetness. The second glass poured, I wait. Pablo's a hard one to find if he decides he's lost.

O

After I finish the first blenderful of margaritas, I make a second and retire to the living room. After the second, I turn off all the lights. Strawberry margaritas are my comfort now. By the dregs of the third pitcher, I am in a stupor and don't care where Pablo is. I don't need this. If I wanted worries, I'd go live with my mother. She has worries to share.

Sounds from the kitchen filter through the tequila haze. Propped up on the couch, I peer toward the kitchen door. In a blur of movement, a tall, slender figure appears in the doorway.

"Nice of you to come home," I mutter, reaching for my glass. Blast — it's empty. "What the hell time is it? Near dawn—" I squint at the windows. "Too damned near dawn."

Pablo simply stands framed in the doorway, sorrow and re-gret emanating like heat waves off a sidewalk. I scrutinize him. Why the little bloodsucker — I flip on a light. Pablo shields his eyes. His mauve shirt — *my* mauve shirt — is splotched, his pale skin, underscored with healthy, ruddy cast, is smeared. When he lowers his hands, his eyes reflect a deep, dark scarlet.

"It was nice of you to ask me along," I say, struggling to my feet. I shove the pitcher off the coffee table. "I satisfied myself with margaritas, and I'm not the one recently indoctrinated into the ranks of Vampires Anonymous."

Wiping his bloody mouth with the back of his hand, Pablo stalks toward the bedroom.

Outrage overpowers drunkenness. "Don't walk out of this room when we're talking."

"You're shouting," he says, pausing at the doorway. "You're accusing. You're being your usual cruel bastard selfish self."

"Are sure you didn't leave anything out?" I inquire.

"Insensitive — uncaring — guiltless—"

I leap across the room and tackle him. We hit the floor hard, Pablo beneath me. To my disappointment, he doesn't struggle. I wanted to pummel him. Guiltless, my tight ass.

The lean body under mine trembles. Oh, Christ, Pablo, no tears please. The trembles heighten to convulsions. Stretched over him, I wrap my arms around him. We lie on the floor until the threat of sunrise forces us to our separate graves.

2

Dragging myself out of my coffin, I stumble to the bathroom for my evening bath. Unfortunately, this bathroom is a far cry from the luxury — even semi-luxury — to which I am accustomed. The door screeches shut over uneven rot-blackened linoleum. The sink dangles below the medicine cabinet's clouded mirror. The toilet, the pull-chain tank suspended from the wall, sits opposite.

I pick my way through the scattered bloody clothes that Pablo let lay where they dropped. That boy has no concept of wardrobe maintenance.

In the corner sits a claw-footed tub, streaks of rust mar the porcelain. The ancient handles, the H and C long since worn away, squeak like tortured rats when I turn on the water. A trickle spills leisurely from the faucet. At least the threat of destructive running water is minimal. Still, when the tub is full, I twist each handle tight and wait a moment for the water to calm. Bath water may not be the churning ocean, but Andrew doesn't like to take too many chances.

As I settle into the steaming water, I squirm for comfort against the silver bullet lodged next to my spine. Two years ago, at my first Big Confrontation with Steven-Old-Boy, he unloaded a round of silver bullets into me — from my own revolver. No harm done; silver bullets are for werewolves, not vampires.

However, one got trapped on its way through me. I'm one fortunate bat that I'm not limping through the centuries.

At the foot of the tub looms a single pipe with a shower head at the top. Drip ... drip ... drip fall the droplets, rippling my bath water. Singly, droplets hardly classify as running water; the gentle ripple they create poses no threat to Andrew's death and limb. All the same, I keep an eye on those droplets. Some night I'll be lounging here and those drops will become engorged to a full-fledged spray — a merciless cascade of no-stopping-the-flow-now running water — that will corrode my complexion. Taunted by Pablo's desire to "cure" his vampirism, I'd almost welcome the onslaught of spraying water to put me out of my eternal misery.

Truthfully — I can handle it — I have no cause to be discontent. My existence took a full turn when Pablo joined me on the midnight road to eternity. During the last two years I haven't wrestled with the dilemma. Beauteous boys still abound, but Andrew has been occupied with his Pablo. Finding a mark has become a matter of necessity: pick the least offensive and get it over with. Dead or undead is no longer the question.

I've come to know Pablo in the last two years — all his little quirks, like littering the bathroom with his bloody clothes — and I've become comfortable. Being comfortable isn't a crime. Why try on a new coffin if the one you have, regardless of dents, fits just fine?

On the flip side, Steven-Old-Boy, bonkers bartender, and Eddie, boy-in-cop's-clothing, are still hot on our trail. I know how David Janssen felt; I just thank the moon I don't have to perform some good deed every week. Pablo and I have fluttered the full length of the West Coast and back again. At first, we hit college towns — excuse me, but there's nothing like fresh freshmen. Steven-Old-Boy was onto that routine like mold on a tombstone. Even when I forced myself to vary our patterns, Steven-Old-Boy and Eddie eventually caught up with us.

Death on the run is no sausage on a pizza. Your standards fall off. Before you know it you're living in one quarter of the top floor of a rundown tenement. You try to maintain your wardrobe, but you don't hold a job long enough to make decent money. You're stuck wearing last season's rags which were only meant to last one season anyway. Andrew in threadbare clothes is not a pretty sight. You end up working in a dive of a clothing store stocked with apparel that not even the lowliest of hetero-hicks would be caught wearing on their worst day.

And the droplets become engorged to a full spray of running water that burns the eyes out of their sockets so that the brains leak out and wash the drain.

"Andrew?" The door opens and Pablo peeks in. Pale skin drawn over his tight features accentuates his pockmarks and receding hairline. His blue peepers smolder irritation. "I think an hour in the tub is sufficient," Pablo says, in his most condescending tone. "You don't live alone."

"Yes, dear," I reply, and swear I can see the acid fairly drip off my tongue.

O

The 35-inch-surround-sound-stereo-color TV's eight-inch speakers spit staccato violins in accompaniment to *Carnage Campus*. In the dark living room I lounge on the couch, one of the few pieces of furniture we were able to salvage in our flight from that bloodthirsty bartender. The coffins and those stupid matching stands took up most of the room in Pablo's van. My dead heart breaks for the heirlooms I was forced to leave behind.

Half-watching the dismemberment of nubile coeds and their virile honeys, I scowl at our lair. The jittery blue light does little to soften the room's decay. The wallpaper hangs curling, the carpet lies worn through to the padding. Chunks of plaster have fallen from the ceiling. I suspect that sunlight streams unheeded through those holes. Someday, I'll repair them. I am handy with a hammer. I installed the crossbar on the front door, thick drapes, and opaque blinds. I even managed to brick up the window that leads onto the fire escape.

On the screen, an enticing honey is shedding his clothes. I am entranced. This may be my film; he's going for the belt, the top button of his jeans.

Just as the honey goes for the third button, the screen goes black! I jump to my feet, whirl to Pablo, who holds the TV remote. I consider ripping that smirk off his face.

"Let's go," he says. "The meeting starts in half an hour. I want to get good seats."

Giving up the scenery of *Carnage Campus* for a VA meeting doesn't sound like a fair trade to me.

O

One solemn clutch of stiffs, we and the other pasty deadbats wait in the alley beside the desecrated church. I put on my bravest face, which draws a skeptical look from Pablo. I have made my thoughts known about the entire Vampires Anonymous organization. Pablo is not dumb enough to think I've changed my mind. However, he appreciates that I have tagged along solely to please him. We've become Siamese twins at the palm.

Patient loitering has never been one of Andrew's strong points. I light a cigarette and exhale a thin cloud toward the hazed sky.

An intriguing fresh-faced number with blond hair — moon-streaked or Clairol; no way has the sun been at him — mimics me. Acknowledging my attention with a crooked grin, he ambles over.

"Good evening." He winks.

Pablo sizes him up, then looks the other way.

"John Studnidka," the blond says, extending his hand to me. "New member?" He nods at the church. "Appropriate, isn't it?"

A man with a sense of humor is a relief in this gathering. "Andrew Lyall. Observer. This is Pablo Saldana."

"They call this 'anonymous' for a reason," Pablo snaps.

"It's not like I'm in the phone book," John Studnidka says. He nudges me. "Are you in the phone book, Andrew?"

"I haven't been for eight years."

"Only eight years." That crooked grin heightens a spark in his hazel eyes. "I've been unlisted since—" He counts backward on his fingers; he could use another set of hands. "Nineteen fifty-two or fifty-four — I'm not too good with even numbers. I've always been the odd one out."

In spite of his years, he looks good, a tad loose in the abdomen and pecs perhaps, but his jeans are firmly packed.

Pablo gawks at John. "That's nearly—"

"I know!" John laughs. "It's been rough, too. I used to surf." He nudges me again. "I don't do too much wave-riding now. It plays hell on the skin."

Considering John's warped sense of reality, I am surprised that he would attend a VA meeting. His youthful face lights up, and he swings his arm around my shoulder.

"I come to hang out with the boys," John says, his voice dropping to a whisper. He scouts out the crowd. "I don't believe in this abstinence bull. Full veins are the way to go, not walking around like something out of a George Romero flick."

I wink agreement. Tonight I am glad I allowed Pablo to drag me here. John has restored my faith in the undead and re-affirmed my belief that some of our kind still believe in the good death. Pablo, on the other hand, watches with increasing disapproval. To be nice — what a concept — I extricate myself from John's chummy embrace and nestle up beside my main corpse.

With horror-show chain rattling, the side door of the church swings open. A tall thin blond gestures the throng inside. Pablo starts after the others; I snag John's arm to detain him.

"What do you think of our Aryan archetype?" I whisper.

"Helmut Wagner?" John surveys the man. "Adolf would have creamed for him."

I allow John a two-step lead, then sneer at his back. I hate it when someone else comes up with better quips.

O

The story of one Colin (no last name, thank you, we are anonymous here) drives me to an early exit. Not that I cannot sympathize with him; I don't imagine being average is easy. And everything about Colin seems pretty average. His looks, his hair, his clothes, his body — and, I imagine, other things — are all pretty average. Even his tale of woe rings with an average man's travails of not being able to link up with a decent mark. In this world we have created, even average boys want a buff pretty boy with a wedge-cut to nibble on.

With a nod to John Studnidka, who has spent most of the meeting staring at me, or Pablo, or both of us, and a squeeze of Pablo's hand, I exit during Colin's testimonial. Quiet as a corpse, I creep into the hall. There, I encounter Helmut Wagner.

"The meeting has twenty minutes to run," Helmut, with a trace of German accent, informs me. He blocks my path. "You should stay for the last address. This evening's speaker stirs the soul with his profundity."

Who in this dump still has his soul, sucker?

"I would love to." I glance back into the room; Colin is still at the podium. Perhaps Mr. Profundity is the gent I saw last night. Is enduring Colin's average tale worth finding out? I turn back to Helmut, all cheekbones and blond hair. "Unfortunately, an urgent matter demands my attention."

"We are here to curb such 'urgent matters,'" Helmut says, drawing up to his full height. "You should go back inside."

"You misunderstand! I had only planned to make an appearance to capture the meeting's essence before moving on to my appointment. I assure you, it is all very legitimate." Even though it isn't, you're not the corpse to stop me, Airhead.

Helmut's royal-blue eyes narrow. The thin lips purse in assessment. "You will return tomorrow night?" he asks. "I have not heard you speak. Tomorrow, you will speak." He brushes past me into the meeting room.

Tomorrow I will speak, my gravestone — if I had ever had one. I quickstep it outside, charge down the alley, pull a quick transmutation, and soar starward before Helmut changes his mind.

O

I cruise beneath a smog-shrouded moon. Below, the streetlamps and car lights glimmer dully through the haze. Only a trickle of life moves on the sidewalks. The skyline cuts an irregular pattern against the illuminated clouds. The varying heights of the buildings force me to dip and rise to avoid nasty collisions. Night flight in this city requires good wings and mine are worn down to the vein-laced membranes.

Selecting an uninhabited alley, I divebomb. Rubbish and dirt whirlwinds under the thrust of my wings. A loose door swings open and slaps shut. I'm impressed. Hovering near a trash bin, I concentrate on one wing, then the other, claws, torso. Last — always last — I put the brainpower behind transforming the snout back to my mug. A great party trick, it's also quite effective for scaring witnesses into hasty retreat.

And tonight, I have an audience. Several yards down the alley, tucked neatly in a doorway, stands a rag-draped, scraggly-haired person. Only my keen sense informs me that this shapeless spy is male. In mismatched shoes, he sidles down the alley.

Andrew cannot have this man be witness to this most private act. My hand slips into my jacket pocket, the fingers coiling around the switchblade. I pursue — at first with short steps, then with long strides that propel me at a dizzying speed. I am on him before he can move ten yards. My hand snags a lice-ridden muffler. With a fluidly swift movement, I toss him through the alley. Headlong, he crashes into the trash bin.

I know he's dead, but a trickle of blood, shimmering in the dim starlight, beckons me through the filth. An impatient foot tapping, I stand over the body. I wouldn't call this Andrew's cup of plasma, but the need to feed is upon me.

What happened to the good old days when Andrew could have his pick of the college cuties and wasn't forced to satiate his needs on the city's derelicts? Where are the happy times?

That derelict must have been at the Ripple; my head is swimming more than usual, and I feel a touch of nausea. Regardless, I set about my grisly chore — body disposal. Temporarily I heave the body into the trash bin and bury him beneath the refuse.

Wait, something's amiss. Here it is — the head. I must make certain I get the heads; I don't want to go through the head-snatching business again. There, head and body are both cleverly concealed. I hope the trash collectors don't come before I return. I don't need another newspaper scandal either — Steven-Old-Boy would be perched on my neck in no time.

I fly back to the apartment building. In the adjacent alley, I hop into Pablo's van. I had to give up the Le Baron; it was too conspicuous in this neighborhood. I weave through the streets, peering into the alleys. Andrew wouldn't be a bright lad to forget where he deposited tonight's leftovers.

Here we go. I make a left turn into the alley. Turning off the headlights, I guide the van between the buildings. The path is narrower than I thought. The side mirror sparks against brick. At last I park near the trash bin with the concave dent that the derelict's head made.

The space between wall and van permits me to open the van door a bare three inches. I squeeze out one arm, part of my shoulder; my head just won't make it. Slumped in the driver's seat, I stare through the windshield at the trash bin.

All right, I suppose if you go around killing people for their blood, sooner or later you're going to run into minor difficulties. I can accept that. If my mind weren't so hazed from dinner, I could figure this out in a snap. I glance into the back of the van. Of course, how silly I am.

Half-crouched, I crawl to the van's side door. It slides open easily. Grabbing a tarp, I climb out. Back scraping brick, chin bumping metal, I sidle to the side mirror. When I stoop below the mirror, my knees bang the fender. I'm stuck.

What are my options? I can transform into mist and waft over on the breeze. No good; mist will have trouble carrying the tarp. Changed back into a bat, I could carry the tarp over in my talons. But what if someone else sees me?

Let's face it, Andrew, you already look suspicious stuck between this van and this building. I suggest you do something.

Tarp clamped between my teeth, I grab the side mirror. I hoist myself upward, pushing against the wall with my feet. One tiny effort, I clear the mirror and drop to the alley in front of the van. Then it occurs to me that I could have gone out the back door and climbed over the top.

I never said death with Andrew would be simple.

After spreading the tarp neatly on the ground, I rummage through the trash bin for the derelict. "Body *and* head," I murmur over and over. This is odd. I pause, survey the alley. I am certain this is the right alley, the right debris — I am certain I remember that rusty tomato sauce can.

Where is the derelict — body *and* head?

Don't tell me ... Steven-Old-Boy...

3

"What'd you lose?" The voice comes from behind me.

I freeze, one hand gripping a moldy piece of pork, the other lost among slimy cans and brittle paper. I search the memory banks, blood-clouded as they are, for the pleasant-on-the-ear inflection. The voice, that tone are familiar—

"It must have been extremely important," the voice says, amusement highlighting the words.

I drop the hunk of rotting meat and turn toward the van. John Studnidka, a crooked grin stretched the width of his vernal face, stands on the van's roof. The hazel eyes twinkle impish humor. Shaking trash-bin slime from my hands, I advance, one measured step after another.

"Fancy running into you here," John says. "Do you have any idea what amazing things people throw away these days? I was looking for aluminum cans, bottles to supplement my income—"

"Screw a lid on real tight, Studnidka."

"I can think of better things to screw," John replies.

"My dinner, maybe?" Ooo, Andrew gets so bitchy he delights himself. "But you're both consenting corpses, right?"

Laughing, John leaps off the van and soft-lands in front of me. "I knew you'd get a thrill out of it."

"Thrill doesn't exactly describe what I'm feeling at this exact moment in time. Pissed. Irritated. Ready to maim and destroy — these are the words that pop into my head."

This lad is tickled about something. Laughing heartily, he drops that easy arm around my shoulders and leans against me. His other hand jabbing at my chest, he chortles then giggles then chortles. Finally, he throws both arms around me, pressing his head against my neck, and titters madly.

"I am pleased that your spirits are high, Studnidka," I say, ever calm, ever in control, "but what have you done with the bloody body — and the head?"

"Don't worry..."

Don't worry? Obviously this happy fool knows nothing of my history of pilfered heads — and on occasion a couple of bodies. I shove him away. His face fills with surprise. Visibly, he tries to compose himself. He drags a hand down his face, pulling the grin out of all the muscles. Unsuccessful, he gulps a breath, holds it, but laughter erupts like hiccups.

A sensible voice behind my eyes says to give the lad a moment. You cannot rush these things. Hysterical laughter cannot be turned off and on like TV. It has to work itself out. And when it has, I might dismember him.

"All right..."

"Better now?" I ask.

"Not really!" He covers a short burst with his hand. "Your face — if you could have *seen* your face."

"I haven't in about eight years. Is it holding up?" I'm serious. It's one of those constant worries.

"You know it is," he answers. This, at least, is good news. He plucks at the open front of his shirt. He seems ready to explode into guffaws at the slice of a switchblade. "Now, you asked me a question."

"Are you a vampire or a vulture?" I hook a finger at the trash bin. "Where are the leftovers?"

"Not far." He looks up. All I see are the two buildings, each seventeen or twenty stories, rising toward a vanishing point of yellow-tinted sky. "He's on the roof. Some bums were checking out all the bins for goodies." He gives me a pointed glance. "I thought I'd save them a shock."

"And give me one instead?"

He releases a half-chortle; he swallows, eyes wide with innocence. "I didn't know he was yours."

"Oh, please, pretty liar!"

"You're right!" The half-chortle expands to a robust laugh. "I followed you. I knew you'd come back—"

"If you start that silly laughter again, Studnidka, I swear..." The switchblade flashes out of my pocket.

"Don't be a poop." He nudges my shoulder with his. "I thought we'd have some fun. Those meetings are so depressing. All those misguided boys trying to give up their life's blood. And, excuse me for saying it, but your beau is *très* solemn. He needs a few hours of good ... laughing."

He's hit the coffin nail on the head there. Pablo has become more than morose. But John is purposefully distracting me from my righteous indignation. "I want the body — and the head — back — five minutes ago."

"Don't worry. They're safe." He leans against the van with a convenient forward thrust of the crotch as he crosses his legs at the ankles. "What you are going to do with him? After all, parts is parts — especially after they're drained."

"He wants to go swimming."

"What a marvelous idea!" Pushing away from the van, he reaches me in two strides. Again his arm swings around my shoulders. This time, the embrace presses with intimacy as he drapes one leg across mine and situates certain frontal anatomy firmly against my hip. "Out with the tide — that's very poetic. I'll help. There's this pier—"

"I'll manage." I attempt escape, but he squeezes me tighter in his leg hug.

"I want to help." Such lasciviousness gleams in his hazel eyes. "Then I'll tour you the town. This city is full of surprises and good times — even for us undead guys."

I give him the Andrew thrice-over, from the top of his streaked blond head to the toes of his scuffed tennis shoes. Socializing with gents of my sensibilities — free of the whining tenets of Vampires Anonymous — sounds fine and dandy to me. But can I survive John as an escort? On the upward sweep, my gaze locks on those bouyant features and shimmering hazel eyes.

"No chortling. No giggling. No tittering or all-around general hysterical laughing," I order.

"Dang, you drive a hard bargin." His crooked grin spreading, he traces the straight line of my nose.

With a patient sigh, I allow him to lead me to the missing derelict — body and head.

O

Wherever the derelict's soul has wound up, he's probably viewing this spectacle with spasms of indignation. No doubt he wishes he had not been in that doorway when Andrew flashed from bat to human form. As if things weren't bad enough that I drained his blood and removed his head to prevent his resurrection as one of ours, John has pretzeled the body into a kind of table with the head set upon the crotch-top.

"Do you do this sort of thing often?" I ask John.

"Naw, I just got into pop-art banality," he replies. He cocks his head to one side, squints at his handiwork. "It's symbolic, a new meaning to the word 'head.'" He looks at me quite seriously. "You have to admit, most men's brains are located down there. Even yours and mine."

I'll judge that accusation later. Crossing the rooftop, I stand over John's "sculpture." I succumb to an irresistible urge to nudge the body with my foot. The "statue" remains standing.

"Death-long guarantee," John says, pressing against my back, his chin on my shoulder. "You and Pablo could set it up in your living room. Take it. Consider it a present from *moi*."

"Let us grasp reality by the hand..."

"Three decades of this existence assures one and all that that is not a good axiom."

"...I cannot have this thing smelling up my apartment," I continue.

"I'll supply a can of Wizard," John says, hands gesturing over his sculpture. "A spray here — a spray there — quite a lengthy spray under here—"

"Enough already!"

"You don't like it." He pouts, but laughter threatens around the edges.

"I'll like it immensely when it's safely at the bottom of the ocean."

He rolls his eyes. "No one appreciates good art." He tosses me the head. "Let's go." He picks up the coiled corpse by one arm. "The night's wasting while you're standing there with your mouth gaping." He winks lecherously. "Unless you suddenly have other ideas."

All business, I tuck the head under my arm and march back to the edge of the roof. Not breaking stride, I step onto the guardrail and leap down to the alley. Thank the moon, I land behind the van and not in front of it. I struggle a moment with the rear doors, then jerk them open. I toss the head among the stuff that Pablo likes to collect.

John strolls over with the body balanced on his index finger and looks into the van. "Tarp?"

"There's not a drop of blood left in him, trust me."

"You have a mother like that, too?" He drops the body into the van. "Why did you get out the tarp in the first place?"

"To wrap him up." I scuff at the asphalt with my heel. In a small voice, I add, "In case he got cold."

He laughs. "You are delectable."

"Don't be so sure."

"I'll get the tarp." John's crooked grin twists; his bemused eyes brighten. "In case he gets cold." Leaping over the van, John gathers the tarp and flits back.

Following him through the van affords an advantageous perspective, especially since he has to bend over so far. A night's adventure with John Studnidka — how have I avoided comment on that name? — might prove enlightening.

O

"If you really want 'anonymous,' this is the place," John shouts into my ear. He should know that my hearing faculties are way above average; I could have heard him over the thunderous, rapid rhythms of this pseudo-disco new wave band. "Never the same faces, never the same bodies. Always fresh succulent meat."

Our little Studnidka does not mince words. But he knows of what he speaks. The Club boasts such a varied selection that Andrew's head spins faster than Linda Blair's. Not since that college town where I first tested my wings have I seen such lovelies — for a change, Andrew is not being sarcastic.

Molded to my back, his hands in my front pockets, John forces me through the hot bodies to a clutch of reflectionless boys posing against the mirrored back wall. Always a cautious man, I resist that wide arena of the mirror. What if some clever Bobby notices the cleanliness of the glass behind these suckers? All too soon a mob of angry villagers will be tapping at the castle door. The live ones, however, take no heed of this cold lot on the prowl for initiates into the mausoleum squad.

In quiet tones, John runs through introductions. Hart Laughlin stands tall, blond, and very familiar to my eyes, although I can't quite place him; Lance Broderick towers taller, wiry body, wavy dark hair, clear blue eyes, and a touchable face. I conjecture them both to be recent converts. Who in the sixteenth century named their sons Hart and Lance? Lance could be short for Lancelot — he's pretty enough. A cap of curly brown hair, heavily lidded brown eyes, and wide, full lips set Jay Bauer out from the crowd. Of course, those second-skin chinos draw the lower attentions. Sporting slicked-down blond hair, Christian Fellows glowers at me through his slits of blue eyes. His name sounds like a cult that doesn't welcome our kind.

At the apex of this gathering stands Kane Davies. A dark elegance hangs in Kane's calf-length black jacket, untucked loose shirt, and onion-skin black jeans. Even the black Boks seem formal on his feet. John's voice lowers to reverential tones as he presents me to this wide-shouldered, large-handed creature. The solemn, aristocratic face, accentuated by ever-so-chic short-at-the-temples-long-at-the-crown black hair, cracks a quiet smile of acknowledgement. Something about the brown eyes — possessed perhaps of haunted memories — marks him the eldest, and perhaps, the leader of the pack.

"Gentlemen of the Club, this is Andrew Lyall," John finishes, "observer of Vampires Anonymous."

Whispers flutter. Kane, locking those age-old eyes to mine, meets the description head-on. "Observer," he reflects. "For any particular reason or simply out of curiosity?" His voice rings with a British accent worn away by the years.

"My companion has enlisted," I reply. "Not to the betterment of his disposition, I might venture."

"I wouldn't think so," Kane says. I feel his assessment keenly. The face appears open and innocent, concealing his judgment, but under that thatch of hair beats a calculating, tireless brain. The lips crack again to that quiet smile. "No doubt you could think of better occupations for his time."

Well, doesn't that hit too close to home. I try not to squirm under his perceptiveness. I am far from accustomed to being so blatantly — and accurately — dissected.

"The whole concept does seem ludicrous," I say. "When people of our status relinquish those aspects of themselves that set them apart from the dour population, they do not impress me as protectors of our race."

"A pretty speech," Jay Bauer comments. The heavy eyelids shutter distrust. "It lacks sincerity."

"Abject sincerity is not part of Andrew's game plan," Kane states, eliciting a crude curl of full lips from Jay.

This man's been reading my mail.

"Does Andrew have a game plan? Perhaps Andrew is all show — taters and no meat," Christian Fellows prophesies.

"I think he has the meat," Hart Laughlin says. Jittery thing, he smoothes his hair, tugs at his bejeweled earlobe, plucks at his sleeve, shifts foot to foot to foot. "The question is whether he knows how best to use it."

"Probably just in the obvious way," Jay says, making a gesture with his doubled hand.

If this were a dark alley, I would make a show of tearing off Jay Bauer's heavy eyelids and stuffing them up his nose.

Kane rests his hand on my shoulder. "I think we cruelly misjudge our new friend," he says. "Lance, show Andrew that we are civilized hosts." He motions to the dance floor as a downbeat ditty drifts from the overhead speakers. "A waltz to calm his ruffled pride."

Before I can protest that a twirl around the floor hardly suffices as proper revenge, Lance loops his arm in mine and glides me into the midst of the fevered humans. A strong hand at my waist, the other gripping my shoulder, he whirls me with the music. The blue eyes shine reassurance.

Regardless, my senses linger with the debating deadbeats. I pique my ears to eavesdrop, but Lance pulls me close and whispers distractions in my ear. Sweet promises, indeed, but I am more interested in why Jay Bauer and Christian Fellows argue with a still Kane Davies. Hart Laughlin stares blankly at the ceiling; a patient John Studnidka listens with crossed arms. Lance sweeps me farther away. The boy must have had many a night's practice at beguiling other prospective members of Kane Davies's clique.

"Do you suppose I passed inspection?" Andrew is in no mood for subtlety.

. Lance merely smiles a mouthful of white teeth. He looks beyond me. A hand taps my shoulder. The dance halts. I turn to John, all crooked grin and sparkling eyes.

"Time to cut out," John says, taking my shoulder from Lance. "Later, Lance." He propels me toward the door as swiftly as he propelled me into the presence of Kane Davies.

I steal an over-the-shoulder glance. Lance has rejoined the corpus cluster. Jay Bauer and Christian Fellows glare; Hart Laughlin fidgets. And Kane Davies scouts the room as if I had never entered his thought-provoking existence.

O

When we return to the van, I check under the tarp in the back. The multifaceted derelict rests among Pablo's collection of boxes, cans, bottles, videotapes, magazines, plastic bags, and Christmas cards.

"Can we drop off our passenger now?" I feign lack of interest about my audition with Kane Davies. Whatever the verdict, John will reveal it in his own sweet time — and his own peculiar way. "You mentioned a pier suitable for our deposit."

"I still think he would make a fabulous addition to your living room," John says. His grin does not waver under my scolding scowl. "Yes. And — how fortuitous for us — the pier's near my house."

I swing the van into traffic and follow John's precise directions to the beach. We make the ride in a comfortable silence of old friends who don't have to talk when they're together. I am struck by how easily John Studnidka and I have fallen into this pattern.

The pier to which John directs me is perfect — a few miles out of the city, nothing around, not even a house on the cliffs across the highway. We wish our derelict friend faretheewell. The tide is on its last legs; hopefully, the derelict will journey as far as Mexico before he again touches shore.

"*Bon voyage.*" John pulls out a handkerchief and waves blithely as body and head disappear beneath the waves. "Parting is such — whatever." He grins lecherously. "The night is young — we are eternal. Let's go have some fun at my place."

"Have you considered adding 'subtle' to your vocabulary?"

"With or without eternity before me, 'subtle' is a waste of time." Swinging his arm around me, he guides me toward the van. "We both know what we both want. Let's get horizontal."

When I was alive, such romantic posturing would have left me cold. Tonight — John does have a point. The notion wormed its way into the atrophied brain the moment I laid eyes on him.

Besides, in the throes of sepulchral passion, I can probe John for the result of Kane Davies's inspection.

O

John Studnidka's house is nestled on the brink of a cliff, at the rear of a large estate. Against the living room wall stand several old wooden surfboards, trophies of bygone times. Above the mantle is a blowup of a living John poised on a board in the center of a curl. The crew cut and baggy swim trunks could pass for last year's fashion, but the trim, defined body in the photograph belongs to an extinct era. The man standing beside me has allowed the consumption of too many boys' blood to defeat muscle tone. Yet, the body John reveals as he sheds his clothes isn't bad — I wouldn't kick it out of the coffin.

"This way," John says, dropping the last stitch over a chair. The naked white figure leads me through a door to the bedroom. In the center of the floor is a king-sized bed.

"Something is missing," I say. "Where do you sleep?"

"Here." He opens a wall-length closet. A decorative, although slightly weathered, coffin is wedged on the floor below the shirts and slacks. "I bring my boys up here. Wouldn't want to scare them away, would I?"

"You bring your marks to your home?" I ask.

"Marks? Interesting term, Andrew." He peels my jacket back from my shoulders. "Why not bring them here? They're usually surfers out on their own. Straight ones who want it but don't want it known." He flashes his crooked grin. "It's safer here than in a downtown alley where anyone can pick up the pieces."

"I stand chastised."

"And raring to go," John says as my slacks hit the floor.

"Pick those up, please." I belly flop onto the bed. If one is going to remove Andrew's clothes, one must take responsibility for their care. John struts about the room, searching for hangers. I shift on the bed for comfort. I'm more anxious than I realized. "Forget it. We're beyond raring to go."

"That's the attitude I want to hear." John tosses my clothes into a corner — I suppress a shudder.

With a delighted laugh, he leaps clear across the room. Somersaulting on the bed, he tackles me. We roll up against the wall; he stretches over me. His body is deceiving — in spite of its look of softness, his muscles are firm.

Then — darkness help me — I remember that I'm supposed to pump this corpse for information. I extricate my mouth, gasp a breath, and ask: "What's with the clique you took me to be sized up by tonight?" That's worming it out of him, Andrew?

"Not now, Andrew," John says, his hands working their way from my chest to my hips and back.

"I just wondered what you boys were up to, that's all." I squirm under his weight to afford him better purchase. "Are you a club banded together for some noble inhuman cause — ooo, that's interesting."

"Andrew." He rears back his head, the hazel eyes flashing off-kilter amusement. "We can talk later."

"Curious—"

"You're in, if that's what you want to know. Jay and Christian aren't so certain about you—"

"They're a cute pair," I comment.

"Jay thinks he's Kane's nanny. Christian parrots Jay to stay in Kane's good graces." His roving fingers find a sensitive spot. "At any rate, Kane says you're in, and what Kane says goes. Does that answer all inquiries, or do I have to..." The maneuver, centered at that senstive spot, knocks me breathless.

"Yes. And you can still do that if you like."

In various and sundry positions, John tumbles me from one side of the bed to the other, then to the foot and back to the head. He withholds the threatened delicacies. I feel chastised for my curiosity. Still, the boy knows some tricks — especially this one where we're suspended a foot above the mattress; ooo, what a feeling.

Then he gets into some heavy stuff — a nip here, a nip there. I experience a moment of uncertainty. Who wants needles jabbed in them in the height of passion? Pulling at his hair, I suggest restraint. "I can't go home full of punctures."

"They'll heal," John assures me. Before I can express my doubts, his fangs penetrate the fleshy area above my shoulder blade. Gasping, I struggle, then abruptly relax. An ounce at a time, he sucks out blood, and the pressure — combined with his other wizardry — titillates the medulla oblongata, swells the cerebellum, and enflames the cerebrum. The sensation expands through the body, one sector after another, explodes a fiery numbness at every nerve ending. Andrew can't tell if he's having a coronary or the sexual experience of his existence.

The undead in bed — it's universal. Exhausted dead weight, we drift back to the mattress, our mingled moans reverberating. Before either of us has the sense to take a breather, John attacks again. Andrew is no fool; he complies. Let's face it, John Studnidka's last name is no innuendo. It's blissful fact.

4

Andrew the Slut — the words are chiseled all over Pablo's face and sizzle in his blue peepers. Not even the fact that we have company — Colin, isn't it, Mr. Average from VA? — curtails the accusation. I do hope Pablo isn't planning a scene in front of a guest. The way he sets down his Bloody Mary does not bode well. A stench of trouble permeates the room; I can practically see the wisps steaming off Pablo's shoulders.

"Perhaps I should be on my way," Colin suggests, putting down his drink.

"Don't be foolish," I reply.

"Be foolish," Pablo grunts. Immediately, he turns to Colin. "I'm sorry, Colin. It might be best—"

"Not for me, it won't," I say. "Sit down, Colin. Finish your drink. The battle can be forestalled."

"Always the clown," Pablo states.

"Someone around here has to act half-alive." I retreat to the kitchen and concoct that old dead-nerve steadier — a triple pitcher of strawberry margaritas.

O

Considering our deathstyle, at least we don't have to sit in silence around the breakfast table after a night of quarreling. I leave Pablo to his shuffling in the living room and retreat to the bathroom.

Bath drawn, I settle into the scalding water, allow the thick steam to blot out the seedy world. I shut my eyes, and Kane Davies's face looms before me. I have been touched by the man, in a completely different way than I was touched by John Studnidka. Yet, being who I am, I wonder if I will have Kane Davies as I was had by John Studnidka last night.

Although the conjecture possesses its own pleasantness, it also leaves me concerned. Pablo won't stand for another indiscretion. I wouldn't want to lose Pablo. Yet, between his television-mentality reaction to my tryst and his insistence on attending these VA meetings, he tasks my patience. Perhaps — for now — I should put Kane Davies out of the atrophied brain and concentrate on resurrecting my Relationship with Pablo.

The notion rallies me. I hop out of the tub and dress, selecting clothes that do not overstate my intention, yet reveal that I am on a serious course. Annoyed by the unsatisfactory inspection of my appearance — this no-reflection-in-the-mirror trait really ticks me off — I amble into the living room. Pablo isn't there. Noise rattles from the kitchen.

What I need is the proper mood. I examine my compact discs. I know which one I want — under S — that's row seventeen. I pop in 57S, hit the switches. LaBabs swells smoothly from the speakers. Smoothly swelling LaBabs sets the best moods.

In a skip, I lean against the door frame. Pablo, hung in his limitless black and gray slacks and shirt, cleans up after my margarita spree. He is deliberately ignoring the music and me. I tap a toe on the tile to get his attention.

Gently dropping the blender pitcher into a tub of sudsy water, he glances at me. His peepers say I make an impression. He dries his hands, leans a hip against the sink, and surveys me. I'd feel more confident if I conjured a smile from him, but I suppose that might be asking too much.

I sweep across the uneven linoleum floor, latch onto Pablo, and swirl him around the kitchen. He resists the rhythm of the music — and my Fred Astaire agility. But I see the twitching of a smile at the corner of his mouth. I persist, forcing him to follow my debonair lead.

"I thought we'd go out." I don't beat around the hawthorn bush with Pablo. "Just the two of us — like old times."

Pablo breaks free and returns to the sink.

"You used to like to dance to LaBabs," I mutter, retreating to the doorway. I pick at the chipped woodwork. "You used to like to spend an evening out with me."

He studies me in silence.

"Pablo..." I swallow, forge my way through emotions that leave me uneasy. "I don't want to fight — not with you. I hope you don't want to fight with me. We're a set, remember. I didn't exactly pick you at random, and you didn't exactly reject me and what I offered. You know — twenty or thirty millennia together — you and me, until eternity do we part."

The blue peepers cloud. He returns to the dishes, taking his time with the blender pitcher. I had hoped for a better reaction, considering what it took for me to say all that. At length, he glances at me. "I'm going to a meeting with Colin," Pablo says in a small voice. "I need to go to a meeting."

"Meeting shmeeting!" I shout. As always, Andrew's sensitive to the last. I choke back further words of outrage. "I want us to spend time together. I'm not talking about going on a killing spree. We used to go out — just to be together."

"I *am* going with Colin to a meeting," he says. He plunges the blender pitcher into the rinse water, then sets it on the drain board.

"And what are you doing with Colin after the meeting?" I sneer. "Is there an undead support group to attend? Or maybe a blood bank to rob?"

"Would you please stop saying that word?"

"What word? Dead? We are *dead*, Pablo."

He slams his palms down on the counter. A margarita glass topples into the sink. The glass tinkles against the porcelain, a hundred pieces. Kiss my last complete set of crystal ta-ta.

"Nice dents you put in the countertop." I give up — I think I want to give up, at any rate. But when I look at him, tall and slender, that long hair thinning at the temples, the fragile profile, I remember the first night I saw him and experience the passion afresh.

No, I'm not ready to give up. Tonight, I have no choice but to retreat and replan my strategies. Eventually, I will succeed. Andrew does not succumb easily to defeat.

5

But in the meantime, I need a diversion from homefront travails. Tagging along with Pablo and Colin to the Vampires Anonymous meeting does not fit the bill. Right now, Andrew wants to put Vampires Anonymous into oblivion status. There's a thought to take one out into the night. Andrew suspects that Kane Davies and his clique of corpses has a grudge against Vampires Anonymous, and Andrew is more than willing to join the struggle.

Leaving the van to Pablo, I take the old-world method of transportation to the club where John Studnidka introduced me to Kane Davies. The night is young, and the clique has not arrived. The press of human boys, however, strongly occupies me as I saunter up to the bar. In appreciation, I scan the hot bods, thinking that a mark might prove more profitable than even an assignation with Kane Davies.

"Something to drink, or you just going to salivate all evening?" demands a deep monotone.

I face the bartender, tall, dark, granite-faced. Ever since Steven-Old-Boy, my phobia of werewolves has been usurped by a phobia of bartenders. This one poses so butch, however, that I gladly belittle him with one of my most overwhelming stares. "Strawberry margarita," I order, my voice gone hollow.

"Yessir." He hops to it and returns in seconds with a thick double. I reward his promptness with another stare, and he runs away to find more pacifistic customers.

Andrew has such fun sometimes, I wonder why I ever have a worry. Death could be like this, just one little trick after another, if only ... Well, if onlys are always there; even the undead cannot escape them. If only Steven-Old-Boy had not discovered my secret two years ago; if only I didn't suffer the dilemma; if only Pablo could be happy — at least content — with our existence. If only — to the end of time...

Resuming my admiration of the milling Bodies-by-Soloflex, I spot a familiar face in the crush. Hart Laughlin, one of Kane's followers, wanders across the dance floor, allowing the dancers to jostle him about. A dim smile slants his lips; his gray eyes are shellacked, as if he has just feasted heartily or ... Of course, I should have recognized the symptoms last night: I can't think of anything more depressing than a drugged-out vampire. Hart stops before me, the smile stretching a fraction, and thrusts his pelvis against my hip.

"Fancy running into you," he says, voice oiled and distant. His eyes dance.

"Indeed," I reply. Andrew has a list of things he despises, and drugs are high on it. I back off; Hart likes the position and traps me against the bar. Ordinarily, I would not reject such proximity, especially considering the proportions, but I can smell the drugs, a putrid rot, seeping from his pores.

"Hanging out, or looking for someone specific?" Hart asks. The smile manages another fraction of an inch. "Someone specific will be along — in time. Settle for me while you wait?" His eyelid droops to a half-mast wink. "I have lots of practice. It used to be my living. No more cameras for Hart." He fiddles with the jewels that dangle from his right ear. "Now I make housecalls to keep me in pretties. American Express welcomed."

I combine the clues, filling in what Hart's glazed brain has omitted. Mix it all up with the certainty that I had seen him somewhere before last night. Memory of his face, and his prowess, in more than one erotic video, springs up in my brain.

In spite of my attempt to control it, the remembrance revives the standard reaction. Hart presses closer, assuming — quite naturally — that I will settle while I wait.

"Isn't this a cozy tête-à-tête?" Jay Bauer, the heavy-lidded eyes fuming, the full lips nastily curled, hovers behind Hart. Christian Fellows crowds in for further condemnation.

"Just having a chat and a drink," Hart says, facing Jay and greeting him with that pelvic thrust. "Join us?"

Shoving Hart aside, Jay glares at me. "I don't believe you were summoned," he says.

Summoned? Andrew? I have very serious doubts about the likelihood of anyone possessing such *huevos*.

"Were you?" Christian echoes Jay's authority.

"From where would you summon me?"

"Kane knows," Jay says.

I believe him. Nonetheless, these boys have overstepped the bounds of Andrew's patience and never-ending good nature.

"You could try to summon me from Hell, if you like, or send me back again, if you think you're that talented, but first I'll rip that smug smile off your fat lips and stuff it under your bloated eyelids." Sit on that wooden stake and spin, sucker.

"Well said." Hart applauds. I may well take a liking to him after all, regardless of his fondness for drugs.

Christian Fellows's hackles jump to the challenge. "No twerp deadmeat in sissy clothes—"

Jay Bauer holds up a hand, terminating Christian Fellows's very unChristian tirade. Jay links his arm in mine, guides me toward the mirrored back wall, and offers to buy me a fresh drink. Hart trails, chuckling at Christian's mumbled outrage.

This camaraderie unbalances me. I had expected a similar outburst from Jay Bauer. He grins, brown eyes gleaming under the heavy lids. He drapes an arm over my shoulders, unsettling me even further. My brain snaps to the alert mode.

"Kane seems to think you're an 'admirable bloke,' to quote the man," Jay says when the drinks have arrived.

"You don't say," I reply, at a loss for better words. The compliment from Kane Davies — even filtered through Jay Bauer's sardonic inflection — constricts the verbal processes.

"Indeed, I do," Jay says. "Christian here does not, however, appreciate the qualities that Kane discovered in our short meeting last night."

Long hands coiled around his glass, Christian Fellows stands ready for a tussle. I would say that all he sees is my blood and guts splattered liberally across the glass behind me.

"Our other friend..." Jay nods at Hart, lost in the swirl of dancers before us, "...sees little more than the flesh." The heavy lids drop as he gives me the twice-over. "A trifle on the thin side — my humble opinion only."

For whatever that's worth, Airhead. In the pretext to lift my glass, I shrug off his arm. The ploy is recognized. Jay knows I'm not duped by his tactics. I enjoy a moment of superiority along with my margarita. Jay is anxious to continue, as if he must have his say — before Kane Davies's arrival?

"Varied, accurate, and inaccurate assessments all," I say, mustering an indifferent mask. "But they are bred of primal emotions set afire by the mere impudence of my presence." I grab a quick breath to unleash the rest of my spiel, hoping I can maintain an onslaught of nonsense to hold Jay Bauer's verdict at bay until I can contrive an escape plan.

Jay Bauer and Christian Fellows are determined to ward off my association with Kane Davies. If verbal abuse will not send me flying, then more substantial weapons will be drawn. They'll make no move here with the human cuties as witnesses, but once we're out in the night, they'll dismember me and scatter my parts over the metropolis. Andrew will simply cease to exist.

"Your objections are rooted in the superficial," I continue. "You know nothing of the mind — the spirit — the essence of Andrew — to make clear evaluations worth hearing."

As the last word is devoured by another simpering pop dance ditty, I hand my glass to Jay Bauer and step away from the wall. I may achieve success. Jay and Christian hover open-mouthed, overpowered by Andrew logic. My foot inches forth for step two.

Hart Laughlin clamps his hand around my arm. "You really know how to put the sanctimonious in their place." I struggle for freedom — too late. Jay Bauer and Christian Fellows shake off their stupors and close in — no doubt for the kill.

"We know one indisputable fact." Jay presses my glass back into my hand. The condensation drips icily down my cold skin. "Your wretched, weathered companion is a regular at Vampires Anonymous, and you have been there on several occasions."

We have hit the crux of the matter, and confirmed Andrew's suspicions. Kane Davies and devotees are rivals of that organization for the faint-hearted undead.

In my own defense, and as protection against flaying by these sepulchral enthusiasts, I state, "Little man, to think that someone of my aesthetics and long association with the delights of a starlit evening would be susceptible to doctrines of abstinence propagated by these toothless simpletons shows a decided lack of perception." I forge onto the difficult task. "As for Pablo — weathered or not hardly signifies, since he is twice the corpse you'll ever be — he suffers a momentary deficiency of mindful presence. When he opens his big blue peepers to the ludicrous jargon thrust upon him by these VA carcasses, he will wing back to the fold of bats on the go."

"On that simple statement you expect us to change our minds?" Jay Bauer asks.

"We should stick to our original plan," Christian says, his thin face a marble death mask.

Hart jabs a finger at Christian's chest. "You can't go around chopping people to little bits because you don't like the cut of their coat." He flicks the collar of Christian's jacket. "Especially when it's cut better than yours."

"He's trouble—"

"Not here," Jay says. His hand grips Christian's shoulder until he cringes and backs down. "This isn't settled, Andrew Lyall. I'm not influenced by your pretty speeches. Chaff is easily separated from wheat. But — and don't let this go to your head—" He has the gall to tap at my temple. "I may be willing to give you a second thought." He glances at his diamond-studded wristwatch — ostentatious, but not unimpressive. "For tonight, you have earned a stay of execution."

"In other words, you're out of time because Kane Davies's arrival is imminent," I say, not about to let him off the hook.

The full lips twist to a parody of humor. "Your existence dangles from a weaker thread than that." He steps back, nudges Christian Fellows toward the Club's entrance. "Hart, you are needed with us." He turns into the crowd.

"I'm thrilled." Hart lingers a moment. Something flickers behind the glassy gray eyes. "He's not in charge," he says. He gropes the air for words. "But he has considerable influence with those who are." He grins, no doubt pleased with his lucidity, then follows the other two.

Left alone — and still in one piece — I gulp my melted margarita. I worm my way back to the bar, intimidate the bartender for a quick refill, and down it. The tequila haze dulls palpitations of dread. Andrew is in trouble — again.

6

The best defense is to ignore the threat — a goodly piece of Andrew advice. How best to ignore the threat? Andrew stays

– 49 –

away from it. I occupy myself with the everynight mundane albatrosses — such as work.

Besides, the weekend has ended. If I wish to keep up the rent on my tenement penthouse, I must attend the dreaded job to earn the needed cash money.

In my need to elude the unflagging Steven-Old-Boy, I have sequestered myself in a slum shop. Located on the ground floor of a crumbling building, the store boasts through its windows a moldy display of clothes from a previous administration. Within, racks and shelves are burdened with loudly patterned synthetic shirts with wide collars and trousers with two-inch cuffs.

"Clothes not even the lowliest hetero-hick would wear on his worst day," to quote some venerable source. Yet, to my horror, residents of these parts actually purchase these rags — to wear — in public. Have they no aesthetics? Have they no televisions so they could at least wear last year's fashions? Suppressing distaste, I assist these fashion-senseless humanoids in their selections. I am amazed I can still lift my head in the society of my own kind.

Come to think of it, right now, I can't — without the chance of losing it.

My sole consolation is that I have not been reduced to draping my own thin, yet appealing, frame in these travesties of taste. True, my wardrobe has seen better days, but please! Andrew wear a lime green acrylic sweater with contrasting canary yellow and bruise violet piping under one of my jackets? Drive a stake through me — hold me out in the sunlight — cut off my head and other more important body parts and just spare me.

"Nice place!"

I have no trouble connecting that amused tone with its fresh face. I drop the shirts I have been stuffing into a cubbyhole.

"Too gnarly, Andrew." John Studnidka's voice vibrates off the high, blackened ceiling. "Jay said you worked in a dump, but this place..." I turn to him. John's hazel eyes glimmer their usual off-kilter humor. The urge rises to slap him even sillier among the rayon socks and plastic ties.

"What an unexpected nuisance," I greet him. I crouch down to pick up the shirts. From the gleam on his face, bending over at this time would be inopportune. "Don't you have to run?"

"I just arrived," he says. Laughing, he spreads his arms wide to encompass the establishment. "Dang, boy, I could have a *field* day here. I had a shirt just like that!"

"You can have that one for a mere twenty-two ninety-five."

"That's a little steep." He surveys me head-to-foot, with a lengthy pause in between; his smile curls up at one side. "What time do you get off — work?" If he becomes any more delighted with himself, I may scream right here in front of God and all his ill-dressed children. "I missed you last night."

"Pity." I wander away to perform an unnecessary duty.

"I thought you'd come to the Club. If not to see me, then to check out Kane again." A large hand gropes under my coattail; I should have known better than to turn my back to him. "I waited for you. None of the guys saw you—"

"Perhaps you should talk to Jay or Christian or Hart," I suggest, facing him. His hand is still extended, and I fall right into his palm.

John Studnidka's laughter rings. "I doesn't matter since I got a grip on you now."

Andrew is in no mood for John Studnidka's chortling. Besides, I cannot allow him to lead me onto the happy trail to his house again. I want to patch my Relationship with Pablo, not rip it open wide enough for a hearse to drive through.

"Ask Jay Bauer and Christian Fellows if I wasn't at the Club last night," I say, extricating myself. "Hart will verify the interesting chat I had with those two carcasses — if he can clear his mind of drugs long enough to think past his—"

"Hart never thinks past that. It's his living." John has stopped laughing, not even a titter threatens to erupt. "What conversation did you have with Jay and Christian?"

"We indulged in an intriguing question-and-answer session about me and Pablo and VA. Your friends—"

His smooth face seeming to age its true fifty-odd years in a dizzying flash, John Studnidka departs with the speed of the undead. I am left conversing with an orange vinyl coat. Andrew seems to have hit yet another frayed nerve.

O

Another night in the fashionless industry draws to a close. I escape into the night and prowl this seedy neighborhood. I don't know where to go or what to do. Pablo has gone to a meeting with Colin. No way with hell rising on earth will I set foot near the Club where Kane Davies's delinquent deadbats flock.

From around me echo the moans and mutterings of the street inhabitants. A high note rings that halts me in my tracks. Andrew must be hearing things. I take a step. Andrew is not hearing things. Somewhere close at hand shrills the cries of an infant — or at least a child. I try to isolate the sound, but the howl reverberates off the high buildings, ululates above then below the derelicts' racket.

After a last plaintive whimper, the sound is gone.

Flustered, I linger in the street. All the hairs at the back of my neck stand on end in anticipation of that cry's reawakening. Minutes pass. I shake my head at my stupidity. What child would be out at this black hour?

I walk on, still uncertain of my destination.

A scream — gender undecipherable — bounces around the dark buildings and resounds off the yellow-tinted clouds.

I falter to a stop. Then, more disconcerted than ever, I scurry on. For I swear that after the piercing shriek has faded, I hear the lost child's laughter.

O

I flutter back to the cave — so to speak. That cry, scream, and laughter buzz in my ears. I secure the crossbar over the front door, turn on all the lights, and cower on the sofa. My shoulders convulse intermittently, my head throbs, even my eyes sting. Those sounds taunt me.

I cannot sit still for long, even when in the grips of — all right, I'll say it — fear. As much as I hate to admit it, that laughter frightened me. I can think of several earthly monsters, even werewolves and demented bartenders, that I would rather face than the owner of that tiny laugh.

I head for the kitchen. Too shaky to assemble the blender, I pour tequila, margarita fixings, including whole fresh strawberries, over ice in a big glass. Swirl it once and gulp it down. Golly. That's a deadly rush I don't recommend.

I reel a moment around the kitchen, then stagger back for another. This time I swirl it twice to mix in the tequila a bit more. I sip this glassful. Apparently suicidal after my scare, I carry my "drink" out onto the balcony. The four boards that pass for the floor creak under my weight. I lean against a post; it wiggles, setting the chicken-wire guardrail to singing. There's a fair breeze, high enough not to carry the alley's perfumes. Swigging my concoction, I stare at the church, two blocks away, where Pablo and his vapid friends are congregated.

It's out there somewhere, Andrew, probably still laughing.

Stray, rabid cat — that's what it was.

Not on your grave, buddy-boy.

I gulp the last of the tequila, then fish out a liquor-soaked strawberry. I chew it to a pulp and make a decision.

If Pablo won't come to Andrew, Andrew must go to Pablo. I have consumed enough tequila not to care that he is at the desecrated church of the vampire temperance society.

With a couple of strawberries for the sky, I flit off the terrace. I've had better response from my wings, but I manage to avoid a head-on with the building across the way. I soar up its face, knocking on every third brick with a phalange. The sky breaks over the roof. I veer off in one direction — oops, wrong way — a quick swerve toward that crumbling spire. My flight plan could use improvement. I should have taken some wind variance and updraft calculations; I'm getting knocked around like a pinball up here. Whoa, I passed that sucker. You had better spiral it down and land before you crash, Airhead.

The alley is deserted; from within the church my sharp hearing picks up a rich voice. I take a moment to collect myself, and finish my strawberries.

But wait; something's amiss. I trace the terrain of my face. What's all this fur? My nose isn't quite this flat and flared. I grope at my ears — pointed and wide. Idiot! Never drink and fly — trust Andrew. It screws up the transmutations.

I shake my head vigorously, take inventory again. Now we doin' a jig on the head of a coffin nail. Andrew's got his face back — the human one. Quite content, I stuff both strawberries in my mouth and saunter inside to the assembly room.

The meeting is in full rigor — excuse me, vigor. Lights are low. These boys could see a distance in the blackest pitch; dim lights will not enhance anyone's anonymity. I scout around for Helmut. An encounter might prove disastrous; Andrew has had enough disastrous encounters already this week. There's my Aryan hunk of dead flesh, right up front beside the podium.

But hark! what side of luscious meat at the podium speaks?

A tall fellow, he has nice broad shoulders one could get a grip on. His gray silk shirt drapes over an expanded chest, clings to the strong biceps of the arms. At the cuffs, long-fingered hands gesture. The face strikes an interesting contrast to the boys in the room. The speaker's face has seen more winter nights — and possibly days. I think he was well into the prime years when he joined the fly-by-nights.

I would not exactly call this gent's face a good face. The planes are correct; the eyes, violet even in the frail illumination, are set perfectly to each side of the classic nose. Andrew's point is that the face is not good in a moral aspect. The lines around the eyes and mouth, that split the forehead below the mane of thick gray hair, seem to have been etched from the nastier emotions.

I tear my fascinated gaze away from the speaker to search for Pablo. A bigger crowd than usual has turned out tonight. VA must have had a recruitment drive. I can see it now: the undead walking door-to-door, "Come join us at VA, and stop that messy blood habit," then pressing a copy of *The Mausoleum* into their convert's hand. In spite of myself, I giggle. Several sets of dead eyes flash toward me.

"Won't you come in and join us?" The speaker, hands gripping the edges of the podium, burns my brain with his penetrating stare. "Come in. There's an empty chair here." He gestures to the front row. "My name is Maxwell, and I am a vampire."

"Fancy that," I reply, then belch further opinion.

"You have come for our help," he says, rounding the podium. "We will see that you don't—"

I shake my head. "Strawberries ... actually..." The belches have altered to hiccups. "Tequila ... soaked..."

"You need our guidance." Maxwell, his violet eyes on me, pauses a foot away. "I smell the foreign blood in your body."

"Do ... tell..." I push up my sleeve and examine my veins. "Looks about ... a quart or two low ... to me. Feel the need—"

"We do not speak of that here," the man says. The creases of the brow deepen, the wrinkles circling the eyes fold inward, the lines to each side of the mouth gash his face from nostril to chin. His voice rasps: *"Never do we speak of it here."*

His vampiric mesmerizing tactics needle my atrophied brain. Fortunately, those tequila-soaked strawberries have marinated my gray matter so that his bewitching commands have no effect. Still, his change of face and voice scare my hiccups away.

"Sure you do." I encompass the entire room of stiffs. "I've heard half these rotters talk about the need to *feed*."

The lines of the face deepen and contract. His grimace originates in pits of Hell unseen by the purest evil. The spellbinding violet eyes blaze. *"Never."*

Andrew, even in his present state, realizes the prudence of acquiescence. I bow — just a tad. "Whatever you say."

"Shall I handle this, Maxwell?" Helmut, all six feet of lean, mean corrupted muscle, stops at Maxwell's elbow.

"Everything is under control," Maxwell says, the rich tone resurrected from the gravel of the crypt that had held it a moment ago. He straightens his shoulders, the dim light shifts across his face. He has put the horror-show mask away.

"I came for Pablo," I say, "then I'll be out of your fur."

"Pablo?" Maxwell tilts his head toward Helmut.

"Tall. Thin black hair. Blue eyes," Helmut rattles.

"That's right. Blue peepers. That's Pablo." I crane past the two of them. "Yo, Pablo! Let's hit the sky."

Hissing curses, Pablo skirts the back of the room. His expression has become nearly as ghastly as Maxwell's.

The expression quickly vanishes when he turns to the tall fellow. "Excuse the interruption, Maxwell," Pablo apologizes. "I think I should escort him home."

Ever sympathetic, Maxwell nods. Yet, as Pablo vise-grips my arm, Maxwell touches my sleeve. "Join us tomorrow. In lower spirits. Benefit from our experiences. Why torture yourself this way?" His hand slides up and down in front of me.

"My fly open?" I press chin to chest to check myself out. I don't look too tortured. "That's just a loose thread."

"Come on, Andrew." Pablo drags me into the hall.

"See you 'round the cemetery!" I shout over my shoulder.

The door of the room quietly closes, shutting us out.

III

HEADS OR TAILS

1

F ace buried in a mound of pillows, Eddie Cramer screams. No pain-filled wail of terror — a howl of total sexual euphoria jangles up the spine to wrack his brain to convulse his body. His hands claw past the pillows, fingernails scrape the scarred wood of the headboard. The sensation differs little from the intercourse. He opens his mouth, dragging in a lungful of feather-soured air. He unleashes another scream — longer, more exhausting. He slings his head side to side in the pillow mound and forces the last breath of the shriek from his bowels.

O

Sweat mats the frail patterns of hair to Eddie's chest and stomach. His groin and legs are sticky, irritating. His every breath gags like dust. His throat hurts; his lungs burn. Taking inventory, he finds his entire body bruised and scratched.

Head lolling over the foot of the mattress, Eddie views the motel room as upside-down. An orange-carpeted ceiling, scratched molding, dark paneling on the wall's upper quarter, patterned wallpaper to the acoustical tile floor — what a universe this would be. What a universe this is. Topsy-turvy — the description fits his life since taking up with Steven Verruckt.

During the last year, Steven has dragged Eddie along a serpentine trail up and down the West Coast, with brief junkets into southern Canada and northern Mexico. Tirelessly, Steven grunts his maxim: *Don't lose scent.* His speech has become more erratic and his voice more grating with each passing month.

Little remains of the good-looking college graduate who once bartended in yet another Village bar. Possessed by the hunt, Steven skulks through the night, a gaunt figure with hollow eyes and sallow skin. His mental faculties have degenerated in conjunction with his appearance and speech. Eddie has watched obsession usurp rationality. The mania plots Steven's existence. Nothing predominates the pursuit of Andrew Lyall.

How deep and wide are the bowels of hell? Eddie wonders, studying his topsy-turvy universe. How much deeper can we go? Eddie's universe cartwheels as he turns onto his stomach. Where will the hunt end?

In an abyss that will devour us all with sulfurous flames.

Dragging himself with his hands, he slides off the bed onto the floor. Dull pains thump through every muscle. He pushes to his knees then hoists himself to his feet, quite a chore for an old man of thirty. He imagines himself in five years — if he survives that long — bent and crippled with a plethora of mechanical attendants to get him through the day.

When was the last time he saw daylight? They travel by night. Andrew and the blue-eyed Latino, Steven and Eddie — all are creatures of the night. Listen to the maniacal music they make. Each possesses a dissonant orchestra. Each lags one note behind the other, yet remains part of the same symphony of darkness.

Standing before the clouded mirror, Eddie pushes dark-brown hair, overgrown to his shoulders, back from his forehead.

Extra lines mar his brow. Scanning his face, he spots a crease, a bag, a discoloration of skin. He skims the curve of his throat, razor-burned raw thanks to Steven's disposable razors.

The reflection of his gray eyes stares him down. *You are an accessory to nocturnal pursuit,* they accuse; *you are a partner to Steven's obsession. You want to find Andrew Lyall, vampire, as much as Steven. Why else have you spent a year of your life with a madman?*

"I want to find Andrew. But I don't want to destroy him," Eddie tells the eyes. "I want..." Thoughts desert him. Uncertainty and fear keep his reasons for tracking Andrew Lyall at bay. His hands rove down his triangular torso. "I want..."

"You want more?" Steven, hair plastered to his skull, stands naked on the bathroom threshold.

Eddie does not dignify the remark. "Are you finished in there? I'm sticking to myself."

"Go 'head," Steven says with a gallant flourish at the door. "There might even be hot water."

Eddie hurries toward the bathroom. After one of their trysts, he doesn't like Steven's company. Once, upon a cliff darkly, he thought sex with a madman might prove too uninhibiting. The theorem verifies itself anew every night — sometimes with the dusk then again with the dawn. Yet, he continues to submit, on occasion willingly. Now, after a year, he doesn't like to look into Steven's face — a different type of mirror in which he might view himself.

"Won't be here when you come out," Steven says.

Eddie pauses.

"Got a lead," Steven replies to the unasked question. "Follow it up. Don't lose scent."

"You do that." Eddie retreats to the bathroom, leans back against the shut door. He shudders.

A hundred different ways, overlapping, large and minuscule; on the bathroom mirror, on the shower stall, the tiles, the ceiling, walls; any surface, rough or smooth, anything filmed with the steam's residue — Steven has scrawled the word *Andrew*.

O

Although his Timex reads three in the morning, Eddie wanders the streets. He stays alert. Eddie's no fool. If Andrew and the blue-eyed Latino are vampires, then other vampires might be haunting any town or city. Eddie carries protection: his service revolver, tucked in its holster under his police jacket, and a silver crucifix, in a front pocket for easy access.

The neons of a bar shimmy up ahead. Through the door, music vibrates. Tight-skirted females flit into the bar. In no humor to ward off tight-skirted females, he passes the place by.

And he will have to ward them off. Eddie's face draws attention; so does his body. He makes no attempt to disguise it since leaving the police force — a society of lawless legal bashers, he decided after they tried bashing his skull. He now wears clothes that turn heads. Why not? He hasn't changed that much in the last year. An occasional tryst in a dark back room satisfies needs that tumbles with Steven — too unrestrained, too detached from reality — do not. Eddie carries life-protection for these occasions as well. Eddie's no fool.

A red light halts him at a street corner. Memories bump against his back. He wants to brush them off, but they demand his company. Who else will listen to them? In numerical order, they parade themselves behind his eyes.

One memory quotes that Eddie Cramer was once a police officer who liked to bash the heads of the pretty boys he also liked to — that memory tastes sour. Eddie calls the next number.

Memory Number Four flails its arms for attention. Forget Memories Two and Three. Look behind Memory Number Four. The light turns green; Memory Number Four jumps off the curb.

This tableau still has Eddie in his blue uniform, his cap pulled tight against his heavy eyebrows. Jumping firelight from the street riot illumates the alley. Ahead, a man runs toward the next street. Eddie chases the him. At full tilt, his legs cannot bridge the gap between them. By the time Eddie reaches the alley's end, the man has outdistanced him by blocks. The man is a blur in the night, then gone around a corner.

Andrew, Memory Number Four whispers.

Yes, Andrew Lyall, vampire.

Eddie staggers to a halt. The memories, caught unaware, advance without him. Good riddance.

The night of the riot, Eddie suspected that something was not quite right about Andrew Lyall. Not even competition runners possess such speed.

What a wonderful gift, Eddie muses.

He pushes away from the building he has sagged against. What is the line — or bastardization of it — that any filmland vampire hunter worth his wooden stakes knows by heart? *Vampirism is not a gift; vampires are the living dead.*

Yet, curiosity about Andrew Lyall holds Eddie in a cold palm. *Are the edges of reality smoother under the veil of night?* Enchantment makes promises meant to be broken. *Marvels do exist in the night. Every edge is silk smooth. Come along. You're no fool, Eddie. Don't ignore the experiences of the night.*

Again Eddie stops in the middle of the darkness. In his pocket, his right hand clings to his silver crucifix. It offers no strength against his fascination with Andrew Lyall. Eddie stares at the sky, clear and twinkling with stars above this tourist town by the sea. No solutions hover there. No protection can be found against the phantasm of Andrew the Vampire that, stealthy as an incubus, seduces Eddie's dreams and torments his soul with thirst.

O

With a soundless cry, Eddie thrusts himself out of a nightmare — one of many haunted by Andrew Lyall. Teasers of dawn peek around the edges of the motel room drapes. Eddie leans on his elbow in the bed; his eyes cast about the gray-hued room. He's alone. He lets out his breath.

Then he sits up; his hand coils around the revolver on the mattress beside him. No, he is not alone.

In a shadowed corner, a figure crouches over Steven's monstrous green ice chest. Eddie tries to open his mouth to demand identification. He is disappointed by a feeble squeak.

"Go back to sleep," Steven's voice growls.

"What in the hell are you doing?" Eddie shouts, his voice returned with a vengeance.

"Nothing," Steven replies. He shuts the lid of the ice chest. "Nothing to concern your empty little head." He wades out of the shadows into the growing day's light. Blue eyes glazed, he taps his chest, grins. "I'll take care everything."

"I feel so secure." Dragging the sheet up his sweat-drenched body, Eddie curls up fetal.

The bed rocks, a hand fumbles at his hip.

"Don't touch me," Eddie hisses.

"You'll beg for it come dusk," Steven's voice croaks in his ear. "*Scream* for it."

Eddie lets a roundhouse fly, connects with Steven's head. The bed rocks again; a thud upon the carpet. Eddie waits for retaliation. Steven shuffles toward the bathroom. A wedge of light breaks across the room, then narrows to extinction.

O

On a mission for nature, Eddie stumbles out of bed. The travel alarm clock informs him that afternoon has wasted. In the other bed, Steven tosses and tussles with his own nightmares. On tiptoe, Eddie crosses toward the bathroom, then pauses.

The monstrous green ice chest sitting in the corner snags his attention. What does Steven keep on ice? Eddie kneels in front of the chest. His hands skim the cool aluminum, then join together around the extra-heavy-duty padlock that seals the ice chest against Eddie's curiosity.

2

"Wake up, sleeping copper."

Eddie, climbing the steep hill of consciousness, opens his eyes. Above him, starkly highlighted by blue television light, looms Steven's sharp-featured face. "Go away." Eddie buries his face in the pillowcase to hide from the light and Steven's eyes.

"It's time to rise," Steven states, "and grasp the night by the balls."

"You grasp it by the balls," Eddie says, lifting his head, "I'll nip at its heels later." He pulls a pillow over his head.

Steven flings back the blankets. Cold air assaults Eddie's naked body. "We got places to go and dead people to see," Steven insists. He hauls Eddie by the ankle off of the bed.

Eddie belly flops onto the floor. He flips onto his back. "I'll have your head—"

"Not tonight. We got places to go and dead people to see."

Eddie squints up at the silhouette towering over him. "Dead people?" A gauzy portrait of Andrew Lyall forms in his mind.

"Told you last night, have a lead," Steven says. "You never listen." Shaking his head, he lounges on top of the ice chest. "Andrew isn't the *only* one. Smoked out another — right here in this tourist trap. Know how to bait 'em and hook 'em." He mimes a cast and reels in a monster.

Eddie cringes against the footboard. "You're not suggesting that we have a meeting with a vampire this evening."

Mouth pursed, eyebrows arched, Steven offers a look of wide-eyed innocence.

O

At the darkest edge of town, a ramshackle building advertises refreshment. *Cock ails — Steaks — Lobs ers — Ch cken* blink from the sign on the roof. Steven whips his Jeep into a parking lot occupied by several Harleys, a couple of four-wheel-drive mini-trucks, and a pickup on tires fit for a 747.

Shutting off the engine, Steven jumps out. Eddie remains in his seat. Chasing vampires in the dead of night is one thing, going into this restaurant strains the bounds of reason. Another Harley roars into the lot; a tattooed gorilla lumbers inside.

Steven marches across the parking lot.

"Steven." Eddie hops out of the Jeep, nabs Steven's sleeve. "I don't think this is a good idea."

"It is too," Steven states. "*He*'ll be here. Watched him three nights. He's always here." He flips a hand at the Harleys. "He likes 'em rough and tough for the tumble." With the grip of the insane, Steven hauls Eddie toward the door.

Gravel crunches underfoot; footsteps rebound off the wooden porch. Pulled by Steven, the screen door screeches open. The main door echoes the protest. Beyond the threshold, shadowed heads turn to stare. Out of a dark corner looms the maître d', all butch wax, grizzled beard, and dandruffed tuxedo jacket.

Eddie steps back; Steven detains him. "Table for two," Steven says. "Near back, please, close to the bar."

Eyes shifting, the maître d' consults a ledger on a rickety podium. He plucks a pencil stub from the confines of his beard and makes a check on the page with a flourish. "Your usual table then, Mr. Verruckt. Right this way." Tucking stained menus under stained armpits, he ambles toward the back of the room.

At a secluded booth, Steven palms the maître d' a folded bill. "Thank you, Jacques."

"He'll be here soon," Steven, consulting his Casio watch, assures Eddie. "Two scotches — no rocks," he says when the waiter, none other than the maître d' in a different coat, appears. He swings a thumb at himself — "Lobster" — then at Eddie — "Chicken."

"No doubt," Jacques says, his eyes lingering on Eddie. He vanishes as silently as he appeared.

"What kind of place is this besides a dive?" Eddie whispers, glancing after the man. "If you tell me everyone here is dead, I'll throttle you."

"Not everyone. Calm thyself..." Face stone, Steven stares toward the front of the restaurant. "Enter our little walking dead man." The words almost pass by Eddie's ears.

In Eddie's opinion, nothing seems little about this easily six-foot-five specimen standing with feet set apart, his leather-gloved hands on slim hips. His face, framed by medium-length, light brown hair, belongs to a kid; from the neck down, he's pure adult male. Beneath the worn leather jacket, chest muscles strain the burgundy t-shirt. The man's faded jeans undulate below the belt with each step; kneecaps peek through shredded slits. Scuffed brown boots clomp across the wooden floor. The man leans forward on the bar. The seat of his jeans, as shredded as the knees, reveal enough flesh below the pockets for Eddie to choke on his chicken.

"He'd give a rise to the dead," breathes Steven. "Those eyes hide vile practices." He fidgets. "Makes me squirm."

Eddie didn't think anything remained on the planet to make Steven anxious, much less squirm.

"You talk to him," Steven says, jabbing Eddie's arm.

Eddie glances at Steven, then cowers against the booth. He shakes his head. "No. You want to know something, you talk to him. Don't give me that madboy look, Steven."

"It must be *you*," Steven insists. "Here." He pulls a folded paper from his jacket pocket. "Show it to him." Steven presses the paper into Eddie's hands.

Eddie lets the paper fall to the table.

"Buy him a drink," Steven says. Picking up the paper, he hands it and a ten spot to Eddie. "He likes bourbon."

Hand quivering, Eddie takes paper and money. For a moment's delay, he unfolds the paper. A lump catches in his throat. A photocopied enlargement of Andrew — from a college yearbook? — captioned "Captain of the Shopping Club" stares back.

"Quit wasting time." Steven taps the paper. "Go."

"All right!" Slipping the photocopy into his breast pocket, Eddie scoots out of the booth. He edges toward the tall man, ill-prepared to buy a drink for one of the undead.

"Two bourbons," he says, voice holding out, when he leans against the bar beside the man. The bartender sets up two shots. Eddie pushes one down to the tall man's elbow.

Dark-chocolate-brown eyes slide in Eddie's direction and pivot the head, then the body. The man smiles, exposing nice white teeth. Picking up the shot, he mocks a toast and tosses the bourbon back. The shot glass hits the bar. Eddie orders two more, then remembers to drink his own.

"Stanley at your every service." The tall man leans an elbow on the bar, swings out a hip on which to rest his hand. "You're not the usual species of clientele this establishment draws." He picks up the second drink. "A toast to..."

"Eddie." The glasses clink. Eddie gulps the bourbon, waves for another setup. "I'm passing through. A friend of mine used to live here. He might yet." Eddie fumbles in his pocket. The picture seems stuck. "You look like someone he might get to know," he adds to cover up the lapse.

"Allow me." Stanley's fingers brush the back of Eddie's hand; Eddie suppresses a shudder for their chill. Stanley pulls out the paper, unfolds it, then tears his eyes from Eddie's to study the photocopy. "He does look familiar, but not from here."

"Do you remember where?" Eddie asks. "I was looking forward to getting in touch again."

"City." Stanley slips the picture into Eddie's pocket. The long fingers skim Eddie's exposed chest. "It was definitely a city." The fingers trail downward; Eddie swallows hard. "I don't remember which. They all look alike after a while."

"Shucks," Eddie whispers. Having obtained the information, Eddie concentrates on how to escape before Stanley's roving fingers go past the point of no return.

Someone taps Eddie's shoulder. Hands folded in front of himself, Eddie faces Jacques.

"Your friend says that if you aren't outside in ten seconds he'll cut it off and feed it to this gentleman," Jacques says.

"Thank you," Eddie croaks.

"What a shame," Stanley says at his ear. His breath smells sweet with liquor yet feels like winter. "I could have spent the entire evening drinking with you." His hands work some quick magic that steals Eddie's breath. "Come back — alone — some night. I'm an experience that'll take you to heaven."

More likely hell, Eddie thinks.

"I'll do that," he says. Stanley's hands grip him a moment longer — promises meant to be broken — then release him. Eddie makes a beeline to the door.

Don't look back.

He does anyway.

O

Around midnight, a fetid ocean breeze whips across the restaurant parking lot. Across the street, Eddie shivers in the Jeep's passenger seat. Behind the wheel, Steven seems impervious. Warmed by rampaging psychotic anticipation, Eddie imagines. Tearing his gaze from Steven's shadowed profile, Eddie resumes his surveillance of the restaurant. Inside, the tall man in the leather jacket lingers still. Eddie sits up. He, too, is suddenly warm. The lights on the roof flicker, then go dark.

"Time's at hand," Steven murmurs. Face turned toward the building, he reaches into the back of the Jeep. He drags a sledgehammer with the broken handle into his lap. Another grope in the darkness produces a long, thick, sharp wooden stake.

Eddie doesn't need to ask the cliched "What's that for?" Steven has pounded the virtues of the stake into Eddie's brain. A demented master of the arts, Steven has lectured Eddie phrase and verse in every intricacy of the vampire's destruction.

Five — ten minutes fritter past. Light breaks through the windows to alleviate the restaurant's black exterior. A battered truck and a mammoth Harley stand deserted in the parking lot.

"Is he still inside?" Steven rests his chin on the steering wheel. Eddie swears he can see the crooked gears toiling behind the squinted eyes. "No, would be messy inside..." In his lap, Steven's hands stroke the wooden stake. "He's not inside ... Damn!" He sits bolt upright. "I'm blind!" He shoves Eddie out of the Jeep. "Used the back door! I'm stupid blind!"

Sprawled on the gravel, Eddie pushes to his knees. Steven scrambles around the Jeep. The duffel bag of weapons over a shoulder, stake and sledgehammer in one hand, he hauls Eddie to his feet. Eddie staggers after him.

They dash around the restaurant. Behind the building, tall grass rustles on the dune crests, the glimmering ocean surges to a horizon capped with thunderheads. A sharp breeze churns up sand and cold mist.

Steven races ahead. Then, as if captured by a whirlwind, he spins around and tackles Eddie. Eddie shoves Steven away and tries to stand. Steven latches onto the crotch of Eddie's jeans and drags him back to earth.

"He's just over dune," Steven warns, "ready to put the bite on."

Eddie glimpses the thrashing grass beyond which wait Stanley and Jacques. Rough wood scrapes Eddie's palm. Steven has thrust a wooden stake into his hands. Eddie drops it.

"You will use it!" Steven hisses. "Can't back out now."

"There has to be another way," Eddie argues. "Do you think he'll lie down on the beach and let you drive this into him?"

Steven grins. "Got a good fight ahead, Eddie-old-boy-in-cop's-clothing." Steven creeps toward the top of the dune. Hoisting his wooden stake, Eddie follows.

Highlighted by moonlight, Stanley stretches over Jacques. From the wide shoulders, down the back, to those smooth, shiny buttocks, Eddie's gaze trails Stanley's working muscles. At another time, a single response would suffice for this tableau. Yet, Steven waits bloodthirsty beside him. The gory purpose of their plan rides high in Eddie's mind. They are about to stake one of the undead — a vampire — a distant kin of Andrew Lyall.

With a nerve-paralyzing bellow, Steven, weapons in hand, storms down the dune. Cursing Steven's lack of subtlety, Eddie labors down the shifting sand after him.

A blur of white against dark sea and sky, Stanley leaps to his feet, abandoning a dazed Jacques. Boyish face contorted, he hurls Steven over his head. Steven thuds motionless at the water's edge. Stanley sets his hellfire gaze on Eddie.

"You," he whispers, the word drifting between glistening saber teeth. "I do get to drink of you after all. I shall enjoy your every last drop as you shall enjoy your last heartbeat."

"There must be a mistake," Eddie stammers. He hides the wooden stake behind his back. "We were out walking—"

Stanley chuckles. His clawed hands working, he advances. Wisps of moonlight glimmer off his chest fringed with dark hair, off his slender legs.

Eddie concentrates on Stanley's face. He must remember this look of bestial savagery carved upon a vampire's face. In the future, he will use the memory as a weapon against the phantasm of Andrew — if he survives the present.

"Come here, my pretty," Stanley says. In a flash, he stands before Eddie. With a startled cry, Eddie stumbles back. Cold fingers rake his chest; his flight is cut short. Then the heavy fabric of his jacket splits at the seams; his shirtfront tears loose. Leaving Stanley holding the remnants, Eddie flees toward the ocean. "There's no escape," Stanley warns. "Why run? Why make it painful when it can be ecstasy?"

Icy fingers snag the back of Eddie's neck. Stanley hoists him off the ground, throws him away from the surf. Eddie soars headfirst into a sand dune. A strenuous growl sounds from behind him. Eddie turns, drops to his butt.

"Nice ... soft ... warm ... skin." Stanley's hands skim Eddie's chest, down his stomach. The fingers loop around the waist of his jeans. Eddie watches, senseless yet fascinated, as the buttons pop. "Sweet ... full ... hot ... veins."

"Oh God, I'm history," Eddie says and falls back on the sand, his arms outflung. His head throbs, his limbs are weak. He doesn't have the will to fight.

"Not tonight, deadmeat," Steven's voice rasps.

Stanley howls — a wail of pure agony, not sexual euphoria. He thrashes on top of Eddie, then heaves himself to his feet. His roar vibrates on the wind.

Eddie lifts his head; the universe swims in a haze. At the apex, a naked Stanley spins circles on the sand. A wooden stake protrudes from his back; a fountain of blood paints the night. Grinning in mad defiance, Steven watches with crossed arms until Stanley collapses. Steven wields his broken sledgehammer at the head of the stake and pins Stanley to the beach. A hatchet flashes out of the duffel bag. Whistling a happy tune, Steven hacks off Stanley's head.

Eddie, drunk with revulsion, passes out.

O

With a headache born of nightmare, Eddie revives in the motel bed. For several minutes, he keeps his eyes shut to the activity around him. Drawers open and shut; something heavy drags across the carpet. The door slams. Another minute, just to be on the safe side, and Eddie views his universe.

The motel room has been turned upside down. Steven has ransacked the dresser and chest of drawers. Even his bed has been stripped, the sheets and blankets vanquished to a corner — the corner where the ice chest once reigned.

"Moving on," Steven says, entering from outside. Cool air and afternoon sunlight accompany him. "Get dressed."

Eddie shuffles to the sanctuary of the bathroom. Bolted inside, he retraces last night. Hazy bits and pieces surface. The bump on his head, swollen and tender under his hair, has disjointed the events. Eddie can't decipher which events are reality and which are resultant dreams.

"I'm probably better off that way," he tells his pallid reflection.

O

Steven behind the wheel, the Jeep speeds out of the tourist town by the sea. Chains secure the green ice chest to the rollbar. Eddie is enthralled by the ice chest until darkness shrouds the highway. He scouts for trouble at the roadside — vampires with flat tires.

"Where are we going?" he inquires of his grim chauffeur.

"To the city."

"Which city? The state has several," Eddie reminds Steven.

Steven's hands strain on the steering wheel. "All of them."

IV

ON THE WING

1

*H*alf an hour after dusk, frantic knocks reverberate through the apartment. Having settled in the tub mere moments ago, I wait with muttering impatience for Pablo to play butler. The rapping continues. I trudge to the front door. This had better be good or Andrew is going to rip some limbs from torso.

THUD ... THUD ... RAP ... RAP!!! Jeeze!

"All right! You'll wake the dead!" Where the hell is Pablo? Surely he hasn't flown off to a VA meeting so early.

I fumble with the crossbar. The knocking ceases. I hesitate. Who would be anxious to see Andrew and Pablo? Jay Bauer and Christian Fellows would adore spending quality time with me. Steven-Old-Boy would equally enjoy Andrew's company. I slip the crossbar back into place. I think I'll play dead.

"Pablo?" The din resumes, more urgent. "Pablo!"

I sort through the memory cells for the owner of that filtered voice and find a match for that average tone.

"Just a minute, Colin," I say, again lifting the crossbar. After fumbling with the chains and locks, I swing the door open.

Leaping inside, Colin thrusts me back and slams the door. He resets all the locks and replaces the crossbar. He whirls around, slumps against the door, and stares at me through a veil of mousey blond hair. "Hi," he gasps with feigned insouciance.

"And a pleasant good evening to you," I reply. "Please, do come in. Have a seat. Can I offer you something to ... drink?"

"Is Pablo home?" he asks, his calm veneer deteriorating.

"Pablo seems to be out."

"All hell's breaking loose," Colin stammers. "You know a Lance Broderick, don't you? Don't deny it. Helmut saw you dancing with him a couple of nights ago."

"Helmut sees a great deal with those squinty eyes."

"Lance Broderick was *captured* last night," Colin says. He sinks onto the sofa. "He's so much dust."

Wait-stop-hold-please. Captured? So much dust? Golly...

I join Colin on the sofa. "Let's go at this one incident at a time. Who captured Lance—"

"Humans!" Colin wrings his average little hands. "Maxwell is right. The humans know now. We don't stand a chance if we—

"Humans don't clip my wings!" I avow. "How did they catch him? Where?"

"Policemen overpowered him in an alley."

"Let's have details, Colin," I press. How on earth did the police know about Lance and how to destroy him? I think I smell a bonkers bartender. "You must know some details to come soaring in here in such a snit. Give me the whole story."

"All I know is what Helmut told me."

Such a bloodbath of information Helmut is.

"Spill it, Colin."

All the gory details spurt forth as if Lance lay on the coffee table with the stake freshly pounded. Colin certainly evokes some ghastly images. Perhaps the intricate details come *via* Helmut. I can see him programming the scene into his Aryan brain cells as clearly as I can see the horror Colin describes.

In a shadow-strewn alley of the Intriguing Faction Borough, a squad of police came upon Lance Broderick and his mark, a Japanese number with a body a samurai would commit *seppuku* for. The two were tight in the clinch, Lance probing the amber-hued throat with his teeth. Billy clubs pelted the pair until the mark was senseless and Lance, bruised and streaked with blood, was cornered. Still he struggled, spitting curses and clawing.

Imprisoned by crucifixes, he was overpowered. The policemen pinioned Lance in the filth and drove a billy club into his chest — through his heart. The Japanese's blood, so freshly consumed, sprayed the white corpse. Corruption devoured flesh and bones.

Colin's precise narrative complete, I slump back on the sofa and stare at the shadowed ceiling.

Lancelot, your dust scattered on a cool even breeze, may you sleep the eternal quiet.

O

Leaving the unnerved Colin with a bottle of red wine, I retreat to my bath. Where better to think than lost in the hot steam? First, my thoughts leap to Kane Davies. What reaction has Lance's destruction wrought? Will vampiric rage consume the Intriguing Faction Borough and destroy each and every policeman?

Second, surprisingly, I consider how the implications of Lance's destruction — that the police know enough about us to track us down and destroy us — affect me. My marks usually pick up their tickets for oblivion in some deserted alley. I could as easily end up with a billy club in my chest. In the future, more caution is advised in the selection of picnic grounds.

Shamefully last, I think of Pablo. For the thousandth time, where is he? For all I know ... No, Andrew doesn't want to even consider that. He's safe, probably at the desecrated church, lamenting the loss of our secret society's secret with that hysterical contingent of the undead, Vampires Anonymous.

In spite of earlier resolves — and pure common sense — I decide to dig up Kane and his cronies. I won't rest easy until I talk to Kane about this tragedy.

I climb out of the tub. Bathsheet as shroud, I shuffle into the bedroom to rummage through the closet. My eyes drag back and forth across the flash and color on my side of the closet to the blacks and grays on Pablo's side. My hands snag a black shirt, charcoal slacks, and a commonly cut jacket. My bod slips into them. Clothes as shroud, I waddle into the living room.

Stretched on the sofa, Colin gives me a wide-eyed gander. I point a threatening finger to stifle any comment that might take form in his average brain.

In the kitchen the back door screeches open and shut. Pablo emerges from the dark. His eating habits have improved; there's not a drop of blood on his clothes.

"I wondered where you were." Andrew plays nonchalant. "Our color's rather high tonight, isn't it?"

If he weren't so stuffed with blood, I'm certain Pablo would blanch, but he hangs his head contritely.

"Pablo!" Colin exclaims, standing. "Of all nights to slip! Don't you know what's going on in this city?"

Hands clenched, Pablo retreats toward the bedroom. I track him, catch him at the doorway, and apologize. He refuses to look at me. I make him turn toward me and cuff him under the chin; he bares his teeth, flashes me a scarlet glare.

I nod toward Colin. "Don't listen to him." I venture a hand into the strands of his hair. "I don't care. I'm sorry I teased you."

"I care," he breathes. "Can I be alone now?"

"You're alone too much."

"Then I'll go to a meeting."

"Yes, you can be alone now."

He slips into the bedroom. The door closes; the key clicks.

At least he's safe, Andrew. Still, I worry about the boy. To be so distressed about something so naturally part of our existence cannot be good for his mental state. Would an evangelist worry about spewing hellfire and brimstone at a gathering of mindless puddy-dawgs? All right, the analogy sucks in connection with Pablo, but if he keeps this up, the child is going to be sick of heart and mind.

"You're just going to let him pout?" Colin asks.

"A pouty Pablo cannot be reasoned with," I inform him. "Don't try to go in and talk to him. He might tear something off you'd rather not lose."

"I seriously doubt that."

"He's not your beau. Trust me. I know the boy well." I gather a few belongings — keys, switchblade, the usual stuff everyone needs to get through the night — and head for the door.

"Where are you going?" Colin asks. "Are you just going to leave me here by myself?" He flips a hand at the door. "Will he ever come out? What about Lance? What are we going to do?"

Jeeze! Questions, questions...

"Work. Yes. No. Tragedy. Don't know."

I leave him to sort it out on his own.

○

The eternity of my rags-store shift knows no bounds tonight. My sole consolation is that Kane Davies — from the one time I've had the chance to observe — arrives late at the Club. At last, the store manager, a Korean woman fond of blue-and-orange plaid, frees the night slaves.

I hurry toward the alley for a quick transmute. From behind me, I hear my manager lock up. I watch until she hurries off in the other direction.

The alley quivers with shadows blacker than my shirt. I falter at the entrance. That hollow cry and laughter from last night haunts me afresh. What if the Demon Toddler lurks here?

A second later, that cry sounds. Cold dread enwraps me. There's a moment of silence, followed by a scream — with a Korean accent ... laughter...

This neighborhood is not fit for man or vampire. I take wing, not the least bit interested in — and too peepin' scared of — whatever stalks Korean women in blue-and-orange plaid.

O

I haven't traveled far when the flutter of wings closes in from behind me. I spin and hover. Another bat wings an unusually straight — pardon the expression — line after me. I veer south and loop it quick to the west. I glance over my wing. My pursuer copies my maneuver. Obviously, he went to the Harvard Flight School for Gents with Four-foot Wingspans.

Oddly enough, I allow myself to be overtaken. Some company might do me good, provided it's the right company. Since he makes no aggressive moves, I consider myself safe.

I sniff my new companion as we soar wing-to-wing over the city. I detect a familiar scent which has recently intrigued me. I scan the lithe lines of the torso, the graceful curve of his wing, the neat tuck of claws beneath his tail. Andrew must be losing his touch. I'm on the wing with Kane Davies.

With a short yet highly dignified squeak, Kane changes our course. We fly north, leaving the city lights behind. The air clears of smog, and I sip the cool night. Beside me, Kane, eyes shut, drifts with the currents. Above, the scattered stars hang bright. Below, the hills roll downward to long, flat stretches of beach. Kane's wingtip brushes mine, and he leads me down toward the sand.

Scarce inches above the beach, the bat-Kane spins, a tornado of black which is soon streaked with white. The man-Kane stands on the beach, his long coat settling around his body. I circle once, then somersault from the sky. Transmutating in mid-flip, I land on my feet in front of him. He offers his quiet smile.

"I knew you would be looking for me," Kane says, those dark eyes fixed on me.

"I didn't think I had a chance of finding you."

Where to begin? How to broach the subject of Lance Broderick's demise? "I heard the news," I say.

Kane looks across the swells of the evening tide. "Lance will be greatly missed. We knew each other a long time, too long a time to be limited by a number." He turns back to me. "He was my first," he says simply. "He was special. In the end he was careless. That makes the grief no less a burden."

The usual sympathetic amenities would be wasted on Kane Davies. I nod, follow his gaze over the water.

Then a thought strikes me, something that has bothered me since Colin brought the news of Lance's demise, something I had mindlessly overlooked.

"What if Lance wasn't careless?"

The misery that wells in Kane's eyes is not meant to be shared. I want to look away; he holds me with his pain.

"Could one of our own kind wish to see a brother murdered?"

"I was thinking of a more human culprit," I reply.

"Andrew, look beyond your own sphere. Your bartender's arm is not so long," Kane says. "He and the policeman haven't reached the city."

"How do you know about Steven-Old-Boy and Eddie—"

"The boy-in-cop's-clothing?"

Reflections of the surf quiver over Kane's profile. The quiet smile shows itself, then recedes to seclusion.

"How much do you know about me?" I ask. Three nights ago he unnerved me with his assessments. Tonight I feel apprehension. Some things about Andrew should not become tabloid headlines.

"We know a great deal," he says, "about college towns and hills above the bay. We knew about Brett."

"Brett?" I clearly remember his compelling face and marble body of a demon — Brett, dead these seven years.

"We had thought that Brett might make an interesting addition to our society," Kane continues. "In the end, however, I agreed with your assessment. Such cruelty does not deserve the gift of the night."

I held that opinion at the time. I carved Brett up real fine just to make the point.

Kane digs his hands into the pockets of his long coat, draws it close around him. "You died in your bathtub — you were always fond of long soaks."

"You even know how I died?" Andrew is spooked. What are Kane and his gang of cadavers — Peeping Bats?

Kane steps toward me; I resist the urge to step back. "Our network stretches around the world in city and town large and small. We know when one of our own perishes. We know when an initiate rises. We watch each one's progress..."

"Then why didn't one of your buddies help me out those first months?" I demand. "If your network is so omnipotent, why let me botch my first mark so badly that seventy-five percent of the goods went down the drain?"

"You did what we hoped for — survived by your own innovative techniques." Again he smiles, but with a full humor I doubted Kane possessed. "Do you know what John Studnidka does with his marks to prevent their resurrection?"

"With John, I hesitate to hazard a theory."

"That pile of wood beside his house isn't kindling," Kane says. "He stakes every one, then buries them." From complete smile to bemused laughter. "Some day the humans will find his stash. Their horror will be unmatched."

"When they find all those marks, our people will look as bad as all the humans want us to be," I retort.

Kane's laughter rolls with the surf. "You amaze me, Andrew. You are a walking, talking paradox." Seeing my ill humor, Kane controls his laughter. It fades as it came, from bright smile to quiet grin to solemnity. "You are a fascinating study, if that consoles you. Your foibles intrigue — even delight me." The eyes slide toward me. "Such as referring to yourself in third person whenever a thought seems too close to your true self."

"My true self? Who might he be?" I inquire, merely out of politeness. "The walking, talking paradox?"

"That isn't for me to say." He strolls away along the line of the surf.

It isn't for him to say? Indeed. Well, I'm certainly not going to volunteer the information.

I swallow the retort. Tonight hardly seems the time to expose Kane to Andrew Wrath. I fall into step beside him. I feel that he is processing information. I show patience, even though I'm curious about the direction of his thoughts.

At length he pauses. Profiled against the bluffs, he stares at the vast ocean. His face offers no revelations. He sighs, a weary-to-the-core sound that the surf echoes.

"Lance betrayed to the humans," Kane whispers. "I had expected ... But this ... I never imagined..."

"You know—"

"I can speculate." He rests his hands on my shoulders. "I am glad I sought you out, Andrew. You've opened a perspective my grief had concealed. Thank you." He draws his coat around him.

"Wait!" I clutch at his arm to prevent his transmutation. "I want to know who you think destroyed Lance. I want to help—"

"In time," he says. "Go home to Pablo. Help him. Protect him. When I am ready, I will send for you."

In a smooth, micro-second transmutation, his arm vanishes from beneath my hand; his bat form swoops out over the waves, wheels about, then soars toward the city.

Something within urges me to follow, to not let him go so easily. Then, his words taunting me, I desire solely to return to Pablo. I swirl my coat around me and wing home.

Go home to Pablo. Help him. Protect him.

2

I stretch the key toward the lock of our apartment and pause. From within sound many voices. I wasn't informed of any social gathering. When I left, Pablo was pouting in the bedroom. He didn't seem in any mood to toss a party.

I reach for the doorknob; the door is jerked open. John Studnicka greets me with his warped grin. Terrific, it's the chortling corpses' consortium convention. Pocketing my keys, I turn back to the hall. The atrophied brain can't cope.

"Stay and play, Andrew," John says, leaping after me. His arms encircle me from behind; he lifts me off the floor. My feet, taken unawares, keep walking. "You don't want to miss this shindig. *Everyone* of stature is here."

"I don't find that very thrilling." My feet dangle above the floor. "Please set me back upon the ground. Thank you."

Linking his arm in mine, John leads me a few feet down the hall. "Some of VA's top men are in there." He grabs my face and forces me to look at him. "I'm not talking that kind of topmen. Some of Maxwell's elite grace your humble abode."

"Now I am so excited I need to change my slacks."

"Gawd, you can be so dense or stubborn or just plain *airheaded* sometimes I could tear your throat out," he says. He traces the curve of my neck. "But I won't — not viciously. Let me see your arm." He pushes up my sleeve to check the fullness of my veins. "You haven't been out sipping from the night." He pulls the sleeve down. "They won't need to lecture you."

"Not in my own home they won't. I'll shred their—"

"A lovely thought, but it's hardly endearing."

I ask that grinning face: "Is death just a party to you? Do you know or care what's happened to Lance?"

"Don't let appearances deceive you, Andrew." He guides me back to the apartment. "We'd better go in. We don't want anyone to think we have our own private conspiracy, do we?"

We're through the door before I can reply that I think we *do* have our own private conspiracy right here in slum city.

Scattered around the living room are a goodly dozen Vampires Anonymous members — so ghastly pale, these boys. Pablo and Helmut stand beside a squat number with past-the-shoulders wavy red hair whom I take to be a member of Maxwell's elite. He has that well-fed-but-I've-been-there-and-will-save-you look about him. Colin loiters near the television.

One by one they turn at our entrance. Fire lights Helmut's eyes as he recognizes me; his sidekick, apparently trained to react instantly to his moods, assumes a threatening stance. The duo advances, Pablo trails behind; the others part as if Her Maj the Queen were coming through.

"Be casual," John whispers in my ear.

One is casual with relatives — well, with an effort — one is casual with friends; one can even be casual with new acquaintances. Andrew, however, thinks it unlikely that he can be casual with these primordial purveyors of silly dictates. Still, for appearances' sake, I'll try.

Helmut greets me, "Andrew. I remember."

How bloody clever you are. "How gracious of you, Helmut."

"May I present my associate, Louis."

I always wanted to meet a red-haired iguana. "I am delighted."

"We are glad that you have returned," Helmut says, his German accent scented with sweet manure. He throws a brotherly arm around Pablo. "We are worried about Pablo."

"He wants so hard to follow the ways of VA," Louis adds.

"Yet temptation plagues him heavily," Helmut concludes.

"I've been concerned about him myself." Your idiot ideas are making a headless carcass out of him.

"Then we are all working toward the same goal," Helmut states, "Pablo's peace of mind."

With hope and admiration, Pablo watches this glacier-eyed Nazi youth leader. Does the boy truly think a blood-fast will cure anything or make the guilt vanish? By that expression on his drawn face, he does.

"And toward that goal," Helmut says, "we think that you should adopt the oaths of VA — for your own redemption."

Oh, the temptation...

"My nights are rather booked..."

Helmut advances, Louis at his heels. I scan the other boys, all staring at me with savage eyes sunk in cadaverous faces.

I edge back a half-step and press against John Studnidka. Andrew doesn't have another friend in this room. The time may have arrived when I'll swear to just about anything merely to get out of this situation as a whole hunk of dead meat.

"I'll check my calendar and see what I can do."

O

Another sunset and another blade slices at Andrew's Relationship with Pablo. How many more can it take?

"You promised you would go!" Pablo fumes. He storms around the living room; everything that isn't staked down rattles in his wake. "I should have known not to trust you." He jerks around, the blue peepers scarlet with accusation. "Who in their right mind would trust Andrew Lyall!"

Baleful rejoinders whirlpool through my brain; I stop them from flooding out of my mouth. I plaster on my most contrite face. Pablo won't be fooled, but with all this screaming I can't think to defend myself without offending him further.

"Does the word 'calm' hold any meaning to you right now?"

I don't think that statement will secure the mask I've donned.

"Does the word 'integrity' hold any for you?" he shoots back. "I could tear out your liver for lying to me!"

"My liver is probably mush—"

"Shut up! I've heard the last smart-ass, heartless comment from you I'm going to hear!" He stalks toward the door, turns back with his usual dramatic flourish.

Excuse me, I take that back; I'm a schmuck, a cad, a slime,

a soulless dead bloke for saying it. The boy's crying.

"I thought you loved me." Pablo's words crackle. "I thought we were special, heart and mind, the whole bit. You'd rather run off with Stud-what's-his-dick." He opens the door.

Is he walking out on me? I cannot believe that VA is the blade that will slash the Relationship to shreds.

"Don't ... Don't let it go, Pablo..."

"Come with me."

"And be a liar?"

He glares from hell. "You *are* a liar."

He swings open the door. A blur, he walks out.

Believe it, Andrew.

"Pablo ... Don't let it go..."

3

Who can move? Not Andrew.

Stunned. Shocked.

Amazed. Aghast.

Surprised?

Not really.

Andrew doesn't know about emotion beyond the simple words.

I knew the boy was unhappy, upset, discontent, distraught. But I never thought he would walk. I don't consider my charms irresistible enough to tie him to me for all eternity. I thought he would understand and stick it out.

I guess Andrew was pretty blind.

He also refers to himself in third person when he doesn't want to face the truth about himself.

The building rattles with sudden thunder. Lightning streaks above the city, highlighting the ragged skyline. Another thunderclap; rain pelts from the undulating clouds.

Hasn't this turned out to be a lovely evening? Andrew thinks it a good night for suicide. A walk in the rain is the same principle as running water: Let the raindrops drip on your head and watch your skin melt away. It's universal.

Pablo's out there, the raindrops drilling little holes in his head, thinning his hair some more, heightening his pockmarks.

Why think about it? I snatch my coat out of the closet, nab an umbrella, and head for the door. How far could he have gone — provided he travels on foot? I'll just bypass that factor and say he couldn't have gone too far.

On the front stoop, I flip open the umbrella before I am pelted and my fine smooth skin blemished. Where are my gloves? The wind is blowing from every direction, tossing rain hither and thither. I don't want my hands getting scarred.

Rain rat-a-tat-tatting on the umbrella, I walk to the alley. Perhaps Pablo has secluded himself among the trash bins.

"Pablo!" Whoa! This alley has great reverb.

Two blocks away, squeezed between the receding line of buildings, looms the tower of the desecrated church.

Shoulders slumping, I huddle against an onslaught of rain. Need I guess where Pablo has gone to find comfort? Colin and Helmut and all those deadbeat bats with recessive jeans — genes, my mistake — probably know more about emotion than merely the words. Or they pretend that they do better than Andrew can.

Jeeze, Andrew, let's have a little self-pity *soirée*. Straighten those shoulders, boy. Show some intestinal fortitude. When did you transmute into a flying milksop?

Gripping the handle of my brellie, I march into the alley. In moments, my walk has surpassed most humans' top run. I focus on the spire of the desecrated church. No empty-veined bozos are going to stand between Pablo and me — I stand between us enough.

This big mother of a door may stand in the way, however.

In the alley beside the church, I twist and turn the handle to find the door secured against pedestrian entrance. I could slip through any little crag in the wall — quick mist, quick entry.

These folks aren't thrilled with me as it is. Violating their sanctuary with a surprise visit might prove foolhardy.

I knock. Within, the sound echoes ... echoes ... I knock again, more forcefully. If Pablo didn't come here, where did he go? He may have winged over to Colin's, but I have no address for him. Right now, the unhallowed halls of Vampires Anonymous offer my only hope of tracking the boy down.

Surely someone is home. I consult my watch; meeting time is a bare hour away. Someone must be setting up, putting out the packets of plasma for snack time, that sort of thing. I lift my fist again, draw it back for the big pound.

Inside, chains rattle, bolts snap back; the door opens.

What's this? I thought this was a stag organization. I'm not sexist, but I didn't expect to find a woman here, especially one like the one glaring at me. Tall babe with long, wild, streaked blonde hair, she exudes mysterious hetero-female sexuality — the kind that always leaves Andrew grateful that he is resolute about who he is. From her slanted black eyes to the breast-revealing, draped chiffon blouse cinched at the waist of her tapered, calf-length skirt to the spiked heels of her boots, she is woman.

"Meetings begin at midnight," she says without greeting. "The doors are not opened — visitors not welcomed — until one half hour before." She gives the heavy door a light push.

"Wait!" My palm slaps against the weathered wood, halting her retreat. For a moment, we struggle, each pushing against the other's strength. For such a slender thing, she's pretty butch. "I'm looking for a friend of mine. I thought he might have come early to get some advice from the head man."

"Mr. Guthridge does not hold private sessions," she states. "Perhaps your friend's manners prevent him from arriving before the appointed hour and being a nuisance."

Perhaps I should tear off your breasts and give your shoulders some silicone-pumped padding.

"Could I speak to Mr. Guthridge?" I inquire, greasing my tone with polite condescension. "Maybe he has seen my friend and you just weren't informed."

"Highly unlikely."

"Helmut and Pablo are pretty chummy. Do you have objections to me speaking to Helmut? Or are you his watchdog, too?"

Ooo, how the blouse bristles. Flash those eyes, baby; Andrew is quivering in his Italian loafers.

"Your name?" Her voice, already resonant, has dropped even lower, her anger embellishing it with uncontrollable vibrato.

"Andrew. No last names. We're anonymous here."

The door thuds shut. I cock an ear, listen to her snappy, retreating footsteps. Then echoes rebound and resound to mishmash. I wonder if she'll fetch Helmut or leave me standing out here in the rain until I'm soaked history.

The door swings open. Andrew is taken aback. Maxwell towers before me. He must have misted down the hall; I heard no one return.

"Andrew," Maxwell greets me, extending a large hand. "Come in out of the rain. It's very bad for your health."

I cross the threshold, but not far enough for him to shut the door. A welcoming committee waits in the shadows, and Andrew likes his exits clear. The blouse glowers from Maxwell's elbow. Helmut and Louis loiter down the hall, pretending they're not threatening to my death and limb.

"Anneliiese tells me you've lost..." Maxwell hesitates.

"Pablo — blue peepers," Helmut says pointedly — sort of like the top of his Aryan head.

"Yes. Pablo." Maxwell draws out the name as if to stroke it. "And Helmut thought that your differences about VA had been resolved. You still refuse to give us a chance. Pablo has run off. A pity, Andrew. We could teach you so much. In our world, there exists a wealth of opportunity that you ignore. Pablo has seen that. Wants to share it with you. Can you blame him for becoming frustrated with your stubbornness?"

"I just want to find Pablo," I reply. Lectures I can survive without. Too many people have been telling Andrew what to think lately. They've tromped on his last dead nerve. "If he hasn't been here, perhaps you can tell me where Colin—"

"Colin — so ordinary." Maxwell looks earthward as if to contemplate Colin's problem. "Yet so warm and sincere. Not the type I would expect you to court. No. Neither is Pablo."

"Pablo is just my type, thank you." I step backward. I'm getting the oogly-booglies in this place, with these corpses. I especially don't like the way Anneliiese's slanty eyes keep focusing on my crotch. "I'll be off now."

"No need to fly." Maxwell moves toward me. Vestiges of the beast I saw in his face two nights ago linger under his thin skin. My brain tingles with a preamble to his mesmerizing tricks. "We can learn much from you. As you can from us."

"Perhaps another night." I flip open the umbrella to block that bewitching stare and retreat into the rain.

I hurry to the street, beat a path away from the church. I need to talk to Pablo about these bats he's hanging out with. Danger lurks in Maxwell's cold eyes. I have to convince Pablo that Maxwell Guthridge, founder of Vampires Anonymous, and Anneliiese, his right-hand blouse, are not our kind of corpses.

But where can the boy be? He's so adept at losing himself that finding him could take until well past dawn. What do I do if I never find him, if he's run off for good? Andrew rejects that question as too horrific to contemplate.

"Pablo..."

Feeling more sorry for myself than at any other time in the past frantic week, I wander off into the storm-thrashed night.

O

Once upon a time, in a quaint college town, Andrew the Vampire found himself a tall black-haired boy with crystal blue peepers.

Death picked up after that. So the black-haired boy had habits that irritated Andrew immensely. Andrew soon learned to exist with them. He and his Pablo got along famously.

Then, the persistent, deranged bartender Steven-Old-Boy returned from his exile in the land of Lunatic Asylum. Andrew and his Pablo's happy little sphere of pretty college-boy marks came to an end upon a cliff darkly. Andrew and Pablo were forced to flee. Steven-Old-Boy, aided by the deluded Eddie, Boy-in-Cop's-Clothing, hounded them the length of the land.

And in the end, driven by despair, Pablo deserted the vampire Andrew, and, in a way, Steven-Old-Boy was victorious.

O

How convenient it would be to delegate the blame that easily.

Steven-Old-Boy gibbers like the perfect scapegoat — Eddie to a lesser degree. If Steven-Old-Boy weren't tracking us, Pablo probably wouldn't have become disillusioned with our existence. We'd still be two happy bats on the wing, scouting the night for our next meal out.

Convenient? Oh yes.

Then there's Vampires Anonymous. Would Pablo and I have had our spat this evening if he had not been coerced into the vile workings of that organization? Let's extend the blame to Maxwell of the not-so-good face and the blouse, Anneliiese.

Unfortunately, Andrew must hold out his own smooth hands and balance acid blame until it eats through to the bones.

When I first came to this existence — Lordie, eight years ago it was — I struggled a great deal with that nasty emotion guilt, renamed the dilemma. To kill or not to kill; to bring into the night or cut off the head taunted me every time I saw a specimen of humanity that set the veins a-poppin'.

I did learn a few tricks of the trade. The prettiest mark was not always the best mark. Too often I juggled saving beauty from time's cruelty with fear of responsibility and — shudder — commitment. I moved on to boys with zero personalities.

Not even I would allow one of those blokes to rise brain-dead.

Finally, I learned that I could savor the beauties, then let my customized switchblade handle the resurrection issue. How many headless vampires have you seen? In the end, the dilemma became less the emotion of guilt and more an exercise of control.

By the time I met Pablo that control had expanded until it imprisoned other sentiments. Only the impetuous passion deserved release. Death was easier when ruled by "Oh, he's pretty, but I bet he never makes his coffin," or "Isn't he just the nicest thing, but his looks are more than a tad exhausted."

Pablo turned out to be the exception to all rules. So, Pablo is scrawny. So his hair is thin and wiry at the temples. Those blue peepers snagged something inside Andrew and brought it to the surface. Even now the word sticks, but I think Andrew is really in love with his Pablo.

And I let the entire Relationship slide down the Tunnel of Hell. We've been together two years, and already familiarity has given way to indifference. On the outside, anyway — the inside Andrew is generally no one's business but his.

Oh yes, it's quite convenient that Andrew has only himself to blame for the disintegration of his Relationship with Pablo.

Now that you've turned your critical eye upon yourself for a change, I inquire, can you discover a solution for this mess?

Hollow promises that I will turn the world on its ear with proclamations of loyalty and fidelity to the end of time won't cut it. I know — and Pablo will know — that you can't teach an old bat new tricks. I have only so much I can release from the inside at a time. Two years ago, I presented my noblest favor: I brought Pablo into the night to be at my side. Beyond that, Andrew's capabilities founder.

O

The rain shifts. Cowering under my umbrella, I smash my face against a window to avoid a splashing. My gaze leaps across cobweb-draped clothes that could send this country back twenty years. My wanderings have taken me to work. I was here once tonight; I'm in no mood to do another shift.

All is dark and deserted within. Everyone fled early. News of our manager's death haunted the store this evening. Rumors flew around the shop that Our Korean Lady of the Blue-and-Orange Plaid was found in a truly shredded state.

Splashing like the rain, the Preschool Death Master's whimpers echo brokenly. They are not far away; I can almost discern the location. I timidly glance toward the alley.

A tall man hesitates near the alley entrance. His posture indicates that he too has heard the Toddler Terror's lure to mayhem. One step after another, the man snags at the bait.

"Yo! Bud! Wait!" The words pop out of my mouth. The man proceeds toward doom and mutilation. My feet fling me up the street. Who would have thought Andrew would take to rescuing humans? "Don't go in there! It'll kill you." That sounds pretty lame, especially when punctuated by that baby wail.

Half in shadow, the man peers into the alley. "It's a child—" He turns to me.

Lordie! Did I need to see this face — as pretty as it is, even with the gray eyes widening in shock — tonight? What chance has brought this encounter? What deity of off-the-wall humor dogs Andrew's footsteps and drops Eddie Cramer, boy-in-cop's-clothing, into Andrew's path?

"Monster Child," I say, ever so nonplussed.

Beyond Eddie, skittering between the alley's shadows, I glimpse the Infant from Hell. Only a glimpse; the creature flees faster than even my eyes can move.

"Andrew!" Eddie's face beams with delight — for a moment. Something dreadful has transpired since last we met. He stumbles back, his face swelling with fear, until he traps himself against the building. He fumbles in his jacket pocket and brandishes a crucifix.

Eddie, I am shocked by your bad manners. "Put that silly thing away, or I'll leave you to the Prepubescent Butcher." I take two steps to verify the threat.

"Don't leave!" Eddie entreats me.

I peek over my shoulder to be certain that he pockets the crucifix. I face him and smile like an old friend. He manages a grin. I think the boy wants Andrew to hang out, and not solely to protect him from the Itty-Bitty Beast of the Alley.

Yet, what other beasts — more Eddie's size — lurk in the night with Andrew imprinted on the frontal lobe?

"Are you still traveling with Steven-Old-Boy?" I inquire. If I'm lucky, the gents in the white coats dragged him back to the asylum for a longer rest. Last I heard, they badly wanted him back.

"He's around," Eddie replies, uncomfortable with the association. He casts about the street. "He's not very stable. He's pretty far off the edge — violent — dangerous."

"I guess he's still the same Steven-Old-Boy." I wonder if this reunion with Eddie is coincidental. After a year in Steven-Old-Boy's company, Eddie might be just as far off the edge and violent and dangerous. "Are you on a solitary stroll?"

"Yeah." He toes the sidewalk. Something preys on the boy's mind. Something he wants to say, but doesn't quite have the nerve to spit out. I formulate a quick theory. The boy is infatuated — excessively infatuated — with Andrew.

What human would form an infatuation for a vampire? Humans like Brett of the compelling face who tracked me seven years ago hoping to acquire the abilities of darkness. Brett, a living flesh-and-blood demon, wanted to exploit those virtues in pursuit of the finer things — like tearing out hearts and consuming souls; Andrew ended his existence.

But Eddie seems a different tale. Eddie doesn't have ambitions to mayhem or nocturnal orgies of blood. Eddie simply has the hots.

I'm flattered, but I don't have time to cultivate Eddie's attraction. I do want to find Pablo. Maybe, like Eddie, I can't find the nerve to say what I want to, but I can't let the Relationship go without some effort to save it.

"I'd love to stay and chat," I tell Eddie, "but we'll both catch our destruction standing here in the rain."

Eddie pushes wet hair from his forehead. Rivulets stream down his temple; droplets drip from his nose. "You have to go?" Yes, he has the hots in a big way. "Will we meet again?"

"The city isn't that big." I take some backward steps. This meeting needs to end before Andrew's lascivious tendencies take over. "But when we do, leave Steven-Old-Boy at home. I haven't exactly missed him."

Eddie nods. "Guess I'll see you sometime then." He turns, shuffles through the puddles, then glances back. "Soon?"

"Probably." I'm kinda sorry to see him wander off.

Lingering at the alley entrance, I shiver. A noise scrapes close at hand. I peer into the alley. I can't see the Diminutive Slasher, but I know it's in there, watching, waiting.

I snarl into the alley's darkness. With a fleeting sound, the ogre retreats. I duck into the alley, then climb the nearest fire escape. Perhaps I should keep an eye on Eddie until he's safely out of harm's way. I leap from rooftop to rooftop, my hearing piqued to the sound of pursuit from the Mutilater Midget.

Too close to Andrew's neighborhood for comfort, Eddie turns into a ramshackle motel. Poor Eddie, hanging out with Steven-Old-Boy has taken him to lower depths of accommodations than running from Steven-Old-Boy has forced upon Andrew and Pablo.

The rain has finally stopped. Folding the umbrella, I drop into an alley across the street, take careful note of the room Eddie enters. Visions of Steven-Old-Boy as the wild-eyed lunatic prance through my head. Is he in there now? Is Eddie telling him about our meeting? Are they conspiring Eddie's next meeting with me, which they hope will culminate in Andrew's destruction? Or is Eddie the lure and Steven-Old-Boy sneaking up behind me, wooden stake ready for the plunge?

I realize that someone has crept up behind me, but not Steven-Old-Boy. These intruders have more of the grave than the crazy about them. I turn, Mr. Indifference, to face Jay Bauer and Christian Fellows.

"You are fortunate, Andrew," Jay says, strolling toward me, "that we were not the police that took poor Lance by surprise."

"You're lucky I didn't fly off the bat and rip your face off," I return. "To what do I owe the honor of this visitation?"

"We won't play games with you tonight, Andrew," Jay says.

"We won't play games," Christian echoes.

After an annoyed glance at Christian, Jay orders: "Stay away from Kane and out of our business, Lyall. We have things to accomplish. You'll only mess them up."

"Are you getting your hair re-coiffed?" I inquire. "That cap of curls really is *démodé*."

The full lips twist. "Your quips won't save you in the end. This is your last warning. Stay away from Kane."

"I'll see Kane if I please," I state. "Neither you nor your Christian prophet will stop me."

"Let's destroy him now!" Christian lunges.

Jay snags his coat and holds him back. "You will have your time, Christian." Why not just order the Hell Hound to "heel"?

Jay looks beyond me to the street. Sneering, he lifts his hand. "The friend you've been waiting for."

Across the street, Steven-Old-Boy skulks through the motel parking lot toward his and Eddie's room. He does have the air of a dangerous psycho-sister about him.

"Hardly a friend," I inform Jay. "He's more a nemesis — low grade variety. You can find one in any funny farm."

"We know about Steven Verruckt and snatched heads," Jay says, stepping closer. "We also know you allowed him to escape when you had the opportunity to kill him."

"Tell me something you know that I don't already know."

Jay smirks. "Several nights ago your *friend* and the cop with the tush destroyed an admirable colleague. Stanley would still be among us if you had done your duty. In the future, remember that your loyalty is to the vampire race and not prejudice-diseased humans. You don't want to get caught in the crossfire when the time comes to deal with Steven and Eddie."

"Any other sage advice before you leave?" I inquire.

"Watch your back," Christian growls.

"Ooo, you're so original, Christian."

"We will be," he retorts.

"You can look but don't touch."

Chuckling, Jay turns Christian away. They transmute and wing up between the dark buildings.

For a moment, I tap the slimy asphalt with the tip of my umbrella, then I stick out my tongue at their brutish backs.

4

The rain has returned with a vengeance — strobing lightning and nuclear thunder — by the time I return home. Happy to be here, I push the door shut, set the locks, secure the crossbar, and drop my dripping brellie into the brellie stand.

"Pablo?"

The living room lights are out; a single lamp burns in the bedroom. I didn't leave things this way. I prefer — in these times of travail — to return to an apartment blazing with light.

"Pablo?"

Maybe he's turned in early. I consult my watch. With an hour until dawn, there's time to chat. I will not sleep well with all these problems preying on my mind. I'll wake the boy up. We can at least hash out this Vampires Anonymous situation.

But first, the chill of a strawberry margarita might assist in loosening Andrew's tongue so the right words spill out. In the kitchen, I open the refrigerator and—

How many more surprises can Andrew take tonight? This one, however, owns a few more chuckles than some of the others. The refrigerator is stuffed with plastic packets of plasma. I examine one label. AB negative isn't my type — yuk, yuk.

I postpone the margaritas. This development demands that Andrew get right to the boy and to the point. Toting a bottle of red wine, I amble into the bedroom.

In the doorway I pause. A fragrance lingers on the air — sweet, a young vintage, but tantalizing. My nose leads me to the bathroom. I peek inside. Shining through me, the bedroom light details the scattered clothing on the bathroom floor. Splotches of blood shimmer to dazzle my eyes. Pablo had quite the feast — and didn't use a straw.

Swigging from the wine bottle, I walk to Pablo's coffin.

Knock. Knock.

"Yo! Pablo."

No response.

I knock again — forcefully, to stir the boy from his dreams.

"Yo! Pablo?"

He's in there. I can tell the difference between an empty echo and a Pablo-is-inside echo. One more knock, then it's lift the lid time.

"Come on, Pablo, open up."

Setting down the bottle, I lever my fingers under the edge of the lid. A quick breath and heave-ho!

Stench — blood, freshly spilled; rot.

I stagger back. Eyes water, blur everything.

But not enough. In a fraction of a scream, I saw. Too clearly.

Pablo. A stake driven through his chest. His head sliced off, lolling in the corner. Flesh decomposed. Pablo.

My heart implodes.

V

HEADS, YOU LOSE

1

Slumped in a lumpy chair, Eddie Cramer divides his attention between the snowy TV and the green ice chest. Eddie slugs back the dregs of his beer, crushes the can. If only crushing that padlock was as easy, then he would know why the ice chest reeks as badly as network television.

"I'm better off not knowing," Eddie whispers to the television. He has told himself that too often in these last months.

Plodding footsteps sound from outside. The doorknob rattles; the door is flung open. Carrying several plastic shopping bags, Steven stomps into the motel room. Tossing Eddie a strange look, he crosses to the ice chest.

Perhaps he will open it.

Steven sets his packages onto the ice chest. Pilfering a beer, he opens the can, spraying Eddie with foam, and chugalugs. Grimacing, he drops the can into Eddie's lap. "Beer's cheap."

"Christ!" Eddie exclaims as the beer foams over his crotch. He fumbles the can upright. His jeans are soaked through; the beer is gluing together his parts. "Why the hell do I put up with you?" Grabbing fresh clothes, he marches to the bathroom.

"To find Andrew." Steven grins.

I have found him, Eddie gloats to himself. He slams the bathroom door, flicks the lock. *And I'm not telling!*

Eddie strips off his shirt. He peels down his jeans: a process similar to flaying the skin off his legs. From abdomen to knees, his skin is varnished with beer. He steps into the shower stall. Sliding the bar of soap over his skin, Eddie wonders if life with Andrew would be as irritating as life with Steven.

He lifts his face into the hot spray of the water, scalding those thoughts out of his mind.

Andrew does not possess life, he tells himself for the thousandth time.

Dressed, Eddie emerges from the bathroom. Staring at the television, Steven lounges on his bed. The packages sit on the ice chest — but not exactly as before. Where there had been four shopping bags, there are now three.

Steven is watching; Eddie returns to his chair, opens another beer. What was in that shopping bag that Steven needed to maneuver him into the bathroom before he could stash it in the ice chest? The next time Steven makes a nocturnal journey, Eddie is going to get into that ice chest and ease his curiosity.

Eddie scans his companion. In the flickering light, Steven looks bad: hollow eyes, pasty skin, sunken cheeks. If Eddie had not seen him moving around in sunlight, he would swear that Steven has made the jump from human to—

No, not Steven. He is a maniac with a mission: Find the vampire Andrew Lyall, and any and all others on the way, and drive a wooden stake through all their hearts. After that—

After that? A memory of Stanley at the beach surfaces. Eddie hoped it only a sick dream; now he's not so certain.

After that, Steven chops off the vampire's head.

"What are you looking at?" Eddie demands, nerves frayed raw under Steven's stare. Living with Steven has taken its toll. Tonight, with that ghastly image of Steven and his hatchet in mind, Eddie doubts the association will last much longer.

"The usual thing," Steven says, getting off the bed. He tugs off his shirt. "It's funtime."

"I don't think so," Eddie returns, jumping to his feet.

Steven grabs for Eddie; his ragged fingernails scrape Eddie's chest. Eddie twists free, shoves Steven away.

Steven leers. "Come here."

"Blow off, Verruckt."

"That's the general idea."

Snatching up his jacket, Eddie retreats toward the door. "Verruckt — German, isn't it?" He twists the doorknob, steps outside. "It means *crazy*."

He jerks the door shut on Steven's smug expression. The night is frosty; Eddie shivers. He struggles into his police jacket. With a glare at the door with the lopsided number, he storms toward the street.

Eddie halts. "Tricked again, Eddie," he says, whirling back. As easily as he was tricked into leaving Steven to put away his package, he was tricked into leaving Steven alone with the ice chest. "We'll see who's smarter, the cop or the crazy."

After a single step, Eddie halts again. Footsteps clatter nearby, hesitate, then scramble closer. Hand slipping into his pocket — damn, no gun, no crucifix — he scans the parking lot, but he can't see another soul. The footsteps sound again — from the roof.

Backing away from the building, Eddie searches the motel's rooftop. Behind the sign, a figure crouches.

"Who's there?" Eddie calls. He reminds himself of a B-movie ingénue — one about to be splattered across the screen.

The figure scurries down the roof's incline. At the eaves, it hesitates, head cocked, body tensed. The figure leaps off the roof.

Eddie jumps back. The fearful reaction recedes. The stealthy figure is Andrew.

But not the Andrew Eddie saw last night, not the Andrew that dominates Eddie's fantasy realm. Poised against attack, this Andrew wears clothes stained with blood and soiled with earth. The swept-back hair hangs disheveled, oily. The face holds Eddie's attention. The pallid skin is drawn, plagued with twitches in the left cheek. The eyes are haggard, laced with veins. This Andrew has suffered the vile torments of hell.

This Andrew should be gotten off the street before the police haul him in for questioning.

"Andrew," Eddie says in a light tone. He approaches cautiously. This Andrew is jittery and best not taken by surprise. "What's happened? Can I help?"

Andrew turns guileful eyes on Eddie. "Yes. Where's Steven-Old-Boy?" The voice drones thin and ragged. "Is he here? Or out ... hunting?"

Eddie refuses to look toward his room, where Steven is ensconced for an evening with his ice chest. "He's out."

"Andrew doesn't believe you." He edges forward.

"Let me take you home?" Eddie suggests.

"Andrew doesn't want to go home," he returns. "Andrew wants to see Steven-Old-Boy." Andrew steps closer. His hand fidgets in his pocket. "All you have to do is ask me in, Eddie." His eyes flicker toward the door with the lopsided number. "Extend the invitation so I can go in and cut off the bastard's head."

Eddie backs away.

"Extend the invitation, Eddie." Andrew's hand flashes out of his pocket; his switchblade snaps open. "He destroyed Pablo. I want to cut off his head the way he hacked off Pablo's."

"It couldn't have been Steven," Eddie says. "When was Pablo destroyed?"

Andrew trembles; his hand coils knuckle-white around the switchblade. "Last night..." His gaze drifts; his features soften from rage to lacings of grief. "I found him at dawn..."

"It couldn't have—"

Andrew slices the air with the knife. "It was Steven-Old-Boy!" The words echo. "He cut off my boy's head! Only Steven-Old-Boy is that demented."

"He would have told me," Eddie says. With a vampire's speed, Andrew could have Eddie by the throat before Eddie could see him move. "He would have gloated, shared his victory."

"Victory!" Andrew snarls. He whirls toward the motel room. "Steven-Old-Boy! Come out and play! It's—"

Eddie clamps his hand over Andrew's mouth. Andrew shrugs him off; Eddie staggers backward several yards.

"Steven-Old-Boy!"

Lights come on behind several windows; Eddie thinks he sees Steven's shadow on the curtains of their room.

Eddie grabs Andrew's arm, flings him toward the street. Andrew stumbles, howls, lashes with the switchblade. Eddie dodges the blow, tackles Andrew from behind, and drags him out of the parking lot. Andrew struggles, knocking Eddie off balance. For every two feet Eddie gains, Andrew steals one back. But Andrew is weakening, perhaps from the exhaustion of fury or grief. Eddie hopes Andrew doesn't get a second wind.

They lurch into the street, crash to the asphalt. The switchblade skids out of reach. Eddie snatches at it. Andrew clubs him, knocking the wind out of him, and crawls over him. Picking up the knife, Andrew steps toward the motel once more.

"Steven-Old-Boy!"

"Jesus!" Eddie gasps, rolling onto his back. He catches Andrew's ankle. After a moment's struggle, Eddie jerks Andrew's leg from under him. The back of Andrew's head smacks the asphalt. Although dazed, Andrew clings to the switchblade.

His back searing, his breath tearing, Eddie clambers to his feet. He loops his arms under Andrew's and drags him across the street into the alley.

And Andrew gets his second wind. Springing to his feet, Andrew attacks; his knife slashes in an endless arc. Eddie reels away. He has saved Steven, however temporarily, but he will be so much sliced cop before Andrew is through.

Then the knife is gone. Andrew thrusts Eddie against a building. "If not Steven, then who?" His cold hands coiled around Eddie's face, he picks him up. Andrew's livid face — a twisted mask of murderous intent — hovers inches from Eddie's. Andrew's fangs extend themselves, poised and waiting to strike.

"Who..." Andrew mutters, his voice a breath caught in a whirlpool of breeze.

The hands release him. Eddie slides at least a foot down the building before his feet hit the ground. Andrew walks to the other side of the alley, stands there, his shoulders quivering.

"If not Steven-Old-Boy, then who? Who else would want to murder Pablo, Eddie?" Andrew looks at him. The rage is exhausted.

"Let me take you home," Eddie says, moving toward him. He reaches out his hand. "Please, Andrew."

"Pablo isn't there." Andrew wanders down the alley, away from the motel. "Pablo is under the ground."

Anguish squirms within Eddie, stinging his eyes, constricting his throat. He chokes a painful sound.

Andrew breaks into a trot; he transmutes. The huge bat veers toward a fire escape, then wings up between the buildings.

Eddie watches, alone, lost, without shelter or refuge. Trails of sorrow burn his cheeks.

Where can he go? He cannot cope with Steven after this. Hands shoved in pockets, he shuffles under the fire escape toward the universe of the next street and its possibilities.

"Eddie..."

Turning, he scans the alley: rubbish and dumpsters and pools of stagnant water. "Andrew?" Eddie calls.

Laughter rebounds off the buildings, tumbles down from — the fire escape. Two men stand upon the rusty iron frame. The nearest, a story above Eddie, has slicked-back blond hair. The other, balanced on the railing three flights up, has dark curls tousled over his forehead by the breeze.

"Don't any of you people make normal entrances?" Eddie demands. The bravado is forced. He betrays it. Sidling along the opposite building, he retreats toward the motel. He keeps his eyes trained on these two; they mean mischief.

"And waste our talents?" the curly-haired man returns. "Set your aspirations higher, Eddie." He grins. "But then, you have, haven't you? You require just a nudge to realize what you want."

"What I want is one night of peace and quiet," Eddie counters. He sloshes through a puddle; cold, slimy water seeps into his running shoes.

"What you want is eternal nights of peace and quiet." The man's tone is that of a schoolmaster correcting a shy student. "We have been watching, haven't we, Christian?"

"We have been watching," the blond man parrots.

"Such an emotional outing with our comrade Andrew," the man says. "What did we conclude, Christian, from that tender scene?"

"Eddie longs to stand at Andrew's side," Christian replies.

The curly-haired man strolls along the thin railing. "But as Andrew is — shy — we think two worthy matchmakers need to prod this union closer to consummation."

"Matchmakers." Christian grins lecherously, rubbing his hands together. "Just leave everything to us."

"I'll pass." Eddie runs toward the motel. His water-logged shoes seem to weigh a ton, slowing him to a brisk walk rather than a desperate dash. His lungs labor for air. Eddie doubts that he will reach the street — forget the motel.

Sound flutters around him; dark forms swirl through the alley. A monstrous bat hovers ahead of him, then transmutes. The curly-haired man waits with open arms.

Eddie skids to a halt. He glances over the shoulder. The blond advances, cracking the knuckles of each of his fingers.

Eddie's brain races, but there is no reference point for eluding two vampires in a dark alley. Both wait for Eddie to make the next move, flagrantly confident that whatever scheme he concocts, they will outmaneuver him.

On the ground, close to the curly-haired vampire sits a 32-ounce can. Will a projectile make a good a diversionary tactic? Anything is worth that old copper try.

Eddie leaps the last yard, scoops up the can. Inside, thick water sloshes. Still in stride, he swings the can up and around. The can, a putrid wake streaming behind it, thuds against the curly-haired man's chest. Drenched, he recoils against the wall.

Eddie races into the street. A horn blares. He barely dodges a speeding bus; the fender scrapes his hip. Reeling, Eddie topples, smacks his hand hard against the asphalt to keep his balance. Curses of gross mutilation and destruction roar after him. Eddie flees at full-out limp.

The beat of massive wings bears down on him. Claws scratch his scalp. Eddie careens into the parking lot. Ahead, the door with the lopsided number urges him on.

He'll be trapped, easy prey.

No. What did Andrew say? *Extend the invitation so I can go in ...* Could it be logical that without invitation these dive-bombing bloodthirsty bats cannot enter the motel room?

Eddie crashes against the door.

Let it be logical!

He wrenches the handle.

Chill fingers scrape down the back of his neck.

He flings open the door, stumbles inside.

The fingers retreat.

Slamming the door, Eddie slumps against it. Then, he gasps back a scream.

Steven sits on the floor, the treasures of the green ice chest lined up on the veneer coffee table. Fresh blood still glistens around the ragged throat of the first head — the shopping bag's mysterious contents. The next head is extremely withered, skin flaking, eyesockets shrunken. One is no more than a skull freckled with dried meat. Last is Stanley, the boyish face sallow, his lips shriveled back from monstrous fangs. Shaking a scolding finger, Steven converses with each in turn.

2

"Didn't Mother teach you to knock?" Steven inquires. Rising, he hefts a blood-rusted hatchet from the floor and cocks it at Eddie. "Perhaps will teach you a lesson you won't forget."

Eddie cowers against the door.

His grin lackluster, Steven approaches. He carves at the air as if he's drawing the pattern before cutting the material.

The door is struck from outside; Eddie is jolted forward into Steven's arms. Someone's mother taught him to knock.

Eddie, open up, the curly-haired man's voice coos through the door. *Let us* all *the way in.*

Eddie tears his gaze from the door. Steven's dull eyes hover inches from his. "We got company," Eddie manages. "I think they've been dead awhile."

Come on, Eddie. Three light taps. *Open wide.*

A spark ignites in Steven's eyes; pleasure twists his grin. Lodging the hatchet in the door frame, he shoves Eddie aside.

Eddie bangs the back of his leg against the coffee table. He spins around and faces the dead eyes of Steven's collection.

Tossing his duffel bag onto his bed, Steven sorts out two wooden stakes. He thrusts a stake, point first, toward Eddie.

Eddie falls back. "Can't we discuss this!"

"It's for them," Steven states, jerking his head toward the door.

Cautiously, Eddie takes the wooden stake from Steven.

"Get them," Steven whispers, "on my signal." He grins, winks. Wooden stake poised, Steven reaches for the door handle. His fingers caress it, close around it, and gently turn.

Eddie. Let's play. Don't be coy—

Steven jerks the door open. He stabs his weapon through empty air. "Fuck!" The parking lot is deserted.

Releasing a sigh of relief, Eddie drops his stake.

Eddie! We won't forget you. The curly-haired man's voice drifts through the open door. *We've promises to keep.*

"Come back!" Steven shouts into the night. "Fight!"

Traffic noises are the only response.

"Chicken shits." Steven shuts the door. He twists the key in the lock, secures the chain, then levers his hatchet out of the door frame. Hatchet in one hand, wooden stake in the other, he faces Eddie. The dull sheen has returned to his eyes.

"Maybe we'll get them the next time," Eddie croaks. Where did he leave his service revolver — suitcase? No, it's lost among the bedclothes. He takes a side step toward his bed.

"How did they know your name?" Steven asks. He returns to his bed, cutting across Eddie's path. He drops the stake and hatchet into the duffel bag. "How?"

"A lucky guess," Eddie suggests. Perhaps he should make a dash for the door and hope Steven isn't quick enough to drive that hatchet into his back.

"Know your name." Steven drops the duffel bag onto the floor. "That's very strange."

"Maybe they're friends of Stanley's," Eddie says.

Pensive, Steven turns to Stanley's head on the coffee table.

You never should have mentioned Stanley! Eddie scolds himself. Perhaps he can overpower Steven, then escape.

"Maybe that's it." One at a time, Steven picks up the heads and returns them to the ice chest. He skims a hand over Stanley's matted hair before he shuts the lid. "Maybe they followed us." He snaps shut the padlock, then stretches.

"I'm tired. Take shower. Go to bed." Walking into the bathroom, he pats Eddie's arm. "Get them tomorrow night. Get Andrew, too." The bathroom door shuts behind him.

As the sound of the shower fills the room, Eddie stares at the coffee table, its veneer slick with slime and blood, then at the deep wound in the door molding from Steven's hatchet.

"Next time, that will be your face," he tells himself. "The time has come to find new lodgings. Steven can grapple with vampires on his own."

He methodically circles the cramped room to gather his possessions. Suitcase packed, service revolver in his jacket pocket, and his crucifix in hand, he heads for the door.

The curly-haired man and his blond friend could be out there, waiting for just this moment.

Eddie studies the crucifix. How long could he hold those two off with a piece of silver? He spies the abandoned wooden stake on the floor. Scooping it up, he warily opens the door.

As before, the parking lot is deserted except for leaves dancing on a dirty wind.

"So long, Steven," Eddie mouths, stepping outside.

Yet, he hesitates, memorizing the details of the room, the ice chest, the duffel bag; listening to the rattle of the shower. He conjures a picture of Steven's face. The image brings forth a year's worth of escapades, good and bad, mostly insane. Eddie wonders if the chill in his stomach means he will miss Steven.

O

Eddie walks the illuminated side of the street. Staying within the light isn't easy when every fifth or sixth streetlamp is burnt out or broken. He watches his back. He can't decide if he's more worried about Steven catching up or an ambush by the two vampires. Eddie walks as fast as he can considering he is weighted down by a suitcase and a three-foot-long wooden stake.

Footsteps click close by. Eddie ducks into an empty lot and presses against a building. Breath held, he watches the street. The footsteps fade. Shutting his eyes, Eddie relaxes.

"Hello, young lover." The curly-haired man and Christian loiter amid the debris.

Droping his suitcase, Eddie brandishes the wooden stake and his crucifix. "Can't you guys give it a rest?" Eddie demands.

"We'll give you a rest," Christian says, grinning.

Eddie levels the stake at Christian. "I'll give you a long rest, deadhead."

The curly-haired man ambles forward. "You would never talk to Andrew — our kith and kin — that way."

"Andrew doesn't keep sneaking up on me with his teeth sharpened," Eddie returns. "I'm too exhausted for you guys." He grips the stake in both hands. "Beat it."

"Yeah, Jay, beat it."

Eddie tilts back his head. On the eaves of the building stands a third man. "Christ, not another one!"

"We saw him first, Studnidka," Christian whines.

"Andrew saw him before any of us," Studnidka replies. "You shouldn't mess with our young policeman before Kane has decided what to do with him, Jay."

"Perhaps John is right," Jay says, studying the new arrival. "This one isn't worth trouble with Kane."

"I knew you'd make the right choice." John steps off the roof, dropping between Eddie and the other two.

"Jay!" Christian protests.

"Forget it." Jay turns the blond toward the street. "Perhaps another time, Officer Cramer," Jay says in parting.

"Perhaps," Eddie replies, squaring his shoulders.

As the two men leave, Eddie snags his suitcase and edges toward the street. No matter how this newcomer came to his rescue, Eddie has had enough of the undead for one night.

"Not so fast, pretty boy," John says, turning toward him.

Eddie freezes, drops the suitcase, and swings up the wooden stake. "You stay there."

John laughs. "I wouldn't dream of approaching such a desperate, heavily armed man." He approaches, his eyes playful, his grin amused at Eddie's defensive tactics.

Eddie wonders if there are trustworthy vampires. This one did rescue him. He senses no more threat from the man than he feels when with Andrew. Hesitantly, he lowers his wooden stake.

"That's better," John says. He scans Eddie head to foot. "So you're the one who's been tailing Andrew up and down the coast. I'm surprised he didn't wait for you to catch up."

"We have a mutual friend who keeps us jumping," Eddie says.

"The deranged bartender will never get the better of our Andrew," John says. "In spite of what Jay thinks, Andrew will amount to something yet."

"Have you see Andrew tonight?" Eddie asks. Maybe he should mind his own business, but someone has to get Andrew off the streets. John Studnidka, with his obvious admiration for Andrew, seems perfect for the job.

"No." John's grin wavers. "Is something wrong?"

"Pablo's been destroyed," Eddie says. "Andrew's gone off the deep end."

"Hell's fire." John glances north, then back at Eddie. "When did you see Andrew? Where was he going? Hell's fire!"

"A while ago," Eddie replies. He studies the distress on John's face. "Are you all right?"

"No!" John snaps, wheeling toward Eddie. "None of us are going to be all right." He jabs a finger at Eddie's chest. "Including you, young policeman. We're all up shit's creek."

"What's that mean?" Eddie asks.

"I have to find Andrew." Leaping skyward, John transmutes to a monstrous bat and wings north.

"Wait!" Eddie shouts. "Christ! You drop in, then just fly off without a word! Christ!"

He stares after the bat for a mere second. Then, quickly hiding his suitcase, Eddie races north. A streak against the clouds, the bat speeds ahead, almost out of sight. Twisting and turning through the city's alleys and streets, Eddie pursues.

The universe is splitting apart. One chunk, his association with Steven, has already fallen off. But what chasm waits to devour Andrew and this John Studnidka, and perhaps Eddie as well? John's words were a warning. Whatever is happening will swallow Eddie and puke him out with the men who roam the night.

Eddie loses sight of the bat. He dodges around scattered pedestrians, gives wide berth to the street on which the motel is located, and skids to a halt across from a church. He scans the smoggy sky. Hope has almost deserted him when a dark shape veers past the church's spire and soars a parallel path to an alley.

Following the bat, Eddie dodges across the traffic of the next street and into another alley. At the far end, the bat circles above a twelve-story apartment building, then vanishes.

On a hunch, Eddie hurries around the building. In the lobby, Eddie stops before a bank of rusted mailboxes. He reads each plastic label. He's found Andrew's apartment. His finger traces the raised letters of "P. Saldana / A. Lyall — 12D." Eddie supposes that even the undead need to get their mail.

He walks to the staircase. He could climb to the top floor and knock on the door of 12D. And if Andrew or John answers the door? How long will a human survive in a vampire's lair?

Eddie backs away from the staircase. He can get through the night without that answer. Yet, he has to know that Andrew isn't out roaming the streets at the mercy of whoever destroyed Pablo.

Gripped by sudden dread, Eddie runs outside and leaps off the stoop. Whoever destroyed Pablo will indeed be after Andrew. Was that what John Studnidka's warning meant? Perhaps if Eddie gets too close to Andrew, even he, a human, could end up with a wooden stake driven between the ribs and his head chopped off.

Still, Eddie lingers in front of the building. Without seeing Andrew, or finding out that John is on top of things, Eddie can't make himself leave.

Eight years of police experience provide a solution to Eddie's problem. When the front door is not a viable entrance, the fire escape will suffice. Back in the alley, Eddie surveys the iron structure cutting back and forth up the side of the building. The access ladder hangs a floor above him.

Ingenuity is on his side. He pushes a dumpster across the alley, climbs on top. The ladder is still too high. Eddie leaps for the ladder. His fingers slip on the slick metal; he crashes back to the dumpster. Holding painful breath, he lies motionless in case the racket brings the neighbors. No one seems to care.

Another try, more calculated, less blind determination, succeeds. He catches the rung. Squealing against rust, the ladder slides down its tracks, and Eddie climbs on board.

Service revolver at ready, Eddie bolts up the fire escape, undeterred by voices behind the windows he passes or by staring faces that have finally been aroused from the lethargy encasing their bodies. No one gets in his way. His gun gives him rights.

On the twelveth floor, several windows blaze with light; the one leading onto the landing is dark. Crouching, Eddie peers at the window, then places his hand against the cool glass. The window is bricked up on the inside. Who else besides a vampire would choose bricks over bars to seal such an easy access to their home?

Eddie sits down, relaxes against the side of the building, and although dawn is hours away, he waits. Another police practice — the all-night stakeout — gives him stamina for the vigil. Yet, as dawn brightens the hazy sky, no sound comes from within the apartment; the lights in the other windows blaze on into morning. Reluctantly, Eddie admits defeat.

After retrieving his suitcase, surprisingly where he left it, he takes lodging in an old hotel down the block. Not bothering to unpack, Eddie stretches out on the bed to rest — like Andrew — until dusk.

3

In twilight, the neighborhood is ratty, exhausted, ready to be razed and rebuilt. Eddie doubts that a vampire could find a better hiding place. The citizens here won't pay much attention to a night bird. But Andrew would stand out in this crowd. Eddie has noticed that Andrew stands out in almost any crowd. He is perhaps too elegant, too perfectly assembled to be overlooked.

Eddie looks across the street at the twelve-story apartment building. The old Andrew was, at least. The Andrew Eddie met last night has fallen to ruin. Eddie wonders if the new Andrew will ever recover from Pablo's destruction.

Absently, Eddie follows the route of a man across the street. There's something familiar ... Ignoring the stares of other loiterers, Eddie ducks behind a lamppost.

He must be wrong. He cannot see whom he thinks he sees.

He peers around the post through the growing dark. No, he isn't wrong. Scurrying to a nearby stoop, Eddie takes shelter.

Across the street, duffel bag swinging from a shoulder, Steven Verruckt strolls past Andrew's apartment building. He doesn't give the place a second look, but he turns into the alley beside the building and melts into the darkness.

Eddie dashes across the street. He enters the alley cautiously. First, he glances up at the fire escape. He would not be surprised to see Steven creeping up the iron frame to the bricked window of Andrew's apartment. Then, Eddie looks toward the far street as Steven crosses into the next alley.

Full night is only minutes away. Andrew will be awake, emerging from this building. Eddie can't decide if he should wait or follow Steven. Eddie jogs through the alley. Even though he wants to be free of Steven, Eddie must find out why he is lurking in this neighborhood.

Two streets over, a mammoth, decaying church casts its long shadow over the liquor stores, pawn shops, and porn palaces. Human night creatures roam the street. Eddie works his way through the crowd, glancing into each shop. For the life of him, he cannot imagine what Steven would buy from Guido's, and he knows Steven has no interest in *Panting Pretties from Peoria.*

At the far corner from the church, Eddie falters in his search. Night has fallen completely; he has missed his chance to see Andrew, and he has lost Steven. What kind of cop is he to miss two easy-to-spot men within a two-block radius?

"Are we lost?" a woman's voice asks from behind him.

"No," Eddie replies, turning. He expected an overdone hooker. The only extravagance about the woman before him is her streaked hair. Her attire, from the diamond earrings to the calf-length black cloak to her high-heeled boots, says class.

"You look lost to me," the woman insists, circling Eddie. "Another soul lost in the city. I imagine you are here on your own. No friends. No family. Alone in the night."

"Not exactly," Eddie says. Her spiel sounds like a come-on for disappearance off the face of the earth. Eddie slips his hand into his jacket pocket with his service revolver. She doesn't look dangerous, but looks deceive. "I have friends."

"But they're not here," she says, stepping closer. Her heels click on the cement. Her hand rises to skim a strand of hair back from his temple. Her fingers are as cold as—

Eddie backsteps into a deserted side street. His hand clamps around his revolver. She is dead — she's a vampire.

Her smile cool, the woman says, "*Those* kind of friends."

Let her misinterpret his reaction — although her conclusion hits the mark. "That's hardly your affair," Eddie says.

"I can make it my affair." She advances; Eddie retreats. "Spend the evening with me. An evening you'll never forget."

Never means eternity. Her seduction lines are not that much different from Stanley's — *I'm an experience that will take you to heaven*. That translates as hell. But where Stanley would confine Eddie to one hell, this woman would put him through a completely different hell before draining his blood.

"I'll be on my way. I enjoyed chatting with you." Turning, he switches hands and pockets. His service revolver is useless against this woman; his crucifix won't be.

"Don't run off." She swiftly passes him to block his path.

Palming the crucifix, Eddie halts. "I have a life to lead."

"You don't want to lead that life."

"I find it rather enjoyable." He savors the abhorrence that clouds her features. "All those hard bodies and such are fun."

"I'll cure you," the woman states.

"No chance, hon." He edges off the curb, circles the woman.

"You need behavioral modification," the woman suggests, tracking. "I'm an expert."

"I like my behavior fine," Eddie returns. "Yours could use some fine tuning."

He spins and races away. Her clattering footsteps pursue him. She lunges onto his back; they tumble into the street. Eddie's crucifix bounces out of reach. The woman flips Eddie onto his back, straddles him. Her icy fingers snag the front of his shirt and rip it open.

"You should not be wasted on men," she breathes, her hands skimming his skin. "You should be savored only by women — a woman — me." She shrugs off her cloak, pulls open her blouse. She drives her jutting breasts toward Eddie's face.

"Jesus!" he cries. He turns his face away; her nipple impales his ear. Rising to her knees, she finds his belt, the buttons and zipper of his trousers. "Cut that out!" Eddie orders. He levers his hands under her arms and heaves her aside.

He jumps to his feet; his trousers fall around his ankles. Reaching for his pants, he points at himself. "Does this look like it's thrilled to see you? Go find some hormone-driven macho stud if you're so hot. Leave me alone!" He jerks up his zipper.

"I want *you*," she says. Breasts swaying with the folds of her blouse, she crawls toward him. The expression on her face has changed. Bloodlust has replaced the carnal.

Eddie searches the street for his crucifix. It glitters inches from his shoes. He snatches it up.

"And I'll have you — one way or another."

The woman convulses in the throes of some transformation. Framed by the wild hair, the face is caught between human and animal: the structure elongated, the eyes sunken and flaming, the mouth stretched and rimmed with saber fangs. On gnarled hands, the fingers tipped with claws, she advances toward Eddie.

What kind of beast, what deformity of vampirism is she?

He brandishes the crucifix.

Roaring, the creature tosses its head from side to side. The transmutation accelerates, distorting her torso and limbs.

"Jesus!" Terrified by each new alteration in the woman's face and figure, Eddie flees.

A howl from the grave echoes after him.

4

The world is full of vampires. Eddie would not have believed that fact a year ago; now he cannot deny it. His jacket zipped to hide his torn shirt, he strolls Andrew's street. Any one of these people slouching on these stoops or pissing in the gutter could be one of the undead. That derelict with his bottle secreted in a paper bag could be sipping vintage Betty Lou. That woman with her hair in curlers could be waiting for just the right Girl Scout to try palming off her cookies. That fat kid—

Eddie rubs his hands down his face. If he doesn't stop, he'll end up in an asylum — with Steven for a roommate.

The bright move would be to skip town. Three vampire attacks in two nights must be a record. If Eddie hangs around the city, chances are — considering his connections — he'll be attacked again. The next time, he might not escape.

And what about Andrew? he asks himself.

Andrew, even in his present state, can take care of himself. Besides, John Studnidka seems more than willing to do the job if Andrew can't. He should forget about Andrew and hit the road.

The twelve-story apartment building looms ahead. Can he forget about Andrew and hit the road that easily? Eddie draws in a slow breath. Has he abandoned his career and spent a year of his life pursuing Andrew Lyall only to run away when he has found him? Eddie crosses the alley and pauses. He doubts it.

A hand clamps down on his shoulder. Tearing free, Eddie takes a backward step. Before him stands Steven Verruckt.

"Edward, bad boy-in-cop's-clothing," Steven says, "left without good-bye."

"I'm sorry to have hurt your feelings, Steven," Eddie replies. He edges away from the apartment building. Has Steven been there all along, pounding stakes into Andrew and chopping his lithe figure to fragments?

Steven approaches; Eddie recoils. "Won't hurt Eddie," Steven says. "Eddie's my only friend."

Why did he have to say that? All his life Eddie has been a patsy to the deprived and lonely. If Steven had said anything else, Eddie could have walked away. Now, in spite of everything, he feels pity.

"You should stay," Steven says, his hoarse voice lowered to a collusive whisper. "Got new leads to follow."

"Do tell," Eddie says. He leads Steven away from Andrew's apartment building. If Steven hasn't been there, Eddie doesn't want him taking notice of it.

"Found a man," Steven relates, "on mission like ours." His face shines with excitement. "Yes, Eddie! Someone else knows. Someone else hunts. Someone else kills." He pats the duffel bag hanging from his shoulder.

"Where'd you find such a wonder?" Eddie asks. Is it possible that the city has as many escaped mental patients in its population as vampires? "What's his name?"

"You will meet him," Steven assures him. "He's a great man of cloth. Has hunted vampires long time."

"Has he had a great deal of success?"

"Many pounded and..." Steven scratches his neck.

"How very lovely."

"Says he even find me Andrew."

Eddie hesitates, then walks on. Steven seems unaware. "I would like to meet this man," Eddie says. Perhaps his success record includes Pablo — in which case he could very well lead Steven to Andrew. Yes, Eddie had best meet this man and direct him to more worthy objects for destruction — like the woman Eddie grappled with earlier.

"Soon," Steven says. "Now, we go home."

"Oh, I don't think so, Steven," Eddie says.

Steven stops and looks at Eddie with an expression close to disappointment, maybe even sadness. "Why not?"

"I need to be alone for a while, Steven," Eddie explains. "We've been on top of each other for a year. I need space."

"Don't like to sleep alone," Steven says, his shoulders sagging. "It's scary — sometimes."

"I've already taken a room. I'm all settled in." Eddie pats Steven's shoulder. "I'll come by tomorrow. We'll go see the great vampire hunter."

"All right." Steven adjusts his duffel bag while giving Eddie a sidelong glance. "Tomorrow night. I wait. Be there?"

"Cross my heart." Eddie watches Steven shuffle up the street, even smiles and waves when Steven glances back. Christ, now what has he gotten himself into? He should return to his hotel and stay put for the rest of the night. He can't walk down a street in this city without running into some kind of trouble.

A half-block from Andrew's building, Eddie crosses the street. He tarries at the curb, making certain that Steven is gone before he enters the hotel where he has taken lodgings.

Maybe he doesn't walk into trouble after all. Maybe, in this city, trouble follows him.

○

In his hotel room, Eddie tries to sleep, but Andrew — one moment calm and neat as a pin, the next raging and ragged — dances as an unstable phantasm behind his eyelids. Eddie flips onto his stomach, but the apparition cavorts in the folds of the pillowcase, in the faded patterns of the wallpaper.

After leaving Steven, he was tempted to return to Andrew's building. This time, Eddie would have climbed the inside staircase and knocked on the door of 12D. He would have told Andrew that Steven has found a dangerous benefactor.

But Eddie's tightly bridled fear of Andrew has gathered strength and kept him locked in his room. He tries to control the fear with memories. Two years ago, Andrew's openness saved Eddie from a miserable life. Three nights ago, Andrew rescued him from an unknown beast. Most vividly, Eddie remembers last night, when Andrew was broken by sorrow. Eddie knows that within the vampire Andrew lingers a soul more human than those of most living men.

More dangerous memories — of a lustful Stanley, of Jay and Christian, of that bestial woman — connive against that conviction. Each pursued him with a single purpose — to feed upon his blood. Eddie's encounters with them have reinforced a fact that he never wanted to confront: At any time, Andrew might decide that Eddie will make an appetizing meal.

Eddie knows Andrew's M.O. When the blood is gone, Andrew removes the head and is done with it. He leaves behind only the shell, the rest is someone else's memory.

Crawling out of bed, Eddie crosses to the window. He stares through the streaked glass at the city. Yet, he cannot stop worrying about Andrew, somewhere in the night, wild and careless in his grief for Pablo.

VI

BAT-IN-ARMS

1

Dusk. Another night. Alone.

I stand in front of Great-Great-Grandmother's mirror. No one stares back. No one is there. The glass reflects only the solitary coffin shoved against the wall.

Solitary.

Hunger is upon me. I don't remember the last time. I go to the kitchen looking for a substitute. All the tequila is gone. Bottles are shattered on the floor, stains streak the walls. I open the refrigerator.

On one shelf are neat stacks of plasma packets. Pablo's. I stare at them, remembering. *Pablo's.*

I tear the shelf out of the refrigerator. Metal clatters on linoleum. The packets scatter, undulating. From my jacket, I produce my switchblade. On hands and knees, I slash, stab. The plasma showers my face, saturates my clothes. The kitchen looks like a slaughterhouse.

But I am not moved to drink. The odor of this blood is nauseating. This blood is tainted. It came from those airheads at that church. I will not drink blood meant to change who I am.

I glance at the ice-encrusted freezer door. I might want what's in there. I pry the door open with a screwdriver. I chisel at a solid block of translucent ice. Slivers of ice cool my face. Metal strikes metal. I chip around a dark shape. I wedge my revolver — encased in ice — out of the freezer. Where did I hide the silver bullets? Maybe they're with the bath oils.

O

My clothes join his in a stack beside the toilet. I got rid of the coffin — I buried him. I can't get rid of his clothes. Especially not the last ones he wore. At the closet, I scan his black jackets and slacks, the charcoal shirts. Would I complain now that he always wore black, that he always looked the part of a corpse? Not now. Not now.

I want to wear his clothes. I resist. They were his. I hurriedly don my jacket and pants, run my hands through my tangled hair. I have to find a certain someone. I check the switchblade in my pocket, strap on my shoulder holster with the silver-bullet-loaded revolver — my new companion in the night. I have a favor to repay.

On my way out, the telephone rings. The answering machine clicks on. I am startled by Pablo's voice on the message.

"Pablo and Andrew can't pick up right now. They work the night shift. Leave a message. They'll give you a ring the moment they rise."

And I thought he had no sense of humor about our existence.

"Andrew?" A woman's high-pitched squeal shouts through the speaker. "We were wondering if you're going to join us at work tonight. You're on the verge of unemployment." *Click.*

I turn my back on the flashing red light and cross through the kitchen to the balcony. Andrew has better things to do than sell mildewed rags.

O

If not Steven-Old-Boy, then who destroyed Pablo?

The question preys upon my every brain cell. Eddie could be wrong. Steven-Old-Boy could be the one. I should finish him anyway, for old time's sake. The switchblade thirsts for him.

The silver bullet lodged at my spine twinges pain. I pause, wait for the pain to pass. Still, a dull ache remains.

Steven-Old-Boy put that bullet there. I should—

I falter again. My right arm tingles down to my fingertips. The bullet has rarely troubled me. Why now?

Who would implicate Steven-Old-Boy by decapitating Pablo?

I walk on. I will find him — them — and the switchblade will have its way. This Andrew will not be denied.

O

Along the way I feast. No deliberation about the mark, no dilemma about the switchblade's role hampers me. When I am satiated, I turn the razor-sharp double edges against the cooling throat. I leave head and body where they drop.

O

From a distance, I watch the activity in front of the Club. Human boys smoke and drink and frolic, jumping off of and onto the curb, daring the traffic to harm them. Fools. If they knew how fragile the net of existence, they would not tempt the strength of its strands. Andrew has a mind to walk into their midst and explain it all to them in excruciating detail.

But other chores are at hand.

If not Steven-Old-Boy, then I elect Jay Bauer and Christian Fellows. Their threats have been fervent: Stay clear of Kane Davies or else. Jay is bullish enough, Christian mad enough, to carry the threat where it would have its greatest impact.

Emerging from the Club, Christian Fellows teases his way through the crowd of human boys, then walks off alone.

He has a shadow.

I bide my time. I wouldn't want to shock the humans with my plans. Christian leads, I patiently follow, out of the Intriguing Faction Borough. The streetlamps grow dimmer, the prowling humans thin in number. In a neighborhood close to mine, he turns into another street. I speed forth to catch him.

Rounding the corner, I find Christian waiting. Expression snide, he leans, cocksure, against a building.

"What do you want, Lyall?" he demands. He lifts an eyebrow. "Did you think I didn't know you were following? Your perceptions are weak. What does Kane see in you? I wonder."

Hand in pocket, I approach. "Pablo's dead."

"No shit. So are you, asshole."

"Destroyed. I wonder how that happened?"

"No shit!" Christian leans back his head to stare at the sky. "Wonder, wonder who popped the stake in Pablo." He slides his eyes toward me. "Real messy, was it? Blood and guts and the whole nine yards, was it? What a tragedy."

"Handy with a hatchet, Christian?" I stop in front of him.

He doesn't look at me; he's fascinated with the smog clouds. "Lopped off his head, too? That's Pablo in pieces."

"Who held the stake, you or Jay? Who struck the blow?"

"Man, that's one dead boy who's better off dead."

I lunge, grab his lapels. "Which one of you cut off his head? Which one of you had the balls?"

"Were those cut off, too?"

I toss him against the wall. He smirks as if I'm no threat. I don't need the switchblade for this.

My hands grasp his throat; he doesn't fight. He'll be sorry. Fingernails tear flesh. A flare of panic now. Yes, Christian, panic. Too late. I claw, rip; skin splits, muscle shreds. Bones crackle. Hand on his shoulder, hand under his chin, I tug. No time for screams now, Christian. Did Pablo have time to scream? I snap the neck bones and cartilage. One final jerk — I toss the head to the ground.

Everyone laughs at Andrew's boasts. No one thinks Andrew capable of atrocities. Let them laugh now.

I perform each threat I've ever made. One arm pops from the socket. I tear off with the hand; the limb falls, shattered bone, tattered flesh. The other arm breaks in quarters. I splinter the right leg, shread the left. I fling a fragment over my shoulder, hurl a part the other way.

That's Christian Fellows in pieces.

One last thing. I kneel over the ravaged torso, rip open his shirt. I poke into the chest. The fingers dig — deeper, snap the ribs one after the other. I pluck out his heart, smash it into the gutter, and stomp that sucker flat.

O

Next, Jay Bauer.

O

I fly home to change clothes. I am drenched in Christian's blood. I try to scrub off the gore with a towel but only smear the blood. Although reluctant to waste time, I draw a bath.

The scalding water is a comforting shroud. The heat permeates my skin to my insides, warming my full veins. Lethargy seeps through me, weakening me. My head lolls, my eyelids droop.

And behind the lids, I can see him, tall, black-haired, blue-eyed. Pablo. My daze carries me back to a bar beneath a deserted warehouse, where I first saw him as a fading, tormented beauty in a den of grubby humans. He touched me.

I miss him.

I force my eyes open. I have lounged here too long. Night is not eternal. Pablo's other murderer still haunts the night. I must deal with him.

After drying, I force myself to shave and comb my hair. If I am going into the Club this trip, I must not attract undue attention. Once inside, I will corner Jay in a quiet back room.

In the bedroom, I halt near the closet. A sound comes from the living room. Has Kane Davies's network already discovered

Christian's parts and come to judge his executioner? I snag a pair of slacks and slip into them. Switchblade in hand, I peer into the living room.

Helmut has dropped by unannounced. He looks up, take a step across the room, stops. His expression reveals uncertainty. Then he tames his features to compassion.

I enter the room. "Next time, knock before misting your way under my door." I keep the switchblade at ready.

"Andrew. You have no need of that with me." He gestures at my weapon. But his movements are guarded. "I came to check on you. We are all devastated by Pablo's ... fate." His eyes shift from mine, then back. "We're concerned about your state—"

"Of mind?" I point the switchblade at him. "You people deal in states of mind, don't you? Vampirism is a state of mind. Humanism is a state of mind."

"We want to help."

"How kind. Look at me, Helmut. Guess my state of mind."

"Perhaps if you came to a meeting—"

I fling the switchblade across the room. Sailing past Helmut's ear, the blade lodges in the woodwork.

"That is my state of mind, Helmut. Take that message back to Maxwell."

"We've done nothing..."

"You destroyed Pablo's state of mind." I walk toward him; with effort he stands his ground. "What are you doing here? How did you know about Pablo?"

"We know—"

"You know too much, Helmut. You know about Pablo. You knew about Lance Broderick. You described that scene in pretty lurid detail to Colin." I stick my face close to his. "Do you know about Christian Fellows?"

Mute, Helmut shakes his head.

"Bits and pieces, Helmut. That's what happens when someone crosses Andrew. Bits and pieces scattered hither and yon."

He can't quite believe, but he's worried. "I only came to..." With a gesture of defeat, he turns toward the door.

I grab his sleeve, toss him against the couch. Helmut knows that he's entered the danger zone. I jerk the switchblade out of the door frame. Helmut scrambles backward along the couch, then leaps to his feet. Backing against the wall, he tries to summon his Aryan air of superiority. He fails miserably.

I flip the switchblade from one hand to the other. "Why are you such a bloodbath of information?"

"Why does Davies know so much?" Helmut returns.

I grip the switchblade and take another step toward him.

"In our sphere, one can find out anything one wants," Helmut mutters. "Davies knows all about you — all about us. What makes you think he puts his knowledge toward noble goals? Perhaps, Andrew, you shouldn't judge others by appearance."

"I haven't judged you by appearance." I am all assurance. "I judge you by your deeds, by the company you keep."

"Then you have poor judgment." He sidles along the wall toward the door. "Kane Davies knew about Pablo's destruction, too — before you did. You had best think about that."

Is it possible? I stare at the switchblade. Since Jay Bauer and Christian Fellows destroyed Pablo, then Kane could well have known before I...

Helmut takes advantage of my distraction. When I turn, he is at the door. His shape is transparent; mist oozes around his feet, then streams out under the door.

I wheel toward the bedroom. Andrew has questions for Kane Davies as well as cold steel for Jay Bauer.

O

They stand as they did the night I met them, against the Club's mirrored back wall, Kane Davies at the apex of their formation.

But their number has been reduced. Lance Broderick has been destroyed by the police. That's still a mystery. Who tipped off the police about Lance? The same worm-bait that murdered Pablo?

And, of course, Christian Fellows is absent. That's not a mystery. Andrew takes sole credit.

As I approach through the gyrating human boys, John Studnidka steps away from the wall. Kane detains him; John looks ready to tear off Kane's hand. With a nod, Kane sends Jay Bauer and Hart Laughlin to greet me.

Jay halts me with a half-shove. "The nerve you possess."

"You are a bad boy, Andrew," Hart says, fiddling with his earrings. Tonight, his eyes are clear of drugs. Still, his lips twist and turn on the verge of an airheaded grin.

"We found Christian," Jays says, his voice sharp with disgust. "Only you would stoop to that kind of savagery."

"And you're so well behaved." I push him aside. "I'm going to talk to Kane."

Jay grabs my arm, his fingers digging. "Kane doesn't want to talk to you." The brown eyes gleam beneath the heavy eyelids; the full lips smirk. "Ripping Christian apart was your downfall. He was one of Kane's. Didn't know that, did you, smart boy? You may as well have shoved a stake into Kane."

"I'll shove one down your throat." I jerk my arm free. I stab a finger at his chest. "You're next, fat lips. Limb from limb. Eyelid from eyelid. I'll enjoy it."

A few humans falter in their dancing. Obviously, they've never heard vampires locked in a verbal duel. From their faces, they don't know whether to laugh or run screaming for shelter.

"This isn't a good idea." Hart edges between Jay and me. "Andrew, Kane is pretty upset."

"He's going to destroy you, smart boy," Jay says.

"Shut up," Hart snaps. He places his hands on my shoulders. "Give it a couple nights' rest, Andrew."

"I'm going to talk to Kane." Shrugging free, I make a circuit past Jay toward the back of the Club.

"Not here!" Hart shouts.

I am bowled over from behind. I leap to my feet and lunge at Jay. We clash. I go for his face. Jay fights dirty; he tries to knee prized anatomy. I lock a finger around his bottom lip, puncture the soft flesh inside with a fingernail. Jay clamps onto my wrist and tries to break it. I stomp on his foot.

"That's enough!"

A hand clamps down on my shoulder, an arm wraps around my torso. "Andrew!" I am dragged back, held firmly against a body I vaguely recognize. Turning my head, I hiss into John's face.

Hart has snagged the collar of Jay's shirt. Lifting him off the ground, he tosses Jay into the gathered spectators. The humans cower as Jay regains his balance and whirls around.

"This will stop now." The authority of Kane Davies's voice rings over the thunderous music. His face hard, his brown eyes smoldering, he steps between Jay and me. "Jay, go outside."

Gingerly, Jay touches his mouth. "Kane won't always be around, Lyall." He pushes his way toward the door.

Deliberately, Kane Davies turns to me. He draws a slow breath, shoves clenched hands into the pockets of his long coat. "Let him go, John."

I am released, yet John remains close behind me.

Around us, the humans slowly revolve back into the rhythms of the music.

"I want some answers from you," I say to Kane.

Kane merely stares at me. Whatever he thinks, whatever he feels, he keeps well guarded. Then, he turns his back on me.

"Don't walk away from me." I try to follow, but John latches onto the waist of my slacks and holds me fast.

"John," Kane says in departure. "Come with me."

"Shouldn't I—"

"Now, John." Kane doesn't pause. "Hart will stay."

John walks around me. His youthful face lacks its usual warped humor. "Will you behave?" he asks. "This is serious."

"You think I'm not?"

"Kane is getting impatient," Hart says, placing his hand on John's shoulder. "Go on."

John glances toward the front of the Club, where Kane waits. Turning back to me, John says, "We have to talk."

"Kane won't approve," Hart says. "Off you go."

With obvious reluctance, and an expression I don't quite comprehend, John departs. At the door, Kane shoves him outside.

I start to follow; Hart detains me.

"You've caused enough ruckus for one night, Andrew," he says. "I'm escorting you home. And home you will stay for the rest of the night."

"I kinda be doubtin' it."

Swinging an arm around my shoulders, Hart leads me to the bar. "First, we'll have a drinkie."

"I'm not in the mood—"

"Two margaritas," he orders of the bartender. "Strawberry, of course," he adds, grinning at me. "Relax, Andrew."

"I don't want to relax."

How can I relax with all these unresolved suspicions stomping around inside my head? How can I relax when one of Pablo's killers still roams the night? Having dispatched Christian Fellows, I crave Jay Bauer's skin under my fingernails. Revenge used to seem a waste of time. I've changed my mind. Settling with Christian and Jay won't bring Pablo back, but it sure as hell will make Andrew feel better.

O

After several strawberry margaritas, Hart and I leave the Club. Hart has succeeded in his mission. I am drunk, hardly capable of ripping open an envelope, much less Jay Bauer's face.

I settle in the passenger seat of Hart's car, lean my temple against the window, and watch the world go by. I spot an all-night grocery. "Stop!" I grab the wheel; the car skids into the parking lot.

Hart shuts off the ignition. He sits dead still, hands gripping the wheel. "Now that we're here, why are we here?"

"I need to pick up a couple of things." I leap out awkwardly and weave toward the store entrance.

Inside, the flourescent lights are blinding. I wish for sunglasses, but I don't own any. Hand lifted against the glare, I search the narrow aisles. At the end of each, I snort a big breath of multifragranced air. Dead flesh isn't on Andrew's list. I don't need bread or doughnuts. Here we go.

I dump my loaded basket at the checkout stand. The cashier gives me the evil eye. I offer a cool grin.

"That's sixty-two eighty-seven. Paper or plastic?"

"Double plastic, please." A straining bag in each hand, I saunter out to the car.

"What's all that?" Hart asks.

"Stuff."

He wrinkles his nose. "Do you smell something foul?"

"No. Let's go."

Back at my building, we spend several minutes stranded in the hallway. I have my keys but, having departed the apartment by the old-world mode of transportation, I left the crossbar in place. With my permission, Hart mists under the door.

"This place is the pits," he says, opening the door.

"Be it ever so roach-ridden." I head for the kitchen.

"What happened here?" Hart scans the blood-splattered room.

"I threw out some leftovers." I heft the shopping bags onto the counter and line up my purchases.

"What the—"

"Too many airheaded bloodsuckers have been making free with Andrew's apartment," I inform Hart. I heft one jumbo jar of garlic power. "Andrew's putting a stop to it here and now." I take off the lid. Hand over my nose, I sprinkle the garlic power over the windowsill.

"Andrew's going to drive all of his friends away," Hart says, backing into the living room.

"Andrew doesn't think he cares."

"Andrew better care." Hart gives me wide berth as I juggle several jars into the living room. He says, "Taking out Christian wasn't the wisest thing—"

"Christian Fellows and Jay Bauer destroyed Pablo," I state. The powder sifts over the rim, sprinkles the back of my hand. Swearing, I shake the granules off before I have permanent scars.

"You can't believe that," Hart says. "Why would they want to destroy Pablo?"

"Because he was my beau. Because Jay wants me to stay away from Kane. That's another thing. How is Kane mixed up in this? Does he know something about Pablo's destruction he shouldn't?"

"That's pretty stupid, Andrew." Hart pulls at his earring. "There are worse creatures in the night than Jay. They're closer to you than you think."

"What does that mean?"

Who in this city is closer to me? My only friend of my own race is John Studnidka, Eddie my only human friend. Do I have enemies, other than Steven-Old-Boy? Without a doubt — Jay Bauer. What about the boys at Vampires Anonymous? They're more irked with me for disrupting their meetings than anything else. Besides, Pablo was a member of that insipid clutch of corpses. Why would they destroy one of their own? I dump a jar of garlic powder across the front threshold.

"The smell is getting a bit thick," Hart says.

"You started this conversation, Hart." I drop the empty jar, twist open another one. "Finish it."

"Just take my advice — for your sake and Kane's — forget your vendetta before you mess everything up."

"Some dead sonofabitch came in here and drove a stake through my Pablo! The butcher cut off his head and left him to rot. I refuse to forget that!"

Hart gags. "I gotta get out of here." He pulls his shirttail up over his nose. "Believe me, Jay and Christian didn't destroy Pablo." He sprints into the kitchen.

"Then who did?"

"Gotta go." Jerking open the back door, Hart jumps off the balcony. I catch a glimpse of heavy wings.

"Damn all of you!" I hurl the jar; it shatters against the wall. The odor of garlic swarms around me, stinging my nostrils, bringing tears to my eyes. "He was my beau. I have rights!"

2

I feel as if I'm suffocating. My mouth and nose seem full of dirt, my eyelids glued shut. I fumble with the locks, heave up the coffin lid. Pungent garlic assaults me in heated waves.

Maybe Andrew's Intruder Deterrent wasn't such a bright idea.

I methodically open every window then drag out the vacuum. I am at the door when a tingling sensation worms its way from my foot into my brain. Pain hits. I stumble back onto the sofa. The bottom of my foot is riddled with garlic powder holes. Wearing Pablo's scuffed hiking boots, I continue vacuuming.

The cleaning done, but that odor still prominent, I settle into the bathtub. This hot cocoon relaxes me. And, as Hart informed me last night, I do need to relax. Not even Andrew can keep up the frantic brain power required for a reign of mayhem.

Well, a little mayhem; tearing one undead airhead apart hardly constitutes a reign.

Already with the quips, Andrew? Pablo's only three nights in the ground, and you're pulling out the smart-ass remarks.

Can the shock and grief of Pablo's demise have worn off already? No, I still feel both deep inside, conspiring toward the moment when they will strike again full force. Lounging in the tub, I realize just how alone I am without Pablo. I never felt this way before I brought him to the night.

But I'll feel this way for many decades to come. There are moments when I forget, when I think of something I want to tell him, when I imagine his reaction to something I've said or done. Then memory rears its shaggy head, points a gnarled finger, and declares, "Pablo's under the ground. Get used to it."

I'll never get used to it. He'll always be a step ahead of me, a thought away, out of reach but right here.

O

I need answers. If Kane has banned me from his exalted presence and has forbidden John or Hart to answer my questions, then I will ask them elsewhere. If Jay and Christian — may he burn anyway — did not destroy Pablo because of me, then I will seek out Pablo's friends and find out whom Pablo might have crossed.

After I dress, I sort through Pablo's personal effects. The things the boy held onto. From the movie ticket stubs, receipts, and matchbooks I sort out a zillion scraps of paper. Most have only scrawled telephone numbers and addresses, not even in Pablo's hand, on their crumpled surfaces. I can't imagine how he would have remembered what number belonged to whom. I search for anything with a name on it, one name in particular. There's an average man in this city Andrew wants to talk to.

When I find Colin's name, number, and address, they are on a neatly printed business card. Colin Patton is an investment broker. I wonder what firm has an all-night branch.

I try telephoning. The answering machine picks up, crackles a boring name-number-and-the-time-you-called message, then beeps into my ear. I hang up. Something tells me not to leave messages for innocent bystanders. Something tells me "Andrew" means "pain-in-the-neck" to just about everyone.

O

Colin's address is on the up side of town, far removed from Andrew and Pablo's residence — Andrew's residence. Upon arrival, I stare up at the luxury condo. Since I haven't been invited into Colin's home, I am stranded outside. Lighting a cigarette, I settle into an evening of pacing.

A car pulls up to the curb. A young skirt in business regalia, complete with molded attaché case, steps out of the highly polished Pulsar. "The neighborhood watch is not going to think much of you," she says, smiling one of those dangerous female smiles. "They patrol every fifteen minutes. They see you twice, they nab you."

"I'm waiting for someone," I reply.

"Who?" she inquires.

"Colin Patton."

Frowning, she gives me a heavy appraisal. "How does he do it? Lately it's been one after the other." She shakes her thatch of bottle-red hair. "He's so ... so..."

"Average," I offer.

"Yes." She circles me toward the entrance alcove. "If you must wait for Colin, you must. But you had best wait inside."

"Is that an invitation?"

"Well, yes, I suppose."

"You are very kind to ask me in," I say, walking up to her.

"You are very welcome." She links her arm in mine, over-estimating the weight of my gratitude, but I allow her to lead me through the front door. "Do you have a name? You're very cute. A little pale, but very cute."

"Don't you find names a nuisance?" I quickly scan the mailboxes beside the block of elevators. There's only one Colin Patton, on the fourth floor. "I must be off now."

An elevator opens, I dash inside. The doors slide shut, and I am whisked up to the fourth floor.

O

Colin put up a better fight than Pablo.

From the threshold, blood splatters the furniture, carpet, wall, ceiling of the condo. The smell hangs too fresh. Edging my way into the living room, I sidestep a thick pool, avoid a splotch on a chair. This is recent business. The killer may still be here. I snap open my switchblade. I pause and listen to a faint sound from the loft. I creep toward the stairs.

A severed hand lies on one step.

I follow a thick trail up the staircase. At the top, I crouch defensively, the switchblade brandished. The smell is denser up here. More blood streams down the walls, soaks the eiderdown of a chrome four-poster bed. At the far corner of the bed, a crimson spring showers the pale carpet.

I gulp, force my lips to part. "Colin?"

A sound, faint and guttural, answers.

Cautious, I round the bed. I halt.

Oh, God. My head spins. Images flash behind my eyelids. An open coffin. A decapitated corpse. A blood-streaked wooden stake. I reel against the bedpost, press against the smooth metal. Bile surges from my stomach. I gag, sputter.

The sound comes again, plaintive. Dying.

I force myself to look down at Colin. Why is this happening? I can't endure any more of this. I can't.

Colin slouches against the bed. More of him is missing than just his hand. His blood pumps out of him, each spray weaker than the last. At his side lies a length of thick, blood-smeared wood. Colin turns toward me. His dull eyes stare. His mouth opens, blood gurgles down his chin.

"Colin." I kneel, pull him into my arms. His head lolls against my shoulder. "Colin, who did this?" As he lifts his head, he slips. I tighten my grip. My hand finds a round, ragged wound in his back. I can feel blood ooze against my palm with each beat of his failing heart. "Who was it, Colin?"

"Hurts. Feel splinters. Can feel..."

"It's Andrew. You have to tell—"

"Digging into me." His handless arm reaches behind him as if to stanch the wound. "Hurts." He chokes, coughs blood over my jacket. "Splinters."

I could lie, say everything will be all right. It won't be. Colin is going. Going to join Pablo.

I hug him closer. I will wait for the end. Then I'll bury him with my boy. "I'll put you beside Pablo."

His body twists in my arms. His left leg kicks without calf or foot. His face turns against my shoulder. He grips my hand.

"Pablo found out." The eyes are focused on me. "Andrew ... Pablo found out."

"Found out what? Not yet, Colin. Hang on. What did Pablo find out? Hang on, Colin. Tell me."

"Ocean ... Village."

He spasms against me. I hold him, even after he is gone.

O

Colin is under the ground.

O

Exhausted, I fly toward home. Discretion advised abandoning Colin's van in a neighborhood far removed from his and mine. The skirt at his building got a good look at me. Fortunately, I had the presence of mind not to tell her my name. Let the police scour that side of the city for someone who's "a little pale, but very cute." I'm too drained to play hide-and-seek with that lot.

My wings are all flapped out. Close enough to home to walk, I dive into an alley and hit the street in human form. It's time to think. I think better on my feet than on my claws.

Here's another mystery for Andrew. Don't these people know I'm no good at this? Maybe they do. Maybe that's why everyone near me is under the ground, and I'm walking around. The killers know I'm not too swift, and they're taking advantage of me.

I can't figure out any of it, especially cryptic last words of average vampires. What did Pablo find out at Ocean Village, a tourist trap with lots of boardwalks and shops planted in the middle of a disintegrating beach district?

One thing hasn't escaped Andrew: Whoever murdered Pablo murdered Colin. But why did they tear Colin up so? I am reminded of Christian Fellows's fortunate end. Were they going to dispose of me by setting me up as Colin's killer? I don't think Colin's destruction would have the same impact on Kane Davies and his clique as Christian's.

Maybe Colin knew — or someone thought he knew — whatever it was that Pablo found out at Ocean Village.

I stop and beat my temples with my fists. Why doesn't something up there connect!

A childish whimper echoes through the street, skittering with the litter in the gutter.

Quiet out there, can't you see Andrew's thinking?

I continue on, nursing my smarting temples. No amount of pounding jars Andrew's atrophied brain to attention.

Again, the whimper wafts on the breeze.

All right, what's the deal here?

"Mama..."

I keep walking. I have enough on my mind. I don't have time to answer the heartfelt sobs of every lost kid in town.

"Mama..."

Okay. I'm not a completely dead monster. I scan the sidewalk opposite me. Nothing. Good, I can — Wait, there's the little critter, cowering in that doorway.

"Mama..."

This kid is in for a surprise.

Jogging across the street, I leap onto the curb.

The whimpers stop.

So does Andrew.

This scenario rings a scary bell. I check out my coordinates. Yep. This is the neighborhood — the slaygrounds of the Midget Mutilator.

I peer through the doorway's shadows. Almond-shaped eyes stare back from a solemn round face framed by dirty blond hair.

Now, Andrew, the voice of reason says behind my eyes, does this kid look like he'll slash you to slivers?

No, but looks can be deceiving. Never judge a book—

Andrew, the voice insists, look at him. He's lost, alone.

The kid's small mouth opens, a whimper issues forth.

"Where are your parents, kid?" I inch just an inch closer.

He shakes his head.

I force a complete step. "You live around here?"

He sniffles, shrugs.

"You're as confused as I am, kiddo." I study him. This is just a lost little boy, not the Infantile Slasher. "Want me—"

Whoa!

The Tyke Terror leaps off the step into my face. Tiny hands lock into my hair. Itty-bitty feet climb my stomach. He makes a bite for my throat.

"Just one minute!" I grab him by the face and hold him at arm's length.

The Preschool Slayer rages, face scrunched up, feet kicking, arms flapping — into wings. He can't quite manage the rest of the transmutation. He spits and hisses up a fit.

"Just screw a lid on it before you hurt yourself."

Growl. Snarl.

"Cut it out, junior. Can't you tell you're attacking one of your own kind?"

That settles him some. The round face resumes its solemn expression. The wings drop at his sides.

"You shouldn't try these tricks until you know what you're about," I say, pulling one wing out to full length — not a bad span for a pint-size vein-drainer. The wing re-forms to an arm. "That's more like it. If I put you down, will you behave?"

Such calculations whirl behind those almond-shaped brown eyes. At length, his mouth a tight line, he nods. Well, since I have him by the face, his body wiggles acquiescence.

"All right. That's a promise. You bite my ankle or take off, I'll get ticked and go home. Got it? Good."

I set him down. The boy's feet want to run, but he can't take his eyes off me. Maybe he didn't know more of us exist. I crouch down in front of him.

"What's your name?" He stares at me in silence. "My name is Andrew. Tell me yours."

"Ryan."

"How old are you?"

He holds up four fingers.

This is sick. Andrew doesn't like this at all. Someone pulled a fast one here, and Andrew thinks it stinks. "Who did this to you?"

"Did what?"

How does one explain vampirism to a four-year-old vampire?

"Who left you out in the dark?"

"A lady. A tall lady."

Bite my tongue, but don't it figure? Throughout our history the skirts have not been able to keep their hands off little ones. I, personally, never touch anything that hasn't aged at least twenty — all right, eighteen years.

"Do you know where the tall lady is?"

He shakes his head.

How fortunate she is.

"Are you really..." Ryan asks, snarling back his upper lip to shows off his fangs.

"Yeah, I'm really..." I do the same.

"Big."

So I've been told.

What do I do now? I could walk. That's easy. I have too much preying on my mind to take responsibility for a four-year-old bloodsucker. Does Andrew look like a babysitter? No. Andrew's gotta walk.

"Take care of yourself, Ryan." I pat his head. "I'm sure we'll run into each other again some night."

I turn tail. I don't get far before tiny footsteps follow. I glance over my shoulder. Here he comes, walking but putting on the speed of our race. I accelerate. The footsteps behind me quicken, break into a clicking run.

You're a beast, Andrew, says the voice behind my eyes.

I have things to take care of, things not even a vampiric child should be involved in.

How long will he last alone in this city?

He's lasted this long.

You're worse than a beast, Andrew. Heartless monster.

This has got to be worse than any dilemma I've faced over any mark in the last eight years. I do wonder how the little tyke will survive on his own. How long will he get away with his crying-lost-child act before someone — like the police who destroyed Lance — stakes him? I couldn't bear finding a kid with a stake in his chest, or with his head cut off.

I wait for Ryan to catch up. He stops beside me and gives me a drilling stare.

"Yeah, what?" I ask, unnerved.

"What'll it be like when I'm this many?" He holds up five splayed fingers.

"Pretty much the same as it is now."

"This many?" He opens and closes both hands about thirty trillion times — in the proverbial blink of an eye.

"Pretty much the same as when I'm this many." I open and close my hands faster than he did.

His round face grows more solemn, the almond-shaped eyes say oh-yeah-and-how-would-you-know? but he lets it drop.

I start walking again. He tags along at my side for a block before tugging at my jacket sleeve.

"Papa."

Nonono. This is too much. I halt, kneel in front of him. "I'm nobody's papa, kiddo. Aesthetically speaking, I don't go in for that sort of activity."

"Andrew, why do we only play at night?"

I look up at the sky. Eternity is beginning to look like one big question mark for Andrew and this bat-in-arms.

"Where's your coffin, Ryan?"

He tilts his head to the side.

"Where do you take your daytime naps?"

Grabbing my hand, he heads back the way we came. At a particularly run-down building, he squeezes through a broken basement window. I resort to the mist-method. When I swirl myself back together, Ryan is staring at me in awe.

"As you grow older, you'll pick these things up."

Lordie, he won't grow older, will he? Upstairs maybe, but physically he'll always be this two-and-a-half-foot-tall corpse. When I find the skirt who did this...

"Where's the coffin?"

He takes my hand again. He leads me through a labyrinth of moldy boxes and shattered furniture to an abandoned boiler room. In a corner sits a crate loaded with soil. Apparently making one's grave is instinctive. Two heavily damaged stuffed animals occupy the crate in Ryan's absence.

He's bound to be discovered here. I'm going to regret this, but I can't turn my back on that expectant face a second time.

O

For the first time since I found Pablo, I wake up refreshed. Grief still presses at the back of my head; I am still furious, still determined to find and annihilate Pablo's murderer, yet I feel calmer. Maybe this calm will allow my brain to work properly so I can figure out this puzzle.

When I crawl out of my coffin, I stop short. In his duds which we pilfered from a reasonably fashionable children's store, Ryan stands before my great-great-grandmother's mirror. The glass is quite barren of his reflection, yet Ryan smiles so wide that the rest of his face seems to have disappeared. He turns to the left, turns to the right, adjusts the lapel of his jacket, brushes a speck of lint from his trousers. Then, face pressed close to the glass, he bares his fangs and laughs.

He realizes that I am watching. The laugh fades, the smile shuts down. He turns and gives me that solemn look.

"Good evening," he greets me.

Lordie, don't tell me that's instinctive, too.

"You need a long soak in the tub before we hit the streets."

The corners of his small mouth droop.

"It won't destroy you." I take his hand and drag him toward the bathroom. "You're carrying around enough dirt to start a landfill." He spits a hiss, transmutes his feet to claws, and digs into the linoleum. "Come on, Ryan." Andrew has the solution. "You don't want to ruin your new clothes, do you?"

He studies his ensemble, then examines his hand, caked and streaked with grime. Pouty, he trots toward the tub.

O

Ocean Village turns out to be pretty much as I expected: a gaudy attempt at urban renewal on the edge of a slum. Surrounded on three sides by cement-block walls disguised by redwood fencing, exaggerated Olde English Shoppes are crowded along boardwalks to the bay. The only strange thing about this mecca of extravagant human vulgarity is the crowds it attracts at night.

Ryan in tow, I tour the boardwalks, read each shop name for a double meaning, peer through every multipaned window for some clue. All my antennae are out, sensitive to any vibration indicating others of my kind loitering among the tourists. All my efforts are in vain.

Ryan, on the other hand, has found plenty to interest him. He strains constantly against my grip. How brightly the brown eyes shine when they lock upon this or that ruddy-skinned tourist. No doubt he has never seen such a wealth of nourishment at his usual hunting grounds. Keeping him at my side takes most of my energy.

Having exhausted each byway, I scope out the wharf where hungry tourists swarm various expensive, haute-cuisine fast-food stands. Leaning against the oceanside railing, I scan the milling tourists. Fat people stuff their faces, skinny people pick apart sandwiches. One woman in straw hat and baggy flowered shorts finds this all magnificently quaint and sweeps the area with her video camera. A little boy looks lost...

Where's the kid? I push away from the railing. He was here a minute ago. On the edge of panic, I search for his towhead, certain that I'll find him chowing on somebody's neck in the midst of all this humdrum activity.

No, thank the stars, he's merely playing ham for the lady with the video camera. The woman encourages him to perform. Ryan stands perfectly still, face upturned and squished into that brilliant smile. At least he keeps his fangs in check. The woman crouches down and zooms in; Ryan crouches down and cranes his head toward the lens. Lady, you're in for a hell of a jolt when you play back that tape. As photogenic as the kid may seem, the undead take lousy — and blank — photographs.

"He's soooo cute," the woman says when I wander over to her and Ryan. "Soooo precious."

Why does that most horrifying of horrifying words "precocious" keep bouncing around my brain?

"You must be his father," she says. "Yes, I see the resemblance. Your eyes are identical. But he must have his mother's hair."

The kid's and my eyes are identical all right — fiery, bloodlust red. As for his "mother," may I never run into her. I have an illuminating lesson of vampiric propriety to teach her, and she won't like it. I take Ryan's hand; he pulls against me. The sheen of his eyes says that it's feeding time.

"Enjoy your video," I say.

Ryan resists. I firmly lead him away from the woman. He possesses more strength than I suspected. He jerks free.

"Ryan."

He leaps to the top of the cement-block wall. I glance around nervously. Did anybody see that? I hurry after the kid. He's on the prowl and the lady in the straw hat is the prey. That fact hasn't escaped her, either. She gapes at this soooo precious kid loping along the top of that ten-foot-high wall.

"How did you get up there?" Her voice quavers fear.

Ryan prepares for the lunge. I race over the few yards separating us. He grins at the woman; his fangs are out. I bound between them. He leaps. I catch him; the force of his jump sends us spinning.

"My word!" the woman exclaims.

Affecting a parental tone, I scold Ryan for pulling a dangerous stunt. He struggles in my arms. I clamp a hand over his mouth to stifle his snarls. Beneath my hand, his face transmutes to a snout. I wrap his head in my jacket.

"He gets a little rambunctious," I stammer. Grappling with his wriggling form, I back away from the woman. "Too much sugar makes kids act like beasts."

Wheeling away, I make a swift exit down one of the less inhabited walkways. Ryan continues to growl and struggle. I give him a swat on the butt. That gets an instant reaction. Face human, he lifts his head from the folds of my jacket and gives me a how-can-you-hit-me? stare. I fight tinglings of guilt and shake a finger under his nose.

"Some things are just not done in public," I tell him. "Discretion is the better part of survival."

"Hungry," he states.

"Well, yeah, so am I, but this place isn't a restaurant. You can't pluck one of these folks out of the crowd and put the drain on them. At the proper time, in the proper place, but not here. Don't give me that look. You have to learn these things."

I set him down, but keep a good grip on his hand. Something in that face informs me that he hears but doesn't quite buy it. I beat a path toward the exit. Temptation here is too great for the tyke, and I might not be quick enough to stop him next time.

Besides, I can't find anything weird going on here. Maybe Colin was just having a flashback to better nights when he spit out "Ocean Village." This place is too mundane to be sinister.

When we reach the exit, Ryan plants his feet and halts. Bristling, he glares toward the far side of the parking lot.

"What is it now?" All I see is a woman leading a kid between the cars.

Beside me, Ryan has transmuted half of his face; his other arm spreads to a wing. The woman and child disappear into distant trees. Kneeling in front of Ryan, I ask, "Is that her?" He growls. "I'll fix her wagon. You stay here."

Ryan latches onto my lapels. "Bad!" he says. "Bad!"

"I can handle her."

He shakes his head to a blur. "Bad!"

"Hey, Andrew." A familiar figure towers over us.

With a mixture of pleasure and annoyance, I look up at John Studnidka, his vernal face stretched in a facsimile of his crooked grin.

"Who's the baby bat?" John asks, leaning toward Ryan.

Pressing against my leg, Ryan snarls a warning.

"I'm surprised at you, Andrew! Is it even out of diapers?"

Howling, Ryan lunges at John's kneecap. John is quick: He snags the front of Ryan's shirt and hoists him off the ground. Ryan manages the arms-to-wings transmutation.

"Cute," John says, "but will it fly?"

Snapping at air, Ryan struggles free and leaps into my arms. He keeps his eyes fixed on John.

"Believe it or not, kiddo, the Stud is probably our only friend," I assure Ryan.

John's smile flashes genuinely. "I didn't think you had noticed." He nods at Ryan. "You aren't his 'father,' are you?"

"No." Ryan watches me intently. "Some skirt did it. I think she was here. I was just about—"

"Here?" John asks. His voice holds a different quality. "This is hardly a hangout for vampiric skirts."

"It's not a hangout for any self-respecting vampire. What are *you* doing here?"

Scuffing his feet on the pavement, he hems and haws.

"Forget I asked. I didn't mean to throw you into a trauma."

He offers me a small smile. "How you doin', Andrew? I wanted to stay and talk to you at the Club—"

"Were either Kane or Jay involved in Pablo's destruction?"

"Hart told you that was ridiculous."

Great, Hart reported our entire conversation to Kane Davies, and anyone else with ears. I suppose he also blabbed about the garlic powder. My credibility is going down the toilet.

"Then who's left?" I demand. "Who would want to destroy Pablo and Colin Patton?"

"Poor Colin. His place was a mess. Did you find him?"

"I was with him, and I buried him. Answer my question."

"Who's left?" He breaks into a real chortle. "You're pretty thick in the head — especially this one." He taps my temple. He glances around as if he thinks we're being watched. Turning back to me, he touches my arm. "Think about it, Andrew. It could be an almost religious experience." He winks.

"Am I suppose to understand that?"

"I just wanted to see that you were all right," John says. "I'll be in touch when I can. Try to be patient. It's not one of your strongest points, but give it a whirl." He gives Ryan the once-over, then pats his head. Ryan snaps at his hand. "Did he learn that from you, Andrew?" He walks off into the night.

And, like a sunbeam in the eye, it hits me. You're real funny, John. It could be a religious experience, as in desecrated church, where Maxwell Guthridge of the not-morally-good face conducts his Vampires Anonymous meetings.

"Andrew is blind as a bat, kiddo," I say to Ryan. I carry him to the van. "I'm taking you home, then I'm going to stake some self-righteous corpses to some desecrated walls."

"The Stud said to keep it tucked away," Ryan warns.

I gape. Baby bats say the darnedest things, and in the most commanding tones. But he may have a point.

As I suspected all along, Kane Davies and his clique want to put Maxwell and his rude cadavers in their place. I'd like to help Kane out and settle my debt with Vampires Anonymous, but too many have fallen already — Lance, Colin, and my Pablo. My interference may cause more needless destructions. If Kane is in command of the situation, I'll have to force patience into my vocabulary and bow out of the picture. For a while.

VII

NIGHT FLIGHT
TO HELL

1

*L*ounging in the low-slung seat of his black Prelude, Kane Davies watches the night through the tinted window. On the CD player, filling the car's interior with marvels, Kiri does Puccini. Although Kane fixes all concentration on the arias, the soprano's phrasing, the flowing swells and ebbs of her voice, his gaze registers each variance of the street's activity: the number and models of passing cars; each person — sex, style of clothing, signs of mood, and whether or not human.

Kane exits the car. Through an exercise of memory, he takes the arias with him. The nuances of the orchestra and the singer's voice accompany him, as the premiere performances of *La Clemenza di Tito* or *L'in Coronazione di Poppea* once followed him from the opera houses of Europe. After locking the door and activating the car alarm, he crosses the street to the Club. Not even the raucous dance number that greets him as he enters can impinge upon the subtlety of "Vissi d'Arte."

From the edge of the dance floor, Kane observes the men caught in a pagan frenzy of courtship. Under the strobing lights, the perspiring faces shine with a message — the same message exchanged throughout the centuries by couples twirling in a minuet or a waltz or this bouncing frolic. *Let this evening of dancing lead us to substantial emotion and lasting concord.*

In the midst of the dancers, Jay and Hart partake of the ritual. Dark eyes hooded, Jay glides a blond man toward heights unscalable with a human partner. With his reputation as an erotic film star, Hart has attracted several partners in a tight body grind. Jay pulls himself from the rite and looks at Kane. Hart remains oblivious, his senses overpowered by drugs.

Kane turns toward the bar. Night is different since Lance's destruction. Lance had appreciated the value of their caste, the lasting, inner accolades it could bestow. The others, like Jay and Hart, will never advance beyond the superficial.

But tonight is not for contemplating Jay and Hart, not for reminiscing about Lance. Tonight his mind must remain clean of all impressions and evaluations. Kane does not want his disposition read as he reads the dispositions of others.

At the bar, Kane orders a drink. He is worn and weary. The drink does nothing to alleviate the strain. He orders another.

Leaning against the bar, Kane spots Helmut Wagner squeezing toward him across the dance floor.

"Helmut. Care for a drink?" Kane asks when Helmut reaches him.

Helmut consults his watch, then frowns. "I did not allow for a social interlude in our schedule."

"I'm certain we can spare a few minutes."

"If we must," Helmut says. "This establishment works against our goals. Lewd behavior propagates participation in activities we attempt to curb." He scowls across the crowd.

"They are only dancing," Kane says. "Your drink." He extends the glass to Helmut.

"Danke—"

Emerging from the crowd, Jay jostles Helmut. Liquor sloshes over the rim of Helmut's glass and splashes his hand. Helmut wheels to an arrogant Jay and a grinning Hart.

"Schwein," Helmut snarls.

"How predictable," Jay says. "I like your friend, Kane."

"Go about your business," Kane says.

"Whatever filthy activity that is," Helmut says.

"What filthy activity do you think that is, Herr Wagner?" Jay asks, stepping closer. His voice drops to a whisper. "Maybe taking one of these young men into the alley and having a feast."

"Leave, Jay," Kane says.

"You wouldn't know about that, would you, Helmut?" Jay persists. "Your organization disapproves of such feasts."

After a glance at Helmut's frozen features, Kane slams down his glass. "Take the space cadet and leave."

"Space cadet?" Hart glances around, laughs. "Must be me."

Jay says to Kane, "This slime you're with diminishes your authority, Davies."

"We don't have time for this," Helmut informs Kane. "We should leave now."

"And where are you off to?" Jay asks, blocking their exit. "Don't tell me. A VA meeting." He jabs a finger at Kane's shoulder. "I certainly am glad Lance isn't around to see this. He'd impale himself on a stake before seeing you go for a cure."

Kane snags the collar of Jay's shirt, jerks him forward. "Don't talk to *me* about Lance," Kane orders.

With a snarl, Jay tears Kane's hand loose. "You disgust me." He shoves Kane back against the bar. Kane's glass topples.

The bartender slaps a towel over the spilt drink. "You boys caused enough ruckus in here last week," he says.

Leaning across the bar, Hart transforms his face to a monstrosity. Gasping, the bartender flees.

"That was stupid!" Kane glares from Hart to Jay. "You're both foolhardy and dangerous."

"No one's making you stay," Hart says.

"That's right, Kane," Jay says. "You want to act like you're a human boy? Let VA brainwash you." Scowling, Jay steps aside. "But don't come back to us when you're dying of thirst. We won't know you."

Without another glance at Jay or Hart, Kane steers Helmut toward the door. Outside in the cool still night, Kane summons Mahler's *Das Trinklied von Jammer der Erde* to calm his mind.

"Your friends would benefit from our meetings," Helmut states. "But they are too dimwitted to realize it."

Kane slips his hands into the pockets of his long coat. "Aren't we running late?"

"Yes. How did you arrive?"

"I drove, as you recommended." Kane crosses the street to his car. "I prefer driving to—"

"Do not consider the alternative," Helmut says while Kane unlocks the Prelude's passenger door. "You will learn these mandates at Vampires Anonymous." He flops into the bucket seat.

Kane slips into the driver's seat, settles comfortably into the leather upholstery. The Prelude purrs to life.

"Reconditioning," Helmut continues. "Purging the mind of the undesirable habits..."

Staring out the windshield, Kane flicks on the CD player, and Kiri does Puccini at full volume.

O

Men crowd the Vampires Anonymous meeting room. In groups, they whisper among themselves, cast furtive glances at new arrivals. All of them are pallid of complexion, thin of figure. Kane recognizes several faces, but shuns them. At the sight of John Studnidka, Kane forces association out of his thoughts.

Helmut nods toward John. "One of your friends, isn't he?"

"He's more an acquaintance," Kane replies.

"As you like." Helmut studies John. "He attends meetings regularly. But look at him — the flush of his skin. He has learned nothing here. He refuses to take direction." Helmut gives Kane a sidelong glance. "He is too influenced by that troublemaker Andrew."

Kane shrugs off the comment.

After a glance at his watch, Helmut wades through the crowd. With a carved smile, he nods to men who greet him, but does not stop until he reaches the front of the room and the squat Louis.

"We had to set up an extra row of chairs tonight," Louis says. With the air of a castle guard, he surveys Kane. "I see you decided to join us."

Helmut places a hand on Kane's shoulder; Kane stands rigidly. "Kane is discovering that our circle is more benign than the circle of his old friends, aren't you?"

Kane nods.

"In the end, all will realize the necessity of our organization," Helmut predicts. "In these times of hedonistic lifestyles and growing martial law over individual existences, our kind must seek a lower profile."

"We have witnessed, in your friend Lance," Louis continues, "that the unrestrained hunting of humans will bring destruction."

"Not only to the individual," Helmut concludes, "but to the entire community."

"Indeed," Kane says.

Helmut consults his watch. "Time to begin. Louis, do we have a seat for Kane, near the front?"

"As you instructed." A hand at Kane's elbow, the short man guides him to two empty metal chairs in the front row. "Save this chair for Helmut," Louis says. "He usually sits up front." He points out three chairs to the side of the podium. "You are his special case. He doesn't want you to feel ignored."

Kane sits down and focuses his attention on Helmut, who positions himself behind the podium. Spreading out a few sheets of paper, Helmut sweeps the room with his cold gaze. Quiet descends, followed by the shuffling of feet and the scraping of chair legs as the men seat themselves.

"I welcome you to Vampires Anonymous," Helmut says, his voice filling the small room. "A special welcome to new members who have seen the wisdom of joining us."

Kane remains motionless under Helmut's gaze.

"Vampires Anonymous is a support group," Helmut says, consulting his notes. "We are here to help each other spurn the need for human blood. The founders of this organization know that this task is not an easy one. But our objective is attainable. By seeking other forms of nourishment, we can stop the killing and become normal members of society."

Kane shifts on the hard chair. Around the room, he senses a collective harmony with Helmut's doctrine.

"The most obvious source for blood is blood banks." Helmut smiles. "But we don't recommend a rampage of theft." The members laugh nervously. "Plasma packets are available through our organization," Helmut continues, the smile quickly put away.

"Another alternative is the blood of animals," Helmut explains. "We recommend domesticated beasts or rats for the city-bound, horses and cattle for those in the rural regions. We encourage members to utilize these sources quickly. The sooner human blood is forsaken, the sooner we will attain our ultimate ambition."

A well-placed pause holds the room. The members are attentive, ready to hear the ultimate ambition. Gripping the edges of the podium, Helmut straightens to his full height. His lean face gleams.

"In the end," he states, "we must abstain from the consumption of all blood."

The aria playing in Kane's mind wavers, out of tune. The men wait eagerly for Helmut to lead them on this lofty quest.

"We must stop the consumption of human blood to restore our humanity," Helmut states. "The only road back to humanity is total abstinence. To the initiate, this intent may seem far-fetched." He sets his eyes on Kane. "Yet, in this country, also in parts of Europe, Vampires Anonymous has been successful in turning our kind from their bloodlust." He glimpses his watch, smiles briefly, and gathers his papers.

"Now," Helmut says, "I invite one of you to come forward and share his thoughts." Again, he looks at Kane.

Kane tears his gaze away to study his hands in his lap. Breath held, he waits through the silence, then relaxes when footsteps move from the back of the room toward the podium.

"I was hoping you would volunteer," Helmut whispers, taking the seat beside Kane.

Kane touches his brow. "My thoughts are too muddled."

"That's the perfect time," Helmut says. "Sharing your confusion would help everyone understand themselves." Helmut places a hand over Kane's. "But I will not force you."

At the podium stands a rail of a man with a haggard face. For the moment, he seems transfixed by some thought his quivering lips are reluctant to form. Louis rises from his chair and whispers sharply to him. The man shakes off his reveries.

"My name is Noel. I'm a vampire," he says, his voice weak.

Kane braces himself.

"Hello, Noel!" the members respond.

"Hi," Noel mutters. "A month ago I advanced from the plasma stage of recovery. I tried rats. Killing a dog or cat seemed cruel." He sways from one foot to the next. "The rat blood made me violently ill. Louis suggested that I try a cat instead. He said that alternative sources of nourishment vary from individual to individual. Cat blood made me sicker." He takes a deep breath. "I've tried dogs, but I can't keep anything down.

"I don't know what to do next." Noel's pale eyes reflect torment. "Louis suggested moving on to total abstinence." He gestures at his skeletal frame. "I've lost thirty pounds. I'm constantly nauseated and dizzy. I don't know how much longer I can go on. My resistance grows weaker as I grow weaker."

"That is why we are here, Noel," says a deep voice from the back of the room.

Kane looks over his shoulder to the tall, well-proportioned, gray-haired man marching toward the podium. The intelligent, striking face veers right and left, brimming with assurance. Kane turns away from the power gleaming in those violet eyes.

At the front of the room, the man swings around and faces the meeting. "Hello, my name is Maxwell, and I am a vampire."

"Hello, Maxwell!"

"You can depend on any of us to help you overcome this obstacle," Maxwell says. "United strength and courage will defeat the burdens of our condition." He places a hand on Noel's shoulder. "Thank you for sharing, Noel. Everyone, thank Noel for bringing up this important topic." The members applaud. "Be seated, Noel. And listen."

Maxwell waits until Noel has returned to his seat. Then, he slams a large hand against the top of the podium.

Kane jolts in his chair. Around him, the other men crane forward, rapt. Kane empathizes with them. Maxwell's face radiates confidence; the violet eyes blaze with passion. His every movement promises seduction.

"We must abandon the old ways." Maxwell sweeps the room with his hand. "Abstinence! Total abstinence at any cost..."

Maxwell marches to one side of the stage, pausing to direct his stare at one man, then another. With each step, Maxwell's lightweight slacks mold to his pelvis, buttocks, legs; the shirt presses against his wide chest; the sleeves flow around his gesturing arms. His fervid gaze never leaves his audience.

Around Kane, the men are open-faced, open-minded — mesmerized. Helmut's sway over these men is mere *obbligato* to Maxwell's dominance. With his show of earnest sympathy, he

– 154 –

draws each man forth to take communion, with his words as the host.

His voice vibrates through the room, a resounding opiate. "In the end, personal victory will outweigh the carnal satisfaction of consuming blood," Maxwell commands. "Fight against the murderous tendencies of bloodlust..."

Kane presses back in his seat, away from that voice. He struggles against an urge to question himself and his existence. He realizes that a beguiling Beast hides behind Maxwell's human mask, yet he cannot tear his eyes away. The Beast's maw yawns open; Kane feels himself slip down the Beast's gullet to drown in the acids of the Beast's gut. Consumed like the other men, he is ready for Maxwell's erosive revelations.

If only I could look away.

Back at the podium, Maxwell leans forward, a confidant to each individual. "You will be more human than any living human. You will have struggled for your humanity. We have all fallen. We will fight our way back to a more enlightened existence. To an exceptional eternity that humans dare only dream of."

Maxwell's words resound in an enthralling baritone that charms the senses. A fever grips Kane. His convictions waver. All melodies are jumbled in Kane's head — everything conducted to confusion. He grasps the sides of his chair. This man, with his physical appeal, entrancing intonations, and sorcerer's eyes, is the allure, the narcotic of Vampires Anonymous.

"You are moved," Helmut says. He rests his hand on Kane's leg. "You shiver with excitement for that higher plane."

Kane looks into the sharp face, the royal-blue eyes shining with fervor. He shifts his leg, but Helmut's grip tightens.

Maxwell beckons others to share their troubles and triumphs.

"Now," Helmut declares, "you must speak. I can see that Maxwell has touched you." He cups his hand under Kane's elbow, urging him to stand. "You must tell all."

Falteringly, Kane rises.

"Yes!" Maxwell cries, extending his hand, reaching for Kane with his compelling stare. "Come forward, my friend. Tell us what you feel!"

Tearing his gaze from Maxwell's face, Kane catches sight of John Studnidka, but as ordered, John shuns contact.

"Go on," Helmut urges.

Kane turns abruptly toward Maxwell. He is overwhelmed by every aspect of the man.

Maxwell steps forward. He entreats Kane, "Join us."

In the craw of the Beast, swallowed naked and whole.

Louis crosses to him. Kane offers no resistance when he takes his arms and leads him to the podium, to Maxwell. Kane gapes at the man, feels the full potency of the violet eyes as they cast their spell. He hears their edicts as if the words are spoken in his brain. Louis releases him. Maxwell takes control — such control. Kane never imagined one man could possess this extensive sovereignty.

I have you, I possess you, I consume you, gloats the Beast.

"Welcome to Vampires Anonymous," Maxwell says. "My name is Maxwell, and I am a vampire." Swinging an arm around Kane's shoulders, Maxwell turns him toward the gathering. "Welcome our new friend."

"Welcome!"

Kane cringes from the explosive voices. The onslaught of noise jolts him. Although trapped by the intimacy of Maxwell's embrace, he feels released from the man's dominance. At the sudden return of freedom and uncorrupted thought, he trembles.

"Yes!" Maxwell shouts, his hand clamping on Kane's shoulder. "I feel the emotion surging through you. Speak, my friend. Your name and what you are." Maxwell takes a seat beside Louis.

Kane gropes at the podium for support. Before him, the expectant faces wait to hear what Maxwell's mastery has wrought within him. He glances toward John Studnidka. This time, John stares back. His smooth face is the perfect touchstone.

The arias flow clearly, note for note, measure for measure.

"My name is Kane Da—"

"No last names are necessary," Maxwell interrupts.

Kane draws a slow breath, lets his hands fall to his sides. "My name is Kane *Davies*," he repeats. He senses instant tension in the men behind him. Helmut watches him apprehensively. "I am a vampire. For centuries, I have traveled the night and watched the successes and failures of the world.

"But what I have witnessed tonight..." For a last time, he glimpses John, whose expression borders on worry. His thoughts will not be quieted, yet he will not drag John into the craw of the Beast with him. "How do I feel, these organizers of Vampires Anonymous want to know." He gives Maxwell a nod. "Who would not feel impassioned and ready to conquer all after such a speech?"

Uncontrollably, Kane snorts a laugh. "Domesticated beasts?" He pins his stare on Helmut. "Horses? My good fellows, real vampires don't suck cow."

Chair legs scrape the floor; Louis advances toward him. Maxwell, his features stone, waves him off.

Murmurs of dissent ripple through the room. The men gawk.

"How can you be shocked?" Kane asks, surveying the crowd. "Why have none of you questioned the doctrines so zealously preached here? Are you so ready to give up the most natural part of your existence? Can you believe that you can become human again? You are vampires. You cannot reverse the process."

He gestures toward the back of the room. "Look at Noel. Look at him! Giving up blood is destruction — more painful and horrifying than the stake or sunlight."

"Thank you for your views, Kane," Maxwell says.

Kane turns to find the man at his side. Lost in his own speech, he has allowed his defenses to drop. In an empty room, would he be able to correct the error? He steps back from the hand Maxwell extends toward him and returns to his seat.

Beside him, Helmut breathes through his mouth. He ignores Kane and watches Maxwell with an expression akin to terror.

"We must thank our friend Kane for his words," Maxwell says to the restless crowd. "I understand them, for, as he said, they are thoughts that enter all our minds at one time or another."

He leans forward on the podium. "They are thoughts of personal corruption that must be overcome." His voice soothing, Maxwell says, "My friends, humanity is a state of mind. Each of us can reach that plane. I have reached it. Louis—" The eyes shift. "And Helmut — have reached that zenith which frees us from the bloodlust. To join us there, you must practice abstinence."

He levels the violet eyes, riddled with sparks of rage, upon Kane. Behind Maxwell's human mask, the Beast snarls. "Abstinence only seems like destruction."

Legs crossed, Kane leans back in the metal chair. An overture that he had thought forgotten drifts through his mind.

2

A preoccupied Helmut beside him, Kane follows the men out of the church. Briefly, Kane chastises himself for his outburst. When he is far from the perceptions of others, he will devise a way to correct the wreck he has made of his own scheme.

As he and Helmut step into the alley where the Vampires Anonymous members linger, Louis strolls up behind them. Kane faces him; Louis turns up the corners of his wide mouth.

"Helmut," Louis says, "if you can spare a moment, Maxwell would appreciate your company." Louis strains the smile further. "But you should wait, Kane. Maxwell won't keep Helmut long." Louis returns to the church.

"Will you wait?" Helmut asks, tearing his eyes from Louis.

"Of course," Kane says.

Nodding, Helmut starts toward the door, pauses to compose himself, then hurries inside.

Kane wanders into the alley, skirts the thinning crowd of men. Some of them stare at him in anger.

From the midst of the group, John approaches. Kane backs away, shakes his head, yet John walks up to him. "What were you thinking?" John demands in a breathless whisper.

"Now is not the time," Kane says. He peers into the church. The entry beyond the door is deserted.

"This is going to blow up in our faces," John states. "I'm not trusted enough to pull it off—"

"Go home or to work or wherever you go," Kane says. "Get away from me. I don't want Helmut to see us talking."

"Jay is going to abort this whole thing when he—"

"You are not going to tell Jay," Kane orders. "I can fix this. Leave before Helmut comes back."

Briefly, John is torn between Kane and the open door. With reluctance, he nods. "Remember Pablo and Colin," he warns. "And Lance." He dashes into the alley's shadows. A huge bat veers near the church spire, then flies off into the darkness.

I will always remember Pablo and Colin. And Lancelot.

From within the church, footsteps echo. Helmut joins him. "You are in luck," Helmut says. His arm drops around Kane's shoulders. "Maxwell is fascinated by you."

"Is he?"

"Yes! He wants to speak to you." Helmut guides Kane through the door. "You are privileged, Kane. Maxwell rarely takes time with individuals. You are a special case."

Kane hides a frown. Earlier, he was Helmut's special case. Being promoted to Maxwell's doesn't set well, especially after the outcome of tonight's meeting.

Bypassing the church's meeting room, Kane and Helmut walk through a corridor. At the end, a cramped stairwell drops into the cellar. Helmut motions Kane ahead of him. A hand on the stone wall, Kane edges his foot down to the first step. The air holds a scent of overturned earth. Helmut close behind, Kane descends the stairs. At the bottom stretches another hall, lined with cob-web-hung doors.

"This way," Helmut instructs, urging Kane on.

At length, they reach a door edged with light. Helmut steps past Kane to knock. Kane takes a quick bearing. The hallway terminates several yards away in another descending stairwell. The scent of earth is stronger.

The door opens, Louis stands before them. The dim yellow light within the room transforms his long red hair to strands of fire. He steps aside, leaving little room to pass. Helmut hesitates, then squeezes through. Kane disregards Louis for the man, just beyond the lamp glow, seated at a massive desk inside.

"Ah, Kane ... Davies," Maxwell says from his shroud of shadow. The light reflects off a ring as he gestures Kane into the room. "I am glad that you could stay. For a talk."

"I am flattered that you invited me," Kane replies.

Louis shuts the door. Helmut remains at Kane's side.

"Be seated," Maxwell says. "Louis, a chair for our guest. Our new friend."

Louis lifts a heavy chair with one hand and plunks it down before the desk. Sitting down, Kane watches Maxwell. The man's face is amused; he enjoys the façade of hiding in the shadows. But the Beast's violet eyes glare through the darkness.

"You gave us a turn this evening," Maxwell says. "Didn't he, gentlemen?" A strong hand rests on the desktop, in the pool of yellow light.

"I didn't think you would object to opposing views," Kane said. "What would the world be if everyone thought the same thoughts or acted upon the same convictions and presumptions? A generic, banal world isn't worth inhabiting."

"I appreciate your candor." Maxwell straightens in his chair. The light spills across the pale face, its lines and creases tight. The violet eyes capture the light, re-ignite it at the core of the large pupils as a vibrant torch. "I only hope your passion has not led any of our members astray, Kane. We work hard with these men. To help them. I would hate to think that your words — so obviously spoken from your heart — have foiled that work or brought misery to even one of my men."

Kane nods.

Maxwell's mouth splits in a smile. He settles back in his chair. "In the future, if you feel inclined to such speeches at my meetings, I ask that you give us warning. So that you may be properly introduced. As a ... devil's advocate."

"Of course," Kane says, standing.

"I have enjoyed our talk," Maxwell says. "I look forward to another, longer discussion. When time permits."

"So do I. Good night." Kane turns toward the door. Louis stands in his path. Helmut, lingering behind the chair, takes Kane's arm to lead him out.

"Helmut," Maxwell says. "I require you a while longer. Kane can find his own way out. Can't you, Kane?"

"Of course."

"Good. You and Helmut can make plans tomorrow night. Or better yet, join us again, Kane. And ... observe."

"I'll do that," Kane says. Louis steps aside, and Kane opens the door into the hall. The door swings shut after him.

Kane retraces the tunnel toward the stairs. He would like to explore the bowels of the church, but leaves it for another time. He knows that after his outburst, he will be watched.

Attentive to the building's sounds, he hears sharp footsteps ahead, descending the stairs, then striding toward him through the twisting hall.

Kane pushes on. Ambush would come from behind, not ahead. Unless this has been prearranged: the chat, cold with undercurrents of animosity from Maxwell, to be followed by destruction by an unknown assailant.

Footsteps clatter closer, bouncing off the pitted walls. A fragrance precedes the hall's other occupant. Then she rounds the juncture and halts, as surprised by Kane as he is by her presence here. He memorizes the attractive face, framed by streaked blonde hair. He extends his senses; they collide with a maliciousness that enwraps her like her flowing cloak.

The woman surveys his figure with her black eyes. A sneer curling her full lips, she nods, then brushes past him, her dry hand touching his.

Wiping the back of his hand against his long coat, Kane watches the woman until she rounds the next juncture. Only when he is certain her retreat is not a ploy does he hurry through the church to the side entrance.

In the alley again, Kane studies the huge edifice. Briefly, he wonders what evil drove out the God-fearing and permitted Maxwell, that woman, and Vampires Anonymous to claim this church.

Or were they the miscreants responsible for the desecration?

Kane senses movement within the church. Coat pulled around him, he leaves the alley. He holds further thought in check until he is behind the wheel of the Prelude.

Driving home, he recalls when rumors of Vampires Anonymous began to circulate, first from Europe, then in the United States. He dismissed the reports, not believing that any of his race would trust an organization that purported to cure vampirism. But, like a recurring motif, the reports persisted from one after another of the major cities. Not only did VA exist, but a rash of destructions and disappearances coexisted with it. When circulars appeared here announcing a new branch and heralding Vampires Anonymous's success at returning vampires to the fold of humanity, Kane, with Lance's agreement, decided to investigate.

Kane selected John for the preliminary reconnaissance, against Lance's warning that John would have difficulty playing the part of penitent vampire. Lance's insight proved valid. In spite of his disregard for VA's edicts, John seemed in no danger. He continued to attend the meetings. Not being a member in good standing, however, John learned nothing of value.

Nonetheless, the infiltration scheme was not abandoned. Lance was to be the next to enter VA's ranks. Just hours after initial contact, he was destroyed. Doubtless the police were tipped off to Lance's whereabouts, and how to destroy him, by one of Maxwell's henchmen.

Kane grips the steering wheel, fighting the insistent dirge in his mind. He was so grief-stricken by Lance's destruction that he could not see the hands pulling the strings of the police. With the assistance of Andrew's objectivity, Kane surmised the circumstances of Lance's murder — and the full extent of the danger.

After Lance's destruction, Jay Bauer argued to end the investigation. Kane, however, was determined to discover Maxwell's goal. Regardless of Jay's objections, and the risk, Kane ingratiated himself into Helmut's favor. Tonight saw the culmination of his scheme. He was escorted to a Vampires Anonymous meeting by one of its highest-standing lieutenants.

And I nearly threw it away!

Kane brakes the car in front of his house. He must correct tonight's mistake, or the rash of destructions will continue.

O

Hands wrapped around a stoneware mug of coffee, Kane walks through the dark house to the living room. The afternoon sun has left this side of the house warm, but the heat is wasted on his naked skin. He is chilled from the inside, colder than he has been in three hundred years. Sitting on the sofa, he sips his coffee. The liquid scalds.

After last night's encounter, he is haunted by Maxwell Guthridge, the powerful Beast at the heart of Vampires Anonymous. If the Beast cannot entice the vampires of Kane's persuasion to give up the human blood they require to survive, then it will stake them to the earth as were Lance, Pablo, and Colin. By whatever methods, the Beast is dedicated to annihilating the vampires of Kane's orientation.

Knowing Maxwell's mission — the Beast's conniving evil — Kane questions his strategems. Should he forget the ploy of joining the organization? Or should he play the role through, insinuate himself into Maxwell's ranks, and attack from within?

The wisest choice might be the direct one. End the coy duel, call Jay, John, Hart — and Andrew — and destroy Vampires Anonymous before it can destroy anyone else. Already the toll has been too high.

Will you end the bloodbath now, Kane, or forge on to prove that you can outwit these monsters?

In the past, he always played through to the ultimate climax. More times than not, he was successful, defeating this foe or that. But there were also appalling turnarounds that left his allies blood and bone. Good men, like Lance, paid for Kane's insistence that risk is a necessity of existence, that all enemies can be vanquished.

Is Vampires Anonymous surmountable? Maxwell and his tribe are resourceful, clever. Maxwell, an hypnotic evangelist against the sins of indulgence, possesses enthusiasm, magnetism. Through his organization, Maxwell has succeeded in luring vampiric men across the country to suicide. Can a full-out assault overpower that cleverness, that magnetism?

Or will the subtle scheme which Kane and Lance concocted prove a more potent conqueror? If Kane can infiltrate the hierarchy of Vampires Anonymous, he might discover a weakness to crumble the organization. Razing the organization from its foundations is what he must accomplish. Simply eliminating Maxwell and his henchmen will not be enough.

After dressing, Kane slips into his long coat, straightens the collar. He checks his pocket watch. He has more than enough time to drive to the church for his rendezvous with Helmut.

For now, he will stay with his original plan. If he cannot correct last night's error at tonight's meeting, then he will orchestrate a direct battle against Vampires Anonymous.

Either way, others will be destroyed. Kane has faced that fact in the past and survived. He will face it again — and again — and not cringe from his responsibility for it.

O

As he walks down the sidewalk, Kane presses the alarm remote, and the Prelude chirps its welcome. Rounding the back of the car, Kane runs his fingers along the trunk. He pauses, looking over his shoulder to the end of the block, where the road rises over a sharp hill. Not far away, he hears the squealing of tires.

"I'll never drive you so recklessly," he says, patting the roof of the car. "Unless I have to." He imagines that the car twitches under his palm, as many a favorite horse used to do.

Kane unlocks the door. Fingers hooked under the handle, he hesitates again. The peeling tires sound closer. He turns toward the hill. Swerving headlight beams slash the sky, splatter the trees with a jittery white glow.

Engine roaring, a pickup truck hurtles over the crest of the hill. The truck bottoms out against the asphalt. Rubber smokes off the screaming tires. The pickup careens down the hill. Kane lifts his hand against the headlights' glare; the truck bears toward him.

Kane leaps over the Prelude. He cracks his foot against the roof, loses his balance. He lands hard on the sidewalk, rolls across his front lawn.

A horrific sound shatters the night.

Teeth aching, ears drumming from the vibrations, he lifts his head from the grass.

The pickup, rammed into the back of the Prelude, thrusts the black car along the curb. The wheels scrape against the cement. Tires explode. The sleek nose collides with another parked car. The hood folds and pops. The trunk buckles.

The back of the Prelude swings away from the curb. The pickup shoots across the street. Bouncing over the curb, the truck rides up the side of a house. One front tire caught on the foundation, the truck hangs at a precarious angle.

Silence stifles the night.

The passenger door of the pickup creaks open. A man falls out onto the ground. Scrambling to his feet, he flees.

Kane picks himself up. Pain stabs his elbow, throbs in his hip. He limps into the street. Glass crunches under his shoes.

Around the neighborhood, porch lights snap on. Voices raise an alarm. People quickly gather. Some, their faces masks of concern, run to Kane with questions for his well-being. Others meander out to gape.

For a moment, Kane remains still, staring. One minute ago — less — he stood beside a sleek car; now only a shattered ruin remains. He approaches cautiously, fearful that the Prelude might convulse in its agony. Hadn't a mare done that — many years ago — after catching a bullet meant for him? She convulsed, rolling her eyes at him as if in a plea for comfort.

Kane stumbles; someone steadies him, suggests he sit down. He draws strength for a grateful smile, yet walks to the Prelude. The car is no less pitiful than the mare. A headlight cover has been torn off, the lamp beneath shattered — an eyeless socket. He brushes his fingertips over the once-silken black finish.

The *glissandi* of sirens fills the night. Kane looks toward the hill, the bordering trees highlighted by flashing red light. Headlights top the crest, barrel down the hill. This time, they stop and splash the wreckage with stark brilliance.

O

Standing in the middle of the street, he watches the tow truck haul the Prelude away. The neighbors shuffle back toward their homes and sleep; the body has been removed and the vultures retire. Hands deep in his coat pockets, Kane shuts his eyes. The image of the wrecked car haunts him like a tormented spirit.

A car pulls up in front of the house. The engine revs, then dies. Helmut Wagner emerges. Face tight, he glances after the tow truck, then turns to Kane.

Kane feels the man's penetrating stare. He shuts off thought and feeling as Helmut approaches.

"I missed you at the meeting," Helmut says. "Maxwell noticed your absence."

"Uncontrollable circumstances," Kane replies. "You've just missed the excitement."

Helmut glances toward Kane's house. "Why don't we go inside? You can tell me about it."

"I think I'd rather go out," Kane replies.

Helmut is thoughtful. "I know just the place. Shall I drive?"

Kane hurries toward the car. "Either that, or we fly."

O

Driving along one of the city's main thoroughfares, Helmut expresses inordinate sympathy for the Prelude. Staring out the window, Kane grunts ackowledgement when necessary. The houses along the street begin to degenerate as they draw nearer to the coast. The scent of sea air mingles with the odor of refuse and decay. Even the glow from the streetlamps seems dimmer.

Ahead of them, at the end of the narrowing street, the sky is brightly painted with light. Kane realizes their destination; he clears his mind of reaction. From his memory, he selects a fugue to mask the details he has accumulated about Ocean Village.

"This place will take your mind off the accident," Helmut says, parking in the crammed lot.

As they stroll along the boardwalks, Kane observes Helmut. Perhaps the blond man will reveal some involuntary sign of Ocean Village's connection to Vampires Anonymous. Helmut merely rambles on about the organization's many benefits for members dedicated to its doctrines. Kane nods appropriately, letting the diatribe bypass him.

He cannot keep from speculation about this place. His agents have followed Helmut, as well as Louis, to the vicinity of Ocean Village. On each occasion, they eluded Kane's spies, but always at a different location: in the midst of the shops, out at the edge of the wharf, and in the parking lot.

Kane is not the only person suspicious of Ocean Village. John has told him that since Pablo's destruction, Andrew haunts the boardwalks, searching for the intangible.

"You're drifting, Kane," Helmut says. "I truly thought you were interested in our organization."

"I am," Kane replies. "I'm still upset by the accident."

"Of course you are," Helmut says. He takes Kane's arm. "You need quiet." He dismisses the village with a curt wave and leads Kane toward the parking lot. "We can go to my place. It's not far. We can continue our discussion in peace."

Leaving his car behind, Helmut leads Kane to the far side of the parking lot, then into a patch of trees.

Not far indeed — the connection is not Ocean Village...

Several yards from the lot, the trees thicken, and the ground drops sharply. Helmut warns Kane to watch his step. The blond man's hand tightens on Kane's arm. Is the hold to assist Kane or to keep him to their course?

"What was that?" Helmut asks over his shoulder.

"I didn't say anything," Kane replies. He must guard his thoughts more carefully; Helmut's perceptions are strong.

Through the fractured shadows, Helmut's expression is bewildered. "I thought you said something."

He stares at Kane a moment longer, then pushes on through the entanglement. The ground levels, but the going is still difficult. Helmut locates a narrow path, rough with rocks and sprouting scrub. And again, the path descends.

Into the craw of the Beast, Kane's thoughts whisper.

The roar of the ocean increases. The air is sharp with salt. Refracted light off the waves spears through the branches.

"Here we are," says Helmut.

Secure in a small inlet, a cottage stands on an outcropping. A narrow pier extends toward the sea. The rising tide washes against the far piles. To the south Kane can discern the lights of Ocean Village.

"You live here?" he asks.

"Why not?" Helmut returns. He grins. "You aren't afraid of water, are you, Kane?"

"Not at all."

"Good. Come in." Helmut leads Kane onto a wooden verandah which circles the foundation to the pier. There, a weathered door opens into the cottage. The main room reeks of decay. The furniture stands moldering in thick grime.

"Shall I light a candle?" Helmut asks, crossing to a littered table.

"I can see well enough," Kane replies. "You're not much of a housekeeper, are you, Helmut?"

"I can find a clean blanket to throw over the sofa if dirt bothers you," Helmut says.

Cottony gray stuffing and springs protrude from the sofa. A large roach preens on the stained armrest.

"We can talk at the table," Kane suggests. He pulls out one of the straight-backed chairs. A rat gnaws at the woven seat. The rodent peers up at Kane, then resumes its work. "I wanted to know more about your alternatives for nourishment."

"It is not complicated," Helmut says. He places a hand on Kane's shoulder. "Come, sit over here." He guides him to a cot under the raggedly curtained window. His hands slip around the collar of Kane's coat. "Let's be comfortable."

Kane shrugs off the coat. While Helmut hangs it up, Kane surveys the cot. The blanket and pillowcase look clean, smell fabric-softener sweet.

Helmut's hands skim Kane's shoulders, the long fingers pluck at Kane's gray-and-black-striped shirt. His chest presses against

– 169 –

Kane's back. His breath tickles the hair at the nape of Kane's neck. Helmut glides his hand across Kane's chest.

"Does Maxwell approve of this kind of persuasion?" Kane asks, shrugging against Helmut's embrace. "Or is this your own method of induction?"

"Forget about Maxwell and VA," Helmut whispers, unbuttoning Kane's shirt. "You are too tense."

"Lewd behavior propagates participation in activities we want to curb," Kane says, squirming free of Helmut's experienced hands. He turns, his calf bumping against the edge of the cot. By his expression, Helmut does not appreciate having his own words thrown back in his face. "We came here to talk."

"The evening is young," Helmut says. His hands smooth up Kane's chest, over his shoulders. Kane's shirt falls. "We will have ample time to chat." He nuzzles his face at Kane's throat and eases him down onto the cot.

Kane is repulsed by this seduction, yet he suspects that to stop it will ruin his last chance to infiltrate Vampires Anonymous. He braces himself to play the game through.

Helmut stretches over him. From outside, the surf drums counterpoint to Helmut's quickening breaths. Kane tries to switch positions. Trapped beneath Helmut, he has no control. Helmut wraps his legs around him, pinning him to the cot.

Helmut's caresses become abrasive. His fingernails rake up Kane's sides, scraping his skin.

Kane tenses. The intent of this seduction has become clear. He has crossed Maxwell, and Maxwell wants him destroyed. More, Kane realizes that this cottage is a death house and Helmut the executioner. How many other dissenters, lured by Helmut's show of concern, have found destruction here?

Helmut nips at Kane's shoulder, at his neck. Kane levers an arm under Helmut to throw him off. Helmut digs his fangs into Kane's flesh. The fangs clamp deeper, then rip. Agony stings Kane's eyes. He thrashes beneath Helmut's weight, but cannot free himself. Then Helmut rears back. Blood streaming his chin, he clamps a hand around Kane's throat.

Through the numbing pain, Kane realizes that he was foolish to underestimate the strength of Helmut's hatred.

Helmut lifts his right arm. In his hand, he grips a long wooden stake. A spider clings to the carved point. Kane grabs at the stake. Helmut clubs him in the face. Gripping the stake in both hands, Helmut hoists it high. Kane freezes, gaping at the point quivering above him. Beyond it, Helmut's face, bright against the gloom, wavers in its expression of animosity.

Then the stake streaks down — a blow to his chest, as if from a sledgehammer, followed by a moment of complete numbness. Pressure grows from his chest, spreads from his torso into his legs and arms, into his head. Pain shoots daggers of fire through him. The numbness returns, centers at his chest, creeps through him as each nerve perishes. Thoughts burst through his mind, too swift to be understood. A roar swells in his ears — the sound of the surf amplified to deafening decibels. From within the maelstrom, a frail note sounds, then is overwhelmed.

O

In the craw of the Beast.

O

A frail note reprised. Wavering, it expands to a refrain against a thunderous drum roll. Crescendo ... cadence. But not coda.

Senses return: a scent of decay, a chill of breeze, the rough touch of dirt, a blurred vision of buildings.

With the senses comes awareness.

Of thought.

You have escaped the Beast. Swallowed whole, yet regurgitated.

And of pain.

But the Beast still gnaws at your flesh.

Kane lies among the rubbish in a dark alley. Naked, he shivers against the cold. The shivering ignites the agony that penetrates his body, from his chest and through to his back. He lifts his head. His sight is uncertain, but, combined with feeling, he knows the dark, wet stain upon his torso is blood.

You will not survive. Free, but doomed.

Free — how and why? His head lolls on the ground. An image swirls behind his eyelids, charred into memory — Helmut and his wooden stake. Yet, the stake has been removed. Why?

He wasn't rescued. No one knew he was with Helmut. And a savior would not discard him with the trash of this alley.

For some unfathomable reason, Helmut changed his mind.

It doesn't matter, Kane. Your heart is bleeding; you will expire, disintegrate. Another pile of dirt in a city littered with dirt.

Through the haze of pain, Kane realizes that something is approaching him. He opens his eyes. A form slinks through the alley. Kane groans, pushes a heel against the ground.

The form circles him, moves out of range of his vision. The creature sniffs around his head, paws at his hair. Kane twists away, and the creature skitters off.

Dunkel ist der Tod.

A pall of cold closes around Kane, and the dim sights of the alley flicker out.

Dark is death.

VIII

DEATH'S LAIR

1

After a week of nightly visits to Ocean Village, I have discovered nothing that connects it to the cadavers of Vampires Anonymous. Not to insinuate that Colin's last words were worthless, but if Pablo stumbled onto something here that led to his destruction, I'm a blind bat with malfunctioning radar.

I head toward the exit. Along the way, I scout the boardwalks for a blond pixy playing lost lamb. In spite of my warnings, Ryan still finds this place a smorgasbord of culinary possibilities. Of course, he's only four; I can't expect him to have my sophisticated aesthetics.

There's the little bat, hamming it up for two half-clad surfers. Maybe his aesthetics aren't so unsophisticated.

"Ryan, time to fly," I call, setting an intercept course.

When he turns to me, the smile he has displayed for these blond hunks deteriorates to that don't-interrupt-feeding-time look I'm beginning to know too well.

"This your half-pint?" one of the surfers asks.

"Blood relative," I reply, picking up the scowling Ryan. "Don't be such a fidgit."

"Hungry," Ryan states. "I'll share."

Ooo, how he connives to get his way.

"It was an enormous pleasure meeting you boys," I say, tussling Ryan under an arm.

"Sure thing, dude," the first one says, giving me the thrice-over. "Why don't you join us tomorrow?" His eyes meet mine. "Catch some waves. Party hearty."

"Thrill me."

"Will do, dude." He winks as the two of them saunter away.

Why do I get these invitations when I don't have the time — or to be truthful, the inclination — to accept them?

"Don't spit and hiss so," I chide Ryan as I carry him into the parking lot. "I've told you a trillion times we have to find our marks where we won't be remembered. Quit chewing on my wrist or I'm throwing you into the ocean!"

"I want down."

We have journeyed far enough from Ocean Village that he might not scamper back for his double-surfer entrée. I set him down. His so-hurt-and-pathetic expression almost softens what's left of my gut. I stand firm. He will learn vampiric etiquette.

"You're mean," he mutters.

"If I'm so mean, why do you hang around with me?"

He puckers up his face in thought. After what seems an eternity, he smooths the front of his miniature sports jacket. "You give me nice clothes."

Which is why I allow him to hang out with me. What other four-year-old corpse appreciates good clothes as much as I do?

That's not the only reason I keep him around, but Andrew doesn't admit everything right off the bat.

We continue our walk home — Ryan still hasn't gotten the transmutation trick down, and I don't like driving Pablo's van.

Ryan skips ahead of me. The street is deserted, so there's little chance he'll imprudently put the drain on anyone, or that some creep will accost him. Still, when I lose sight of him, I experience pangs of worry. I know he survived the streets before he took up with me, yet I can't stop thinking of him as this little bat-in-arms lost in a big ugly city.

After several minutes, I pick up my pace. Worry has fostered dread that he's stumbled under the wheels of a bus or fallen down a sewage drain. Dread grows into hysteria when I see him dash out of an alley.

Wings flapping furiously, feet several inches off the ground, Ryan tears up the street. He rams me, bowling me over. Jumping onto my chest, he tugs on my tie.

"Lordie, boy, what is the problem?" I choke. "Is it her?" I still want to get my claws into the skirt that made the kid a vampire. "Where is she?"

Shaking his head, he pulls on my hands and hoists me to my feet. With a distressed look, he drags me toward the alley. The black entrance yawns before us. I stumble to a halt. Ever so sensitive, my nose picks up a scent I've become too familiar with during the last week. I was introduced to it the night I found my Pablo and renewed the acquaintance in Colin's apartment. The smell of spilt heart's blood drenches this alley.

"Who's in here, Ryan?" My voice comes as a strained whisper. "One of us?"

Tugging on my arm, Ryan points toward an overflowing trash bin several yards ahead. My clear night vision locates a naked body in the rubbish. The white skin is streaked with blood that shimmers in the frail night glow. Against my will, my feet lead me closer. Andrew would rather not preside over another expiration, but neither can I leave this man to a solitary end.

Ryan, sniffing the air, approaches the man. The man groans, then squirms as if to escape. He turns his face toward me.

Kane.

Kneeling beside him, I take his hand, lean close to him. "Kane, it's Andrew."

Kane opens his eyes. His hand flexes around mine. I can't tell if he recognizes me or is grasping at any reassuring touch.

Swallowing back sickness, I examine the wound in his chest. Only a wooden stake could inflict a vampire with a gaping wound that exposes broken bone and straining, punctured heart.

Deterioration of the body must have begun before the stake was removed. Kane has aged. Lines mark the once-smooth brow; a network of wrinkles frame the eyes. His cheeks are more hollow, his lips dry and cracked. Gray flecks the black hair. The skin of his hand is splotched, the knuckles swollen.

"Who did this?" I sputter, although I could hazard a good guess. "Do you think you can hang on while I get my van?"

That's better, Andrew, take control. Maybe the wound isn't destructive. I cannot endure another deathbed scene.

Kane swallows hard; his features constrict with pain.

"I'm going to get the van." But how can I leave him here unprotected? I look at Ryan kneeling at Kane's head. "Ryan, you have to stay with Kane."

His almond-shaped eyes narrowing, Ryan nods.

Kane is too out in the open. I carry him to the far side of the trash bin. As I place him gently on the ground, he trembles.

What we need here is a blanket. I scan the alley, while fingering the nub of my jacket. There's not a quilt in sight. I examine my clothes, then the shivering Kane. I strip off my slacks and hand them to Ryan.

"I won't be gone long," I say as I take off my jacket. "Ryan, it isn't polite to gape."

"Big."

"Hold this." I drop my jacket over his head.

After dressing Kane in my clothes, I cuff Ryan under the chin to lift his gaze to my face. "Don't let anyone near him."

The kid takes his post at Kane's side. Lordie, pity the poor soul that gets within a hundred yards of this watch-bat.

O

With a good tail wind, I soar home in a matter of minutes. After throwing together an ensemble, I drop off the balcony to the alley beside my building. The van — Pablo's van — sits forlorn, neglected since my first trip to Ocean Village. I bounce the keys in my hand as I approach. Once I'm behind the wheel, I'll be fine. Getting inside unnerves me. The interior still smells like Pablo, that special mix of soap, shampoo, and cologne. The first wave always hurts.

I unlock the door.

Peculiar, isn't it, that most vampires drive vans? I prefer something a touch classier. But most vampires do drive vans. Coffins fit snugly in the back so there are no frantic calls to Rent-A-Hearse when you need to skip town before the angry villagers storm the castle.

Finally — I'm inside and zooming down the street to where I left Kane and Ryan. Having the mind occupied helps when that first wave of Pablo essence hits.

I relocate the alley easily. Jumping out of the van, I race toward the trash bin.

The most ferocious roar I have ever heard greets me.

Ryan, teeth bared, clings to the edge of the trash bin with his claws. He yowls another warning.

"It's Andrew. Remember me? I took you in, gave you nice clothes."

Ryan jumps off the trash bin. "No one came."

That's good news. Now I can admit I feared that Kane's assailant would return to finish the job.

I brush my hand across the top of Ryan's head. "You did good, kiddo."

He offers me a rare, genuine smile.

O

After making Kane as comfortable as possible in the back of the van, I drive out of the slums toward his house. I force myself to stay within the speed limit. I don't want to explain me of the frantic face, Ryan who snarls out the window at every passing car, and Kane, in blood-soaked clothes, lying on a bed of newspapers in the back, to a policeman.

As I drive, I glance continually back at Kane. My senses tell me he's holding on, yet he looks emaciated, about to give up the ghost, as someone with a more cynical disposition might say. Our race possesses incredible rejuvenation capabilities — knife and bullet wounds heal miraculously — but Kane's wound is so savage ... Can such rending of flesh and heart mend?

At Kane's house, I open the van's side door. Kane looks at me with recognition. I pick him up and carry him to the door. After Kane utters the invitations that allow Ryan and me access to his house, we enter. I carry Kane into the bedroom. Like so many other boys in this city, he owns a bed. His coffin is hidden, appropriately enough, in a secret room. I place him on top of the eiderdown. While I go to find bandages, Ryan resumes guard duty.

Our kind aren't usually squeamish, but neither do we often face this level of barbarity. Fears that Kane won't survive beset me. I put up a brave front as I clean off the blood, but neither Kane nor Ryan is fooled.

Under the bright bedroom lamp, I examine his wound more closely. He has indeed begun to heal; a discolored scar marks where his heart was punctured. The hole in his chest has grown smaller. Still, the process is dreadfully slow.

"Sewing kit," I blurt.

Kane turns his head toward the chest of drawers.

Before I can move, Ryan leaps off the bed, climbs the chest, and roots through the top drawer.

"Bottom..." Kane murmurs.

Ryan drops to the floor, tugs open the drawer, and crawls inside. In a moment, he leaps out with an old tin box in hand.

"You are a boon tonight," I thank him.

I snap open the box, steady my hands to thread a large needle. With a gulped breath, I slip the needle through the skin at the edge of Kane's wound and draw the thread taut.

Kane groans, grabs at my hand. Again Ryan reacts faster than I. Pulling Kane's hand back, Ryan holds it against his chest. Pressing his forehead against Kane's, Ryan coos comfortingly while I sew the wound shut.

As I return the spool of thread and the needle to the tin box, I spot a small pair of scissors. I take them up, turn them over in my hand. An idea germinates. One thing might ensure Kane's recovery. I seem to be the only available source.

I shrug off my jacket and roll up my shirt-sleeve. The scissor blade is sharp; the gash I make over the artery inside my elbow hardly hurts. Cradling Kane in my other arm, I feed him the blood from my own veins.

In a matter of moments, thoughts swirl and vision blurs. I experience a strange intoxication, unlike that of strawberry margaritas or that of satisfying my own thirst. Warmth radiates from my arm and enfolds me. My head lolls against the headboard. Fragments of memory flutter through my mind, resurrecting sensations and emotions that taste of must. Present concerns fade; I welcome the release. Absorbed, I draw Kane closer. Isn't this what dying was like?

Fingernails dig into my skin, breaking the spell. I force my eyes open. Frightened, Ryan leans close to my face. "Stop!"

Reluctantly, yet knowing the tyke is right, I withdraw my arm from Kane. After bandaging myself, I pull a chair up to the bedside. Ryan crawls into my lap and drills me with his do-that-again-and-I'll-smack-you look. I ruffle his hair, then settle back to wait for a reaction from Kane.

By degrees, color returns to his gray skin. The wrinkles on his face become less marked, even if they don't fade completely. At length he opens his eyes. For the first time, I can believe that he will recover.

O

"I want you to find Jay," Kane says. He sits propped against the pillows of his bed holding a cup of strong black tea.

Jay Bauer won't be extremely happy to see my face. He didn't like me from the outset; he despises me since I did that number on his friend Christian Fellows.

"Couldn't I find Hart or John instead?" I suggest, sitting down on the mattress edge. "We have more of a rapport..."

"Yes, get John," Kane says. "He works at a gas station near his house." He glances at the bedside clock. "Hurry."

"I will." I stand. "Ryan will stay with you."

"Thank you, Andrew," Kane says, grasping my hand. "What you did—"

"Well ... you know." Pulling free, I back out of the room. "Keep an eye on him, Ryan."

I hurry toward the front door. Before I go out, I hear Ryan's voice: "My new papa gave me this nice suit."

And I don't even get upset.

O

At the base of the road that leads to Sybaritic Estates stands a pop-stand of a gas station. From a bat's-eye view, the building looks deserted. Making a pass, I realize that what I perceived as reflections of moonlight are sputtering fluorescents.

Back on my feet again, I cross the road from the ocean side. Inside the garage, a Mercedes is up on the rack, a lamp dangling from its belly. John, however, doesn't seem to be on duty. I creep through the gravel lot, and not just to keep my shoes from getting scuffed. Andrew has learned to be wary of every suspicious situation, and this situation looks suspicious.

– 180 –

"John?" My voice echoes back from the high cliffs, punctuated by the distant rumble of the surf. My hand slips into my jacket pocket where my trusty switchblade waits on perpetual alert. "Hey, Stud, you here?"

Turning slowly, I scan the darkness around me. There isn't much to see—

"*Boo!*"

The switchblade snaps out of my pocket. I spin around. The blade, shimmering under the fluorescent light, jabs out.

"Dang, Andrew, you've put a hole in my overalls!"

I gape at John's face. Pouty, he stares down at his stomach. I've rammed the switchblade to the hilt under his ribs.

"John..." I jerk the blade free.

"No harm done." He laughs. "You should have seen your face. When I scared you *and* when you realized you'd stabbed me."

"Some night, young man..." I warn him. I hold the switchblade gingerly, wondering where I'm going to wipe off the smear of blood.

"Allow me." John swipes it down the front of overalls unzipped more than four inches below his navel.

"You need to call Jay and Hart," I say, back on course for my mission, yet taking the long way around. John's face clouds. He's taking the direct route. "Someone tried to destroy Kane."

Quick tears brim his eyes.

"He's all right," I say. "Ryan and I found him, took him home. He's safe."

"Hell's fire!" He staggers toward the rusted gas pumps, then halts. "You're sure..." He takes a deep breath. "I warned him. After last night ... Hell's fire, I told him this was going to blow up in our faces."

Knowing nothing about last night, I concentrate on carrying out Kane's request. I place my hand on John's shoulder. "He wants you to contact Jay and Hart."

"Yeah. Jay can handle this." Wiping at his face, he turns back to me. "You've done us all a service we can never repay."

"I didn't do—"

"Andrew, humility doesn't suit you." He swings his arm around my shoulders. "Come inside. I'll call Jay. We can't leave Kane alone. We don't know if any of them have access to his house."

"He's not alone. Ryan's standing guard."

John holds his hand at knee level. "Baby bat? Come on, Andrew, who's he gonna scare off?"

"He's little, but feisty."

"Like his old man. Hello, Jay..."

Highly insulted, I cross my arms and lean back against the counter — then inspect the seat of my pants for grease. Let Jay go barging in; Ryan might chew off a few of his fingers. On second thought, maybe Jay should be warned.

"John. John." I tap his shoulder; he brushes me off.

"See you there." John hangs up.

Oops, too late.

O

"Little, but feisty," John says, stopping in the doorway of Kane's bedroom.

"I don't know why no one listens to me," I reply.

Ryan is improving in the transmutation department. This time he's changed not only his feet and arms to claws and wings, but has the better part of his face contorted to a snout. Fangs bared, he holds fort on the footboard of Kane's bed.

On the bed, Kane looks stronger. He has even managed a shade of his smile.

Staying at a safe distance, Jay glowers at the kid. "Who does this creature belong to?"

"He's his own bat," I say, rounding the bed to stand at Kane's side, "but he came with me."

"I should have known," Jay snorts. "Only you would—"

– 182 –

Wings flapping, Ryan leaps. Jay stumbles back against the dresser. He flails his arms at the hovering, clawing Ryan.

"Call him off, Andrew," Kane says. "You've had your fun."

Not nearly enough at Jay Bauer's expense, but for now, it will suffice.

"Yo, Ryan, tuck it in."

The kid drops to his feet and shakes the last of his wings from his arms. Keeping a steady scowl on Jay, he walks to me.

"How are you feeling?" I ask Kane.

He shakes his head. "Strange. I can feel myself healing — my flesh weaving back together." Hands knotted, he winces. "It is not a pleasant sensation."

"You should rest," John says, moving to my side. "Can any of those bastards get in the house?"

"No," Kane says. "Where's Hart?"

"I left him a message," John answers. "Some of his escort chores last until the wee hours."

"Then we'll have to postpone our plans—" Kane says.

"Plans?" Jay repeats, storming to the foot of the bed. "You aren't going to persist in this after tonight—"

"Regardless of what Helmut did to me, we cannot allow Vampires Anonymous to lure men into its trap," Kane says. "I did find out why Ocean Village is so popular—"

"What did you find out?" I interrupt. The mystery of the week is about to be solved.

"It's no more than a way station," Kane replies. "They take men there, then ask them 'home,' which is a deserted cottage in a nearby cove. That's where Helmut staked me—"

"That's the entire connection to Ocean Village?" I ask. I cannot believe that I have been traipsing through that place night after night when what I was looking for was someplace else.

"Why are you still here?" Jay demands. He takes a step toward me; Ryan rumbles a warning. "You've done your bit, Lyall, and we're all terribly grateful. Now beat it."

"You are out of line, Jay," Kane says. "Andrew is as involved in this as the rest of us. Maxwell had Pablo staked as he tried to have me staked tonight."

"This flit ripped Christian to pieces!"

On that subject I stand silent, but unrepentant.

Still, I decide to make things easy on Kane. He's been through enough for one night without trying to make excuses for me. Taking Ryan's hand, I start toward the door. "Andrew never stays where he's unappreciated."

"I appreciate you," John says, grabbing my sleeve. "Kane, either you say something, or I will."

"What do you have to say, Stud?" Jay asks.

"That maybe Christian got what's been coming to him for about two decades," John answers. "Maybe if Andrew hadn't done the honors, some of the rest of us were going to."

Here's a twist. I glance from the stunned Jay to Kane. Kane's eyes are distant, his lips barely moving as if he is listening to something else.

Or is he plotting his next move against Vampires Anonymous? The man amazes me. What motivates Kane Davies? He can think of nothing but continuing his campaign against Maxwell Guthridge, even after his near escape from destruction. My motives are clear-cut — I want the bastards to pay for taking my Pablo away from me. I doubt that vengeance keeps Kane on his course. He is an enigma I'll never comprehend.

Regardless, with plans against Maxwell and Vampires Anonymous in the making, I'm staying close at hand.

2

With an hour until dawn, Ryan and I head home, leaving Kane in Jay's care. Several minutes are wasted shaking off John — not wasted so much as endured — before we load ourselves into the van and trek back across the city.

Our neighborhood is bleak and silent in the early hours. After I've parked the van in the only spot at the far end of our alley, Ryan and I hustle toward our building.

An unusually fragrant smell rises above the odor of garbage. I take a few more steps then halt. An enticing aroma, like spring flowers sprouting in winter's chill, tickles my nostrils.

I step on something sharp. Lifting my foot, I look down at a thorn on the ground.

All right, who's the clown who heard that vampires can't resist picking up wild rose thorns — even if it waylays them until dawn?

Behind me, Ryan, face set in solemn concentration, methodically picks up the thorns and fills his jacket pockets.

I absolutely refuse to even look at those wild rose thorns, which trail all the way to the street. Tapping my toe, I knot my hands in my pockets. I will not succumb to a myth, a legend, a fragment of hearsay handed down generation to generation...

Maybe just one...

I scoop up a thorn. My foot inches me toward the next.

My sensitive hearing hones in on a stealthy sound ahead. With a surge of willpower, I pull back from this compulsion.

Andrew, you fool, you should have known this is a trap — and who is bonkers enough to have set it.

Not twenty feet away he stands, like some macho airhead in a revisionist war movie, toting an Uzi. Eyes sparkling, blond hair tousled around his thin face, Steven-Old-Boy opens fire.

"Hit the deck!" I shout over my shoulder at Ryan.

Bullets pelt around me; I dive behind the nearest trash bin. Steven-Old-Boy's gonna be real sorry if I've ruined this suit because of this stunt.

"Got you this time, Andrew old boy," Steven-Old-Boy gleefully shouts as he rams another clip of shells into his Uzi.

"Steven-Old-Boy, bullets aren't going to be much good against me," I return.

"They're silver bullets!" His mad cackle fills the alley.

Did he say silver bullets? Two years ago, when he plugged me with silver bullets, I explained to him that they are for were-wolves, not vampires. Is he slow or what?

Come to think of it, he probably is.

I peek over the trash bin. Ryan is still engrossed with the wild rose thorns. "Ryan, get the hell out of there," I shout.

Ryan continues on his way until a volley of bullets spark off the ground in front of him. When he lifts his head, his expression of surprise is outweighed only by the bulging pockets of his jacket.

"Silver is useless," I yell to distract Steven-Old-Boy long enough for Ryan to take cover.

Bullets rattle against the building behind me.

As the next volley sweeps toward him, Ryan dashes to the far side of the alley. A slug catches his ankle. He tumbles through the dirt. Leaping to his feet, he scans the grime on his clothes. He snarls at Steven-Old-Boy.

Machine-gun fire strafes through the alley, filling it with smoke. Bullets splatter the ground, then tear into Ryan. His little body convulses; he skids backward in a puppet dance. Then ZAP — Ryan soars down the alley, propelled by the onslaught, and smacks into a brick wall. The kid slides down behind boxes.

I know silver bullets won't destroy one of my race, but they make huge holes. Ryan is so tiny ... My throat clogs; my vision blurs.

In the next second a sound comes from behind the boxes. A chubby hand gropes air. Pointed ears sprouting from his blond hair, his brow and nose matted with fur, Ryan leaps on top of the boxes. His hands grope at his swiss-cheesed, bloodied suit. Eyes blazing, he rages like a frenzied pit bull.

Steven-Old-Boy halts in his advance. Fumbling with another clip, he backs away as Ryan, bellowing fury, races toward him. I detect a touch of panic under the dementia on Steven-Old-Boy's face. Ryan lifts clawed hands. Grunting curses, Steven-Old-Boy drops his Uzi and flees.

"Ryan!" I call, stepping out from behind the trash bin.

He stops and gives me his I-want-to-finish-this look.

"It's almost dawn," I remind him.

Sullen, he shuffles over to me.

At the far end of the alley, Steven-Old-Boy pauses and turns back. "I shall return!" he cries, shaking his fist.

O

In these tumultuous times, my apartment is no longer a safe cave. Too many of Vampires Anonymous's top corpses have been made welcome; it's a tad late to revoke invitations. I have remained this long bolstered by the thin assurance that Helmut and his league of carcasses have to retire for the day the same as I do.

Steven-Old-Boy, on the other hand, has freedom of all the earthly hours. Last night's ambush proves that he makes full psychotic use of them. Before long, he'll come battering down the front door with an arsenal of wooden stakes fastidiously sharpened to pierce my flawless skin.

I don't want to be home when he does, but I can't decide where to go. I don't fancy moving into another tenement. However, as I haven't shown up at my dreaded workplace since Pablo's destruction, I lack the resources to rent something upscale. I do have one idea ... Nah! My options will have to be cut pretty close to the bone before I go that far.

Even though seeking a temporary haven, I must take a few of death's necessities. I park the van under the kitchen balcony. I am in no mood to carry anything down twelve flights of stairs. Heedless of the neighbors and any other nosy humans in the vicinity, I signal Ryan to start dropping the suitcases.

Arms open, I watch the first one descend, a square speck that grows larger and larger ... That's no suitcase. That's the kid's crate. Uumph! I stagger against the van, praying my arms won't

– 187 –

be wrenched from their sockets. I should have done increased momentum calculations for a twelve-story drop.

Setting the crate on the ground, I whisper to Ryan, "Something lighter this time, kiddo."

If that huge shadow up there is my coffin, I'm going to have the kid's head on a plate.

Wait just a bloody minute!

"We're not taking the TV!"

Ryan's round, white face breaks through the darkness around the balcony. He pushes the TV a bit farther; the balcony creaks.

"Do wooden stake and mallet mean anything to you?" I ask.

With immense reluctance, he drags back the television.

Suitcases pelt down from the balcony. I barely catch one, drop it to the ground, then shimmy back to catch the next. By the time the plastic bag of tequila, triple sec, and frozen strawberries hurtles toward me, I am exhausted.

And I still have to lower my coffin down. Fortunately, the pulley I rigged when I moved Pablo's coffin still hangs by the door.

A coil of rope drops from the balcony. I barely cover my head with my arms before the rope hits me and loops around me, head to foot. I struggle to untangle myself. "Give me some warning, for pity's sake!"

Laughter drifts down from the balcony.

"You're pushing it, kiddo," I warn. "On *my* signal, got it?"

Tugging the rope taut, I give the signal. Overhead, Ryan shoves the coffin onto the balcony.

The boards that make up the balcony groan; loosening rivets squeal.

"Pull!" Ryan shouts. "Pull!"

I haul up the coffin. The boards continue splintering, the chicken wire rattles. The balcony collapses under the weight of the coffin.

"Heads up!" Ryan yells.

With Ryan clinging to the lid, the coffin drops. The slack in the rope is jerked up; I am yanked off the ground. Exerting all my strength, I regain my footing. Chicken wire and wood fragments rain around me. One particularly sharp piece of wood javelins into the asphalt near my foot. Horrified at almost being impaled, I release the rope and jump way back.

"Whee!"

"Lordie!"

With the rope singing through the pulley and Ryan along for the ride, the coffin torpedoes toward the alley. I dive for the rope; it burns through my hands. I dig in my feet, coil the rope around my hands, and pull, Andrew, pull! I halt the coffin's descent, but I swear my arms are three inches longer.

Hand-over-hand, I lower the coffin to the alley. Ryan, grinning from ear to ear, jumps up and down on the lid. "Again!"

O

Andrew's options seem cut pretty close to the bone. After driving in circles for an hour — all the while trying to keep Ryan from climbing onto the roof — I steer the van up a road to a cliffside house.

I extinguish the headlights. The horror of what I am doing may generate a better idea, and I may want to retreat before my presence is detected.

Parked in the dooryard, I remain behind the wheel. Ignoring Ryan's questioning stare, I survey the house with its stack of kindling. Light burns behind the windows, and although no shadow crosses the curtains, I know someone is at home.

"Are we going to sit here for eternity?" Ryan asks.

"Sarcasm is not an attractive trait in four-year-olds," I tell him. With a painful sigh, I get out of the van. Ryan, hefting his crate, follows. "We may not be that welcome."

Trotting up to the door, he gives it a swift kick.

When John Studnidka opens the door, I can't tell whether he or Ryan is more astonished.

Ryan looks up at me. "Him?"

"Mind your manners." I give John a halfhearted grin. "He didn't mean it."

"Sure he did," John replies, eyes glittering with amusement. He nudges the kid's crate. "I think I like the looks of this."

"Don't get anything up too high," I warn him. "This is a desperate decision. I seek *only* sanctuary for the kid and me."

John's face brims with innocence. "Would I force anything on you to repay the extreme kindness on my part for inviting you both inside?"

Ryan doesn't need to be asked twice. Pinning John with his I-don't-trust-you-and-probably-never-will stare, he carries his crate inside and scouts out a dark corner.

As John helps me carry in our luggage, I pointedly explain the need for this drastic move. He expresses profuse sympathy.

"It is rather opportune that you showed up," John says after we've crammed Ryan's and my gear amongst his clutter.

"Not that opportune," I reply, carrying the margarita fixings into the kitchen. How am I going to make him believe that if I had my druthers, I would have set up housekeeping in a roomy terrace apartment in the Intriguing Faction Borough?

"Sure it is," John insists, jostling me with his hip.

From underfoot, Ryan growls at him.

"Gawd, he's just like you," John says. "But to the point. You saved me tracking you down. Kane wants you to join us at his house. He still has grand plans for eliminating VA."

I shiver with excitement that Kane wants me included in his relentless fight against Vampires Anonymous. Pablo's destruction needs to be avenged. I'd feel better about accomplishing that feat against Maxwell and his henchmen with Kane Davies behind me.

"How is Kane?" I ask.

"Recovering. We're to meet at eleven." He studies Ryan. "Do you think baby bat can manage on his own for a while?"

"No," I answer more testily than necessary. I search the cupboards for a container. I open one door, and an avalanche of Tupperware assaults me. I give John a derisive stare.

"I'm not leaving Ryan alone, not even here," I state, dumping the strawberries into a four-quart bowl. "I've stumbled over too many bodies in the last week to risk it. Final word."

Kicking John, Ryan sticks out his tongue.

"He can get away with that, junior," John warns. "I'm not sure yet whether you can."

Snarling, Ryan huddles behind my legs.

"He barely obeys me, he's not going to listen to you." I consult my watch. "Nine thirty. Any suggestions for entertainment while we await the appointed hour?"

John's face contorts with lechery. "Several, but we'd have to put baby bat outside."

I knew this was going to be a bad idea.

3

I think a splinter of wood has worked its way into Kane's brain. What else could possibly explain the scheme he has formulated? Sinking into an overstuffed chair, I gape across the living room at him. Pale, Kane sits on the sofa, the new wrinkles around his eyes and mouth heightening the world-weariness of his expression. A smirking Jay Bauer and fidgety Hart Laughlin flank him.

Ryan tugs at my sleeve. "What's a derelict?"

John places a hand on Ryan's head to silence him.

"Someone who doesn't wear fancy clothes," Jay replies.

Ryan wrinkles his nose in distaste.

Kane's brown eyes are trained on me while he awaits my response to his proposal. Apparently my dumbfounded stupor doesn't signify.

"Why me?" I manage.

"We thought you wanted to help stop Maxwell," Jay says, crossing his arms. "Here's your chance."

"Be silent, Jay," Kane says, not taking his gaze from me. "They won't suspect you, Andrew. They'll be watching all of us." His large hand gestures to himself and his allies.

"I have a grudge against them," I protest. "How can you be certain they aren't watching me?"

"Nothing personal, Andrew," Kane replies, "but I don't think they consider you much of a threat."

Oh, no, that's not too personal. Even after I tore Christian Fellows joint from socket, no one considers me much of a threat. 'Oh, don't worry about Andrew,' *both* sides are saying, 'he's just a flit in a colorful suit.' I've built myself an unflattering reputation: Andrew, the Benign Vampire.

"Andrew," Kane says, "we need to know what's in the church's sub-basement. Jay and Hart haven't been invited inside. I want John at the meeting for appearances' sake. As for myself—"

"You're not going near that place again," Jay interjects.

"I'm still weak, or I would do it myself," Kane says. "You've been inside, Andrew. You've come in contact with all of them and know their scents. You'll go in while the meeting is in progress. It won't be that dangerous."

Who said I was worried about it being dangerous? The part that sets my skin acrawling is this disguise idea. I'll sneak into the desecrated church to snoop around; I'll even face Maxwell and Anneliiese, Helmut and Louis en corroded masse. But must I do it dressed like a vagrant?

O

I would rather decompose in a sunlit grave than go out in public looking like this. Unfortunately, matters have been taken out of my hands. To be plainly truthful, Kane has shamed me into it. But the consequences I have faced: Ridicule and Scorn! From my first appearance in this tattered overcoat, these torn and grimy jeans, and this battered fedora, Jay Bauer broke into peals of laughter. Even John Studnidka, my supposed friend, suggested that I should be rolled around in the backyard to dirty me up. The hardest blow came from the kid. Ryan took one narrowed-eyed gander at me and retreated behind the Stud's legs.

Now, out in the night, I wing my way to the desecrated church. Tonight's Vampires Anonymous meeting commences in less than fifteen minutes. From that point, I will have approximately one hour to get into the church, find whatever I can in the basement, and get out. I would prefer a wider margin, but I didn't formulate this scheme.

I did, however, amend it. I never leave home without my revolver since Pablo's destruction. As I hit the street, I check the clip of silver bullets. They won't stop the stiffs of VA, but silver slugs make such big holes I wouldn't load my revolver with anything else. Big holes in the torso, no matter how fast they heal, will give even a vampire a moment's pause — and perhaps give Andrew the chance to escape with his soiled skin. Armed to the teeth, I feel almost safe.

I shuffle through the alley toward the desecrated church. The last of the anemic VA members trail inside. That one's not so anemic. John Studnidka loiters in the alley, too obviously looking for someone. When he spots me where I rummage through a trash bin, he covers his mouth to stifle his burst of laughter, then hurries inside. The door shuts after him.

I continue my charade until my acute hearing picks up, through the stone walls, Helmut calling the meeting to order. I scout the alley for voyeurs, then mist under the door.

At a safe distance from the meeting room, I resume human form. I orient myself. Oops. Sometimes I get confused in the mist state. I mist over the top of the meeting room door toward the rear of the church. I change back to human form — again — these multiple transformations tucker a gent out. Alert to any activity, I hurry through the hall to the basement.

First on my inspection list is the multitude of bolted doors that line the basement hallway. By the time I've misted in and out of a half-dozen empty rooms, I'm bored stiff. At this rate, I won't reach the sub-basement before the close of the twenty-third century. I'll scope out another one, then I move on to hopefully more-interesting locales.

I assume this room deserted, until I notice that it isn't decorated with dusty cobwebs. I scan the room with my penetrating vision. What's this? Maxwell and his lot didn't strike me as computer whizzes, yet this setup seems rather sophisticated for amateurs. I cross to the terminal and keyboard. Of course, I'm no computer whiz either, but, maybe — this switch. The computer hums; the screen brightens.

Impatient, I wait for the program to boot up the system. This is convenient, an easy-access menu with an interesting list of files. Every state in the union is here, as well as several European countries. Let's take a gander at California.

Bakersfield ... Barstow ... El Centro ... Kings City ... Los Angeles ... Santa Barbara ... San Francisco ... *Susanville?*

What are these cadavers up to? Let's try ... this one!

Whoa, children, this doesn't look good. Names, addresses, phone numbers, some with "exterminated" and "cured" bracketed beneath them — the roll call of VA members scrolls up the screen. Andrew understands what this means, and he is one pissed-off bat.

VA members aren't the only boys on this list: Jay Bauer, Lance Broderick [exterminated], Kane Davies, Christian Fellows — should have 'shredded' under his name — Hart Laughlin...

Hold it right there! This is going too far:

Andrew Lyall
3850 N. Hill, 12D
[fly-by-night]

Fly-by-night my tight butt. Where's the erase key? Bingo! Kiss this info ta-ta, airheads.

That was a noise, Andrew. Right out there in the hall, footsteps and voices echo. How long have I been enthralled here?

I shut off the computer and stand dead still.

"I don't know how he survived!" Helmut's voice states — firmly, but with a panicky undertone.

"Liar," a female voice replies — Anneliiese, unless there are other females hidden down here.

The footsteps stop outside the door.

"I told you—"

A thud vibrates against the door, a scuffle follows.

I glance around. Hiding places are at a minimum.

"Take him downstairs," Maxwell's voice orders.

The footsteps, my acute hearing tallies a grand total of four sets, move on through the hall.

I'm supposed to find out what's downstairs. Can this be a good time when the whole festering lot of them are down there? On the other hand, I cannot return to Kane without a look-see. They seemed occupied. Why else didn't they detect my presence?

Certain the hall is empty, I mist back out. I tiptoe after Maxwell and company. When I reach the door to the sub-basement, I pause to assess everyone's whereabouts. With each cold body present and accounted for, I creep down the uneven steps.

I have descended into an entirely different world. The sub-basement is carved directly out of the earth — a very long time ago. But the odor of old earth that assails me is mixed with that of recently turned.

Following the pungent scent of Anneliiese's perfume, I work my way through a mini-maze of low tunnels. At length, I spot dim light ahead. An anguished shout — German-accented — rings out.

Creeping with the rats on the floor, I reach a long, narrow chamber, which is illuminated by smoking torches. Three coffins line one wall. The opposite wall has a number of long shelves newly dug into it — graves for Maxwell's most loyal? If so, I don't have a complete head count and had better watch my rear.

At the far end of the room stands a brazier brimming with red-hot coals. Helmut cowers against the wall beside it. Louis, a glowing pike in hand, hems Helmut in. Helmut's shirt is splotched with smoldering holes. Anneliiese watches with a smug expression. Maxwell, the not-morally-good face creased with anger, towers at her side.

"Don't lie, Helmut," Anneliiese says. "We know you released Davies from the stake." She glances at Maxwell. "I warned you that his proclivities would betray you."

"I didn't," Helmut protests.

Maxwell nods. Louis thrusts his pike into the brazier, then probes Helmut's chest. I cover my ears until his scream stops.

"The man is over three hundred years old," Maxwell says, his voice so low and deep that even I must strain to hear it. "He would have disintegrated to dust. The stake had to have been removed immediately. Only you were there to remove it, Helmut."

Louis rams the pike into Helmut, twists it deep. The fabric of Helmut's shirt catches fire. Louis laughs, strikes again.

"Maxwell," Helmut begs, "please ... don't do this!"

"Please ... don't..." Anneliiese taunts.

"*Schweig!*" Helmut returns, an echo of the old SS commander in his voice. "*I* was his first. You were an afterthought!"

Anneliiese snatches a pike from the brazier, jabs it at Helmut. His wails resound, louder, louder, then cease when she jerks the pike free.

"Maxwell!" Helmut gasps. "I destroyed Pablo and Colin."

"After you allowed Pablo to follow you to the cottage," Maxwell states. "To see too much."

My fingernails dig into the hard earth. My poor boy...

"I've done everything you've asked—" Helmut moans.

"But this," Maxwell says. He hovers in front of Helmut, blocking my view. "You had two opportunities to destroy Kane Davies. You fled from the car accident—"

"He wasn't disabled—"

"You had him at the cottage. You removed the stake," Maxwell says in a silken breath. "Do not deny it, Helmut. I know. Confess your sin."

"No one deserves to perish that way," Helmut whispers. "I removed the stake."

"Good lad." Maxwell lifts his hands to Helmut's face. Helmut releases a strangled shriek. I recognize the sound of splitting flesh and crackling bone. Maxwell steps away from the wall. He holds Helmut's head between his hands. The body leans a moment against the wall, then slumps to the ground. The body and the head fester, then cave in to dust. Opening his hands, Maxwell allows strands of blond hair, all that remains of Helmut, to drift to the earthen floor.

Andrew thinks he has seen enough of the downstairs.

Gingerly nudging rats from my path, I squirm backward along the tunnel. When I think I am beyond their perceptions, I make a mad dash for the outside world. Who cares if they hear me now? Let them try to catch this bat on the run.

O

Back outside, I hit the sky and loop toward my apartment building. What Andrew needs is a nice hot bath. Kane will have to wait for my report. I am not suited to the role of vagrant, no matter how short the play, and I am ready to shed my costume. Besides, I don't want Ryan snubbing me twice in one night.

As I dive toward my roof, I spot a loiterer in the street. That police jacket strikes a memory. I alter course for a closer inspection. Eddie Cramer, boy-in-cop's-clothing, stakes out my building. The ex-copper knows exactly which building to watch. No matter where he wanders, his face stays turned toward those twelve stories of crumbling stone and masonry.

Andrew hesitates to make the obvious correlation, but he can hardly avoid it. How coincidental can it be that last night Steven-Old-Boy ambushed Ryan and me in that alley right there, and tonight Eddie has my building under surveillance? Perhaps I have misjudged Eddie. After a year in Steven-Old-Boy's company, he may well have taken a tailspin into dementia.

The time has arrived to ask Eddie face-to-face how strong his loyalties to Steven-Old-Boy are. I prepare to land — oh, maybe two inches from the boy's heels to give him an Andrew-is-in-command fright.

My keen bat peepers catch stealthy movement in the shadows half a block from Eddie. I recognize that womanly figure, that mane of streaked blonde hair. I snort a quick sniff of pungent perfume. I make another correlation, this one much easier to understand. Anneliiese has her claws out for Eddie.

4

Anneliiese displays excellent taste in choosing Eddie as a mark. But I'll be staked before I'll hover overhead while she samples that hot human flesh. I dive toward the street. If Eddie ever falls prey to bloodlust, Andrew will be the vampire to taste every scorching inch of his body.

In my haste, I hit the pavement farther from Eddie than planned. I glance over my shoulder to relocate Anneliiese. My chilled blood drops below freezing. I curse my sharp sight. What I see in the shadows behind me is monstrous.

Anneliiese is transmuting — but not into a bat. A bat I could handle. Down on all fours, Anneliiese metamorphoses into a full-fledged wolf. At the end of compact, sinewy limbs, her hands and feet contort to paws, tipped with thick claws. Matted fur grows. Narrow at the pelvis, her elongated torso broadens through the chest. Pointed ears sprout from the receding mane of streaked hair. Crowning an extended, thickened neck, the woman's head metamorphoses — brow wide, black eyes round, nose and mouth a snarling snout — to the shaggy head of a wolf.

A vampire capable of assuming a wolf's form conjures big trouble. Werewolves can be stopped with the silver bullets. Vampire-wolves cannot.

"Eddie, run!" I shout, racing toward him.

Eddie turns, a questioning look on his face. He skitters backward, draws a hefty revolver — and points it at me. Lordie, the rags! He thinks I'm going to mug him. Shame on him for judging a person by his clothes.

"It's Andrew!" I shout, tugging off the fedora.

That gorgeous face brims with incredulity. His arms fall to his sides. "No way!"

I skid to a halt in front of him. "No time to check for birthmarks. Vampire-she-wolf on your tail."

On cue, a howl ululates through the street. Here she comes, one hungry wolf — with streaked blonde fur.

"Christ, not her!" Eddie moans.

I snatch at Eddie's arm. He slings me aside, takes aim, and pulls off a round at the advancing Anneliiese-wolf.

"Run!" I push him into the street. He trips; I balance him and turn him toward my apartment building.

"Can't you—"

"Are you crazy? I'm not that far advanced! Get inside. She's still a vampire. Uninvited, she won't be able to follow."

Claws click on cement; she lopes toward us. I drag out my revolver, snap off a couple of shots.

Shoving Eddie ahead of me, I flee toward my building. Eddie outdistances me. This stupid overcoat tangles around my legs. I try to shrug if off — impossible. I hear Anneliiese's paws thudding the ground, gaining on me. I swing the revolver around, squeeze off another shot. She bellows as the silver bullet tears into her shoulder.

I wheel back toward the building. I stumble. No one is conveniently at hand to catch Andrew, bloody hell no. I fall and somersault across the asphalt. Jarred from my grasp, my revolver bounces to the brink of a sewage drain.

Glancing back, Eddie halts. He jumps off the curb, then hesitates. I flip onto my back. The she-wolf leaps toward me. Transmuting, I thrust skyward. Anneliiese nose-dives onto empty asphalt. Legs tangled, she skids into the curb and knocks my revolver down the drain.

The vampire-she-wolf scrambles to her feet. She springs at me, growls when I wing out of reach. She turns on Eddie. He retreats. She bounds after him, snaps at his heels. I dive-bomb, ram her between the shoulder blades. Spin tail and fly! Frothing jaws snap at me.

Eddie takes another shot at her. She twists back toward him. He squeezes the trigger again. A forlorn click responds — out of bullets. Panicked, he backpedals toward my building. The she-wolf lunges. I soar between them, clubbing her hard in the snout with my wing. She tumbles over onto her back. I make a swift pass, gouging her chest with claws and fangs.

Before she can recover, I soar toward my building. On the stoop, Eddie gapes in horror. He lifts his arms. I butt him in the chest, thrust him backward over the threshold. I snap my trans-mutation into reverse. Tangled together, Eddie and I roll across the vestibule floor, thud into the wall.

A wail of fury vibrates around us. We look toward the door-way. Just beyond the threshold, Anneliiese slouches. Not An-neliiese exactly, she looks more like an upright wolf in a bloodied blouse and calf-length skirt. Furry claws swipe toward us, fren-zied black eyes glare.

"You'll burn!" her vibrato voice bellows. "I'll see you both flayed." She presses a palm against the gouged flesh of her shoulder; blood oozes between her fingers. "I'll have your cocks for a feast!"

"Ooo, honey, you can't be that hungry," I retort.

Hissing wrath, she dives off the stoop.

"Such a temper that girl has," I say.

Eddie gapes at me. "She means it!"

"But she's out there, and we're in here," I reply, rising. I extend a hand to Eddie. He stares at it uncertainly. What is that trace of guarded emotion on his face? Does he fear me? If so, does his attraction to me conquer that fear? "Come on, Eddie. I didn't let her get you, did I?"

"You're awfully flip about the fact that I almost got killed — again," he says, allowing me to hoist him to his feet. "Do you have any idea what my life has been like lately? If it's not vampire-she-wolves, it's hormone-crazy vampire men..."

He rambles; I don't listen. Eddie seems to have been through the mill since our last civil conversation; he's all jittery and haggard. I grant concessions for his tirade. Besides, I remember that night after Pablo's destruction when Eddie wanted to comfort me.

"Are you through?" I ask when he pauses for a breath. Something else is different about him, something with his hair.

"I just wanted to make certain you were all right," he states. "The last time I saw you, you were a wreck."

"I'm pulling it together."

"Then I'll go."

"She'll be waiting," I remind him.

Eddie contemplates the door, then turns back to me. "I suppose you have a solution."

"Come upstairs," I say. "You found out where I live, you may as well see the dump. I'll take a bath, you'll have a drink. We'll talk. Does that sound safe enough?"

Thoughtful, he shoves his hands into the pockets of his police jacket.

"Don't you go pulling that crucifix on me again, Edward Cramer," I warn.

Against his will, he laughs. "It sounds safe enough."

Thank the moon. "And, Eddie," I say as we climb the stairs, "get rid of the ponytail. You look like a moron."

O

Although I have discarded my derelict disguise and scrubbed off the grime and smell, I cannot resist a brief soak in the tub. The night has been long; Andrew needs a moment of private relaxation. The mind drifts ... way back...

I open my eyes, disoriented in a fog bank of steam. A handsome Asian man stands naked beside the bathtub. I know the face, I recognize the coolness of the hands that skim my body under the hot water. I am captivated by the wide-pupiled brown eyes fastened to mine. Breath catches in my throat as his hands manipulate me toward passion. The man bends over me, his face at my throat. His lips press my skin, his tongue slithers back and forth. His teeth nip, then embed in my flesh. Searing pain throbs from neck to brain. I thrash, water churns. Strength ebbs, and as my eyelids droop, I wonder why he chose me.

I open my eyes to a tall man with long dark-brown hair. Eddie, his muscular body naked, studies me before climbing into the tub. His firebrand hands draw me to his chest.

"I heard you cry out," he whispers. "Bad dream?"

"A memory. It's too old to say if it's good or bad."

My hands rise out of the water, up the warm triangular muscles of his back. I run my fingers through his shoulder-length hair.

Gazing into my eyes, he pulls my hands away. His hands repeat my gestures, pausing against the pulsating arteries in my throat. From my hair, he skims my brow, my cheek. A finger follows the curve of my mouth. Leaning close, he allows his tongue to mimic his finger.

And he leads me to where I am usually the guide. His caresses seem practiced, as if he has choreographed this moment in a hundred dreams. I submit to him. I would not disrupt the realization of his fantasies.

From the bathtub we move to the living room sofa bed.

His tongue traces the line of my eyebrow, my cheek, my jaw. An arm around my shoulders, he lowers me onto the mattress. While his lips explore mine, his hand burns down my chest, around my hip, up the inside of my leg. His hips scorch my inner thighs. His heat presses into me, driving breath from my lungs.

Ecstasy heightens as we sway back and forth from one to the other's embrace. I am consumed by passion, overthrown by his every nuance of intimacy. I want to tell him; I can't speak. My legs around his waist, I lift him from the mattress, fold my arms around him. I bury my face at his throat to vibrate my gratitude through his body.

His fingers dig into my shoulders; he pushes me back. His flushed face holds panic.

My earlier questions find answers. Beneath his ardor, Eddie does fear that he might be my next mark. At the same time, he cannot resist me, any more than I can resist him.

5

He sleeps. I mold myself against the smooth warmth of his back. Although I have explored every curve of him, I skim my fingertips over his body. My fingers hesitate when they reach his face. I stare at his perfect features; I am struck by sorrow.

An old dilemma returns to haunt me.

Like all human creatures, Eddie will grow old, his perfect beauty will wither. Can I permit such suffering to assault him, this man who has given me so much of himself?

Intoxicated by his warmth, I gaze at his throat, strands of his dark hair splayed across the pale skin. An artery beats just beneath the surface, pulsating, humming the blood from the heart to the brain.

The three alternatives of existence drum behind my eyes: Life ... Death ... Death-life ... Which shall it be for Eddie?

Which might Eddie choose for himself?

"You're not breathing," Eddie says, twisting his head to look at me.

"I am too breathing," I retort. "My lungs are some of my few functioning ... Never mind." I trace the line of his temple, working my fingertips back to his ear, down to his neck.

Eddie springs from the sofa bed, paces about the living room. "I should go," he says. "I was supposed to meet Steven—"

My enjoyment of watching his white figure parade before my dazzled eyes is shattered. I frown. The mention of Steven-Old-Boy reminds me of nagging questions...

"Did you know he attacked me outside this building last night?" I inquire, stretching out on my stomach. Eddie, I see where your gaze is leveled. "Did you hear me?"

"I didn't know," he answers, snitty, as if I just yanked one of his armpit hairs.

"How did you know where I live?"

Lips a tight line, he searches the floor for his clothes. Bend over in that corner a while longer, boy; I like the view. "I followed John Studnidka here," he replies, straightening. "I even climbed the fire escape to see if I could catch you in."

"*You* know John Studnidka?"

"We met ... briefly. He rather likes you—"

Let's put that subject on the back burner.

"And how did Steven-Old-Boy know where I live?"

"Steven Verruckt is the last person on earth I would tell about you," Eddie states, turning. "The man is crazy."

"Pull my leg."

He drills me with a reproach stare.

"I've seen him destroy one — one of your ... brothers." Eddie lowers his gaze. "I've seen what he does after..."

Let Andrew guess. "Wouldn't have anything to do with heads, would it?"

"He chops them off with a hatchet," Eddie says, "and keeps them in an ice chest."

"I'm pleased to hear that he hasn't changed," I say.

"He's met a man," Eddie says, glancing at the window, "a great vampire hunter." He levels dark gray eyes on me. "He's promised to help Steven find you."

I crawl off the bed. "A vampire hunter? Have *you* met this vampire hunter?"

"He'll only see Steven." Eddie places his hand on my shoulder. Concern overflows from him. "The man lives in this neighborhood."

Well, doesn't that just set the table for Sunday dinner? Not only do I have to contend with Vampires Anonymous and Steven-Old-Boy, but now I have another vampire-hunting airhead lurking in the neighborhood. Top that off with rearing Ryan right and sorting out what bloody well looks like a budding Relationship with a very human boy who's half-scared to death of me. What's for dessert, Andrew wants to know, Werewolf Mousse?

O

From the roof of my building, I watch Eddie cross the street. I am anxious about Anneliiese skulking nearby. If Eddie hadn't assured me that he lives half a block away — isn't that convenient? — I never would have allowed him to venture out alone. In front of an old hotel, Eddie waves, then goes inside.

The shutting of the hotel door resounds through the quiet night to rattle my eyeteeth.

The past hours have been a confusing experience for Andrew. Although my relationship with Eddie has been mostly from a distance and has been borderline antagonistic, considering his bosom pal Steven-Old-Boy, I have always harbored a back-brain fondness for the boy-in-cop's-clothing. After all, I gave him a shove out of the closet. That alone creates a bond that even a demented bartender cannot dismember with his hatchet.

Tonight, that bond has strengthened. I have discovered aspects of Eddie which I had attributed to him in my imagination, little things I always hoped might be true. He's caring, he's sweet, he's a little off-the-wall — who isn't? — and he is extremely attentive and talented in the sack.

I, of course, would make that a major consideration.

Staring at the old hotel, I imagine Eddie in his bed.

What has this night of rapture begun? His touch, his kiss, his warmth, and his passion have awakened emotions I thought buried with Pablo. I am drawn to Eddie, I feel as if he could improve me, enrich my existence. My fondness for Eddie teeters on the brink of the Great Emotion which leads to a Relationship.

I am more than hesitant about that. Pablo has only been gone a week and a half. I certainly haven't forgotten my boy; I most definitely have not stopped mourning him. Yet I have been touched by Eddie, almost exactly as I was first touched by Pablo. Eddie is a lost boy in a nasty world; he wants someone he can hang on to, someone he can trust, someone he can love.

But can he love Andrew Lyall, Vampire? Is the passion he displayed tonight deep enough that he can give his heart and body and — lest we forget — soul to this animated corpse? Is Eddie prepared to make the commitment that would complete the bond between us? He would have to give up his life for us to be together as man and corpse. I certainly can't undie to humanity.

If Eddie can sacrifice his humanity, have I learned enough not to make the same mistakes I made with Pablo? I made plenty, too many to detail before dawn.

Am I wiser? Even reaching for my strongest conceit, I cannot say that I am. I don't think I've changed. Mirror, mirror on the wall, who's the most selfish of all? Even the atrophied brain knows that answer. I doubt that I ever will change. I don't have that much faith in myself.

And I'm not certain that I trust myself enough to bring another person into this existence. I destroyed my Relationship with Pablo. Chances are I would destroy any Relationship with Eddie as well. Changes are I would destroy Eddie in the bargain.

If I go for another time around, how do I force myself to make the necessary sacrifices to make a worthwhile Relationship last an eternity?

"Aren't you running a bit late?" Jay Bauer asks when I enter Kane's living room. "John has been back for hours."

I feel as if I'm nineteen, returning home after a night of fun and frolic to find my mother waiting in the dark. 'It's late, Andy.' — *Andy*, can you imagine? — 'Whose aftershave do I smell, Andy? That isn't your brand!'

Ignoring Jay, I saunter to John and Kane seated on the sofa. I glance around the room. "Where's the tyke?"

"He's with Hart," John replies. He wrinkles his nose. "Is that foreign aftershave Eddie Cramer's, Andrew?"

Deja vu!

"No wonder," Jay says in his most lecherous tones. "Mr. Hot-Cop Buns would waylay even Maxwell Guthridge."

Hart joins us. Ryan peeks his head around the doorway. I've never been so happy to see the kid. Nor have I been in more need of a diversion.

"What are you hiding for?" I ask, walking toward him. Wary, Ryan cowers behind the door frame. "I'm not wearing those rags any more. Use your peepers, kiddo. All scrubbed and dapper—"

Sniffing, Ryan cautiously approaches me. Apparently satisfied with my ablutions from my vagrant charade, he leaps into my arms. Still, he studies the shininess of the stickpin on my lapel.

"I won't keep you in suspense any longer," I say, sitting down in the overstuffed chair with Ryan on my knee. "You were right, Kane. The Vampires Anonymous meetings are only the tip of the gravestone. Maxwell is big trouble."

"If he weren't, we wouldn't be going to such lengths to stop him," Jay says.

"What did you find out, Andrew?" Kane asks, ignoring Jay.

"They have an elaborate computer setup in the basement," I reply. "Every vampire of our — shall I say, sensibilities — along with home addresses, seems to be logged in its memory."

His eyes smoldering with the implications, Kane settles back on the sofa. That Maxwell has had every VA member, and non-members such as all of us, followed to their homes prods one's nerves. That any of us can be exposed to the police or ambushed and destroyed by Maxwell's followers — as too many already have been — tugs at the hairs inside one's BVDs — if one bothers with BVDs. That I erased the list provides little consolation since it creates other problems.

"If they use their computer, they'll know they've been infiltrated," Kane says, rising from the sofa. "We need to readjust our timetable. Jay, send out word that we meet here as soon after dusk as possible tomorrow night."

"Excuse me for inquiring," I say, "but what is your plan?"

"We'll catch Maxwell unaware, on his own ground, and destroy him," Kane replies.

"Excuse me again, but isn't castle storming out of fashion?"

Kane levels those dark, age-old eyes on me.

"Do you have a better plan?" Jay asks.

"No, but we don't know how many followers Maxwell has," I say. "That room in the sub-basement has a lot of graves. There could be more in other rooms."

"Kane has everything worked out, Andrew," John says, placing a restraining hand on my shoulder.

"I'm certain he does, but—"

"Andrew," Kane says, "our options are limited. We have to catch Maxwell before he deserts the church. He could have hiding places around the city that we don't know about. 'Castle storming,' as you so shrewdly put it, will have to do."

I hold my tongue, but pardon me for rising from my grave, I think the entire scheme stinks worse than a moldering carcass.

O

"I'm hungry," Ryan states, sitting up in his crate.

"You ate before you went to bed," I return. Wrapping my bathrobe around me, I crawl out of my coffin. How can he be constantly hungry? He gorged himself before we returned to John's cottage this morning. Even in my first year, I didn't put away as much as this imp does.

"Hungry." Following me into the bathroom, Ryan tugs at the tail of my robe. "Now!" He stamps his foot, rattling every window in the house.

"Can't a person sleep in five extra minutes?" John shouts. The closet door slides open. Hanging over the edge of his coffin, he glares through half-dead eyes. "How about some consideration for a worn-out corpse?"

"Screw a lid on it, Stud," Ryan snaps.

Snarling, John drops back into his coffin. The lid slams shut.

"Great, now you've insulted our host," I say to Ryan. "Manners won't kill you, kiddo."

"Hungry," he insists and gives me his I'll-fade-away-if-I-don't-eat-right-now look.

"Patience won't either," I tell him. "I'm taking a bath. You're waiting in the living room. After that, we're all going to Kane's. Then, if any of us survive these castle-storming tactics, we'll see about some chow. Questions?"

Scowling, he storms back into the bedroom. With a glance at me, he pummels the top of John's coffin, then retreats in a blur to the living room.

"What in the hell is the problem?" John yells, thrusting open the lid.

"He's hungry," I reply.

"Already? He's gonna weigh a ton, and his flimsy wings will never get him off the ground," John says, dragging his naked body out of his coffin.

Covering my eyes, I retreat into the bathroom and shut the door. "Keep an eye on him," I call. "I'm taking a bath."

"Need help?" accompanied by fingers drumming on the door.

I recall last night's bath with Eddie. A brief notion to compare aquatic skills worms into my mind. I shake it off. Things are complicated enough without starting that game.

O

Pissing and moaning that I'm starving him, Ryan bounces around in the back of the van. At every stoplight, he peers out the side window for a mark. His tastes run the gamut from the flashy pimp waving down cars from the corner to the drab Bible-thumper preaching salvation through a porn shop door. By the time we reach Kane's house, John and I are ready to open the whippersnapper's veins so he can feed on himself.

As one surly group, we enter Kane's living room. He and Jay, with two early arrivals, plot tonight's scheme over a rough sketch of the desecrated church's interior. Kane points out the available entrances. My interest wanders, distracted by an I'm-famished-and-you-don't-care Ryan in the corner.

Kane's other allies begin to arrive. Singly or in groups, they drift into the living room. Before long, I realize that we have quite a crowd. Sweater boys and leather boys, cowboys and cowgirls, weight-toned women and laced-up ladies, squealing drags and growling butches, clones and space-fashion posers, nearly every conceivable variety of bloodsucker that the Intriguing Faction Borough has to offer is sardined into the room.

Ryan mills through the group, sniffing one after another. He sneers when he realizes that they are all as dead as he is.

"All right, people," Jay says; every man and woman turns toward him. "If we're all here, Kane wants to go through the details of tonight's mission."

"Where's Hart?" Kane asks, not looking up from his sketch.

I do a quick scan. Kane has incredible perceptions to pick out Hart's absence in this roomful.

"Do you want to wait for him?" Jay asks.

Kane shakes his head. I catch a glimpse of irritation on his face. "I want him here."

Without instruction, John goes off to phone Hart.

An uncomfortable silence settles over the room. Even Ryan ceases his roaming and stares at Kane. Without exerting any authority, Kane wields amazing control over everyone around him. I study the men and women. Any one of them would sacrifice themselves for Kane Davies and his scheme.

Returning to my side, John says, "There's no answer." His voice seems a scream in the quiet.

"Find him," Kane says, glancing at John and me.

John locks his hand around my arm, pulls me toward the door.

Ryan breaks through the crowd to follow us.

"You stay here," I tell him.

He kicks the woodwork. *"Hungry!"*

I feel every gaze in the room turn on us. "Stay here. I won't be long." I force myself to confront those disapproving stares. "Would someone please keep an eye on him?"

"Someone will," Kane mutters. "You're wasting time."

Before I can extract do-or-perish promises, John drags me out of the house.

O

On the fourth floor of Hart's apartment building, John and I hesitate. A sour odor lingers in the hall, underscored by something very sweet — blood.

My hand slips into my jacket pocket to keep my switchblade company. Ahead, a door stands open. Flickering light spills into the hall. John races into the apartment. As I reach the door, I hear him, his voice off-kilter, whisper Hart's name.

Just inside, John stands rigid. Across the room, Hart sits on the sofa, facing the television. An orgy fills the TV screen; a suntanned Hart is the center of attention.

I place my hand on John's shoulder. He turns a pale, grief-lined face to me. Why didn't I realize before that Hart was one of John's initiates? "Help him," John says. His voice breaks.

"Stay here," I say. Gripping the switchblade for support, I walk around the sofa. I can't help Hart now.

On the coffee table before the sofa are scattered vials and pill bottles. Everything is dusted with cocaine. Hart's assassins knew what weakness to exploit to make their work easy.

Pinned to the sofa with thin wooden stakes driven through each shoulder and both wrists, Hart has decayed more than Pablo; he was probably three or four years older. A needle protrudes from the crook of his left arm. A rubber tube trails from the needle to a bucket on the floor. Blood fills the bucket, trails down the sides to soak the pale green carpet. Another rubber tube stretches from his right arm to a small electric pump. Two bottles lie overturned on the floor. Picking up one bottle, I finally recognize the sour smell — formaldehyde.

O

When John and I return to the house, Kane and Jay are alone in the living room. Jay paces in front of the fireplace; Kane stands by the window, his hands tight in the pockets of a black leather bomber jacket. Their angry impatience for our lengthy absence imbues the room.

"We ran into some trouble," I say before either one can chastise John and me.

"Where's Hart?" Kane asks, his voice low.

"Hart has been destroyed." John sinks into a chair, his face pale. "They embalmed him, pumped him full of formalehyde."

Stiffly, Kane turns his back to us.

"Good God," Jay breathes. "John, I'm sorry."

"We cannot waste any more time." Kane squares his shoulders, faces us with gleaming eyes. "We join the others now and end this."

"Where is our hodgepodge army?" I ask.

"They've gone ahead to infiltrate the neighborhood in small groups," Kane replies, "I don't want to arouse suspicion."

I can't for the death of me see how that's possible. Even in that neighborhood — my neighborhood — such a diversified collection of walking corpses is going to raise an eyebrow or twenty. Nevertheless ... "Great. Where's Ryan?"

"He's here," Kane says.

"Here where?"

"Andrew, I appreciate your expanding role as parent—"

"Don't make fun of me. Where's my kid?"

"He has to be in the house," John says, standing.

He doesn't have to be in the house. I rush out of the living room, shouting Ryan's name. These gents don't know what they're dealing with. A hungry Ryan is a Ryan not to be left to his own devices. A search of the house proves fruitless. I bound back toward the living room, collide with John.

"He couldn't have gone far," John offers. "He can't fly."

"There you have an excellent point." I drag John onto the front porch where Kane and Jay wait. "When did you see Ryan last?" I ask.

After a glance at a silent Kane, Jay replies, "I don't know. When everyone else left."

The perfect camouflage. Who would notice a two-and-a-half-foot-tall batlet in the midst of that lot?

I hurry down the porch steps.

"I thought you wanted to avenge Pablo," Kane says tightly.

I halt. "I wouldn't expect such a low blow from you, Kane."

"We have a mission—"

"You go about your noble mission. I've got some single-minded ... selfish ... personal stuff to look after."

"Ryan will be all right," Kane says, walking toward me. "He managed on his own before—"

"Once I know Ryan is safe," I growl at him, "I'll come to the castle storming. Not before."

I transmute into a bat and soar toward that favorite fast-food joint of a certain four-year-old vampire: Ocean Village.

IX

WILD BAT CHASE

*E*ddie wakes in darkness. Apprehension envelops him. He lies quiet, listening to the sounds around him — cars in the street, wind rattling the window sash, voices in the hall.

And something else; a quiet sound occupies the room with him — the sound of someone else's breathing.

Sweat seeps from his pores, sticking the sheets to his naked body. Breath quickens; Eddie gulps it back. Barely lifting his head, he scans the interlaced shadows. An intruder lurks there. Eddie fumbles under the bedclothes. Where's his revolver?

Sound scrapes to his left.

Eddie lunges toward the nightstand and his crucifix.

A harsh laugh breaks through the room. "That's no good against me." The nightstand lamp is snapped on. Eddie squints against the dim light. Steven stands at the bedside. "Think vampire got in?" Steven snatches the crucifix from Eddie's fingertips. "Can't without invite. Invite one in, Eddie?"

"I sure didn't invite you in," Eddie says, slumping against the headboard. He drags the blankets up to his chest. "How did you get in, Steven? How'd you find out I was here?"

"Got ways." Chuckling, he wanders around the room. "Got connections."

"Your great vampire hunter?" Eddie asks, sitting up attentively. "Is there anyone he can't track down for you?"

Steven grins.

"I'm overjoyed to see you," Eddie says, squirming under Steven's unvarying stare. "What do you want?"

"Tonight." His grin hardens. "Tonight."

Eddie draws his knees to his chest. Beyond Steven, the worn duffel bag — Steven's bag of weapons in his battle against vampires — slumps on a chair. Eddie forces himself to look at Steven's pallid face. How clearly the intention gleams in his mad eyes. Eddie shudders. Tonight Steven plans to destroy Andrew Lyall.

"What's the plan?" Eddie asks carefully.

"You'll know soon enough. Can't tell you too much." Steven winks. "Can't let boy-in-cop's-clothing out of sight."

"What's that supposed to mean?"

"Eddie's secrets aren't so secret." Leering, Steven sits down on the bed. "Knew where Andrew was all along."

Eddie stretches, yawns. "That's ridiculous—"

Steven grabs Eddie's leg. His sharp-featured face taut, he squeezes until Eddie winces pain. "Don't lie. Why else are you here?" He motions at the room. "Andrew's just down street."

"Coincidence..." Kicking free of Steven's grip, Eddie presses against the headboard. He could continue the innocent façade, create a viable excuse. Steven's expression reveals that whatever Eddie says will not be believed. Steven listens only to a higher source, the great vampire hunter. "What do we do now?"

"Get dressed." Steven stands. "Find Andrew."

"I thought you knew where he was," Eddie says.

"Night time's for out and about. Find him." He taps his temple. "Know where to look."

"I'm not getting up stark naked with you gaping at me," Eddie states. "Wait outside."

"Seen you," Steven says. He imitates Eddie's mock yawn.

"Out."

Shrugging, Steven picks up the duffel bag and walks to the door. "Be right outside. Don't play tricks." The dim light plays harshly over his thin face. "Deal with you like Andrew."

The moment the door shuts, Eddie bounds across the room and flips the lock. Leaning his forehead against the rough wood, he tries to think. Steven's presence, even on the other side of the door, clogs his thoughts.

Eddie sorts through his clothes. Fear churns inside him. Steven has been relentless in his pursuit of Andrew Lyall, vampire. He will be no less relentless tonight. His madness, so much more advanced since they started their quest, pushed further by the great vampire hunter's encouragement, has driven Steven beyond threats. If Eddie gets in the way, he will fall under Steven's stake and hatchet as quickly as Andrew.

Eddie drags his shirt over his head, sits down on the bed to pull on his socks.

How can he stop Steven?

The obvious answer sickens Eddie. Yes, he could save Andrew; he could save himself.

"But I can't kill Steven," Eddie murmurs, rising from the bed, his jeans hanging in his hands. "Not for a dead man. Not even for Andrew."

Not for a dead man.

Leaning against the wall, Eddie tugs on his jeans and stuffs everything inside. Last night is a high-contrast video in front of his eyes. He sees himself in Andrew's arms, sees the passion between them, sees his own uncontrolled response. He watches the reality of his fantasies as if uninvolved with their outcome.

He cannot remain detached. Opposing universes pull at him. From one quarter, daylight reality unfolds its stark evidence: mundane jobs, nameless tricks, horrible illness or degrading old age — eternity under six feet of mud. From the shadow quarter, starlit fantasy slight-of-hands soft-edged clues: short night shifts, choice of the litter, no illness, and eternal youth — eternity under a cloud-smattered sky. And the phantasm Andrew, more real, more substantial, waits in the night.

Solve the case, Eddie. But don't misread the clues. The wrong solution might leave terrors on the loose.

Above all else, the threat of those marauding terrors fills Eddie with dread. They could attack from either quarter.

"Quit jerking off!" Steven shouts through the door.

"I can't find my shoes," Eddie returns over his shoulder. He ties the laces and grabs his police jacket.

He needs two weapons to face this night. From under the bedclothes, he rummages for his service revolver, and from the nightstand, where Steven abandoned it, he picks up his crucifix. Eddie straps on the holster, wrestles on his jacket, and tucks the crucifix into a snug pocket.

He opens the door. Leaning against the opposite wall, Steven waits. "Tonight. Tonight," Steven says with a smirk. Whistling the tune, he leads the way out of the hotel.

O

Topping the rise of a street, Steven extinguishes the Jeep's head-lights and cuts off the engine. He coasts the Jeep down the hill for several yards. The front tires bounce against the curb, jarring Eddie.

"Andrew's here?" Eddie asks, glancing at the modest houses set back from the sidewalks.

"Shush." Leaning on Eddie's leg, Steven sorts through the glove compartment. He pulls out a tattered piece of paper. He twists the scrap at different angles to catch the glow of the streetlamp, then stares at a house with a battered van parked in front. The paper crumples in his hand. "Here."

Eddie huddles in his jacket for the stakeout. Like Steven, he watches the one-story house. Is Andrew in there now? He must be for Steven to wait so patiently. Eddie wonders what chance he would have if he were to make a dash for the inside to warn Andrew. Does Steven carry a gun? Eddie doesn't think so. But, in his bag of tricks, Steven carries a hatchet that would fit nicely between Eddie's shoulder blades.

The door of the house opens. Steven leans forward. Eddie considers snatching the duffel bag and making his escape. He abandons the idea. The men and women emerging from the house would not take him safely to their collective bosom. With light shining through them, the group files out and disperses into the sky. Awed, Eddie stares after the flock.

Jesus! The world is filled with vampires!

Beside him, Steven draws in a sharp breath.

Eddie looks back at the house, certain he will see Andrew. He glimpses a small figure darting through the shadows.

"Little sucker," Steven whispers, lips drawn back from his teeth, "get you, too."

When the exodus from the house stops, Eddie says, "Andrew isn't here. Where to now?"

"Stay here," Steven says. "Andrew'll come."

"How can you be certain?" Eddie asks. "He could—"

"Great vampire hunter knows," Steven replies. "Knows Andrew's cohorts. Knows everything."

"I'd like to meet such a wise man. Where is he?"

"Where Andrew and his like won't find him," Steven replies.

Clamping his hand down on Eddie's thigh, Steven looks toward the sky behind them. He drags Eddie down behind the seats.

To the heavy beat of wings, two monstrous bats soar over the rise. The bats fly directly over the Jeep toward the house.

"Got 'im," Steven breathes.

Up the street, Andrew and John Studnidka knock on the door, then walk into the house.

Climbing back onto his seat, Eddie slips his hand inside his jacket. His fingers curl around his service revolver. Whatever Andrew is, whatever he has done, Eddie will protect him from Steven Verruckt.

Could I kill another human being to save this dead man?

Steven remains in the Jeep, as before, watching the house. His eyes gleam; his upper teeth pull at his bottom lip. A single finger taps against the steering wheel.

One wrong move...

Eddie pries his hand off the revolver.

I'm as mad as Steven.

A tall, dark-haired man, followed by the curly-haired Jay, steps onto the porch. Andrew and John emerge. Quick words are exchanged. Andrew marches down the steps.

The dark man walks to the edge of the porch. He speaks, his words snatched by the wind.

Andrew turns back. Pain fills his face; he tries uselessly to conceal it. Although Eddie can't hear their argument, he senses that the dark man has deeply hurt Andrew. Eddie feels a sudden urge to take Andrew into his arms and comfort him.

With a damning glare, Andrew whirls away. His body closes in on itself, thin membranes unfold from his arms down to his feet. His face contorts to a snout, and a huge bat wings skyward.

"Now get him," Steven states, starting the Jeep.

"But what about them?" Eddie indicates the three men on the porch. Jumping out of the Jeep, he grabs for the duffel bag. "We have to get them, too."

"First Andrew!" Steven jerks the duffel bag away. He slams the stick into gear. The Jeep peels away from the curb.

"Steven!" Eddie grapples at the door; his hands slip along leather and metal. "Stop!" He snags the rollbar; his feet are jerked off the ground. His knees hit the pavement. His fingers slip. But he won't let go. He won't allow Steven to track Andrew alone. Scrambling to his feet, he throws himself into the back of the Jeep.

"Thanks for waiting." He smacks Steven upside the head.

"Was a stupid stunt."

Maybe it wasn't. Eddie looks back toward the house. As he hoped, he and Steven have attracted attention. Heading for the street, John argues with the dark man. Hope dissipates. The dark man drags John off in the opposite direction.

Eddie is thrown against the side of the Jeep as Steven speeds around a corner. He grapples for a handhold. The Jeep leaps forward, hurling Eddie backward. He bangs his head against the spare tire.

"Slow down!" Eddie calls. "You're going to kill somebody."

Steven heaves the steering wheel to the right; Eddie clings to the rollbar. The Jeep squeals around another corner, lurches up onto two wheels, bounces back to the street.

"Don't lose scent..." Steven chants, watching the sky.

Andrew wings against the underlit clouds and hazy stars.

Eddie scrambles back into the passenger seat, fumbles on the seatbelt. He, too, keeps Andrew in sight.

Fly faster!

"You got to slow down, Steven." What logic will Steven respond to? "You're going to kill us. Andrew will get away."

Steven gives him a sidelong glance. He grins. "Won't get away — not this time." He tromps the accelerator.

Will nothing dampen his demented confidence? Will nothing stop him? The service revolver feels heavy under Eddie's arm. A few minutes ago, he thought he could kill Steven — shoot him down to save Andrew. Can he? He has no right to kill another human being regardless of the circumstances.

You were a cop, Eddie. You were forced to shoot people.

Those people were criminals. Steven is insane, not evil. He's not even a bad person — not to other humans at any rate. Steven is driven by an age-old prejudice.

Eddie cannot kill him for that.

Ahead of them, the bat veers abruptly west. Steven hits the brakes, twists the steering wheel, floors it. The Jeep jumps a curb, careens across a wide lawn.

"Jesus!" Eddie covers his eyes.

Wood scrapes metal; splinters and sparks pelt Eddie. He peeks between his fingers. The Jeep jolts back and forth against two houses. The rearview mirror slams against an electric meter; glass explodes. Eddie ducks.

The Jeep vaults into an alley. Steven whips the wheel; the fender scrapes a concrete wall. He rams the stick into fourth.

Cars flash past the end of the alley. Eddie presses back in his seat. Steven leans forward, hands flexing. To the blare of horns and squealing of tires, the Jeep fishtails into traffic. Steven navigates in and out of the tightest spaces.

Parallel with the street, the bat-Andrew soars a deliberate westerly course.

"Be easy now," Steven murmurs. Popped into fifth gear, the Jeep zooms toward the coast. "I know where. Get him now."

The bat tailspins from the sky and disappears beyond a high archway outlined by garish lights.

Steven drives under the flickering words OCEAN VILLAGE. The Jeep screeches to a halt, snapping Eddie's seatbelt tight around his chest and hips.

Grabbing the duffel bag, Steven leaps out of the Jeep. He briefly scans the sky above Ocean Village, then hurries toward the entrance.

"Wait for Christ's sake!" Eddie calls. His seatbelt is jammed. He slams his fist against the buckle. He glimpses Steven running into the crowd of tourists. If he loses him now, he might lose Andrew as well. Eddie squirms from under the shoulder strap. Grabbing the rollbar, he wiggles against the lap strap; it cuts into his crotch. With a final effort against stomach-souring pain, he pulls free.

Jostling the masses, Eddie threads through the maze of walkways. The din of the crowd presses in on him. Even here, with all these shallow-faced people as witnesses, Steven will not hesitate to destroy Andrew.

Eddie can't murder Steven, can't think of another way to stop him. Instead, he searches for Andrew to warn him that Steven is stalking him.

Eddie halts at the edge of a central common swarmed by tourists. He scans the men, scrutinizes anyone under twenty-five with dark hair. In his blindness for Andrew, he looks right into Steven's face — twice — before realizing who he is.

Eddie starts across the common. Maybe he can still steer Steven away from his goal.

Duffel bag over his shoulder, Steven skirts the common. People clear a path for him. He halts; his pallid face contorts with joy.

Eddie picks up his pace. Steven's expression frightens him. Such delight can have but one meaning. Pushing his way through the tourists, Eddie searches the common. Andrew walks toward one of the byways. Eddie presses on toward Steven.

Steven has disappeared. Eddie falters. At the spot where he last saw Steven, several tourists stare at the ground. Climbing onto a bench, Eddie peers over the crowd. Surrounded by perplexed tourists, Steven roots through the wooden stakes, crucifixes, and garlic garlands inside his duffel bag. From the collection, Steven extracts a quiver of foot-long, half-inch-thick wooden arrows and an aluminum crossbow. The tourists stumble back, giving him plenty of space.

"Jesus," Eddie breathes, leaping off the bench.

Steven pops in an arrow, draws back the bowstring. Eddie forges through the mass. Grinning, Steven fires at Andrew.

X

CRAW OF THE BEAST

1

*H*ands knotted in his bomber jacket pockets, Kane studies the pain in Andrew's brown eyes, lining his angular face. Belittling Andrew's concern for Ryan was the wrong tactic.

More than the wrong tactic, it was vicious.

And alienating; beyond Andrew's pain lies hatred.

Is this mission — any mission — worth alienating the people you care about, Kane?

Attempting to mask scarred feelings, Andrew whirls into a bat and soars westward. Kane follows the bat's trail with his eyes. He has misjudged Andrew's attachment to this child. Ryan, offering only devotion, has snagged an iron streak of selflessness in Andrew. That wrong tactic may have cost Kane a good friend. Still, he smiles. Andrew's rhapsody has finally evolved into a fugue.

Squealing tires break the night's quiet. Haunted by memory, Kane wheels about. A Jeep tears away from the curb. The headlights snap on, cutting thick swaths across the asphalt.

"Steven!" Edward Cramer clings to the vehicle.

Cramer hauls himself into the Jeep. Hunched over the steering wheel, Steven Verruckt speeds up the street.

John pushes past Kane. "They're after Andrew!"

"Andrew can take care of himself," Kane says, snatching at John's arm. John tries to pull free; Kane tightens his grip.

In the retreating Jeep, Cramer turns his white face toward them. He expects them to follow. John's willingness to comply buffets Kane. He considers the extent of Andrew's danger from Verruckt; he even wonders if helping Andrew might be more important than invading the church.

Which is more important, the individual or the mission?

Kane wastes no time with the question. Along with his other contradicting talents, Andrew has proven his ability to survive. Tonight, he must be allowed to do that as he always has — on his own. Tonight, all energies *must* be directed toward stopping Maxwell Guthridge. As in the past, the mission takes priority.

"Andrew will come to no harm," Kane assures John.

"How can you know that?" John demands.

"I know Andrew." John could be as easily alienated as Andrew. Hart's destruction has already chiseled at John's resolve. The threat to Andrew further weakens John, exposing the core of his greatest concern — the safety of his friends.

Transmuted, Kane flies point, as much to protect their flank as to keep John with them. Kane glances back at the winged shape hovering over Ocean Village. The complicated melodies of the fugue are underscored by bass counterpoints.

○

The church stands dark behind a high wrought-iron fence. Across the street, Kane, John, and Jay linger under the blinking lights of an adult theatre marquee. An endless lava flow of humans streams past. Not everyone in the throng is human. Occasional sensations touch Kane, recognizable faces pass before his eyes. His people are here as well — awaiting his signal.

Kane trudges through the crowds. Jay and John follow at his sides. Their strong emotions bolster Kane. A protective shadow, Jay is prepared to face any challenge into which Kane may lead him. And John, his smooth face a mask of determination, has regained control. Although his loyalties are divided, his strengths are focused on this mission.

By the time they reach the padlocked gate, a dozen allies have joined them. Kane memorizes his comrades' faces. Not all of them will survive the encounter before them. Candice, who became a vampire while serving overseas during the war, will make it. Her military training almost assures her survival. But how can recent initiates Melanie, with her dyed-black hair and leather regalia, and Simon, with his manufactured musculature and designer fanny pouch, survive tonight's battle?

Kane would prefer to slip unnoticed into the church, destroy Maxwell, and put a neat end to Vampires Anonymous. He knows events will turn against that solution. A bloodbath lies ahead; friends will fall with the enemy. He cannot prevent it.

The men and women form a semicircle around Kane. He twists the gate's padlock. It snaps open; the gate swings wide. The group enters the church's dooryard.

From the top of the wide leaf-clogged cement steps, Kane surveys the street. The humans continue on their sightless journeys through the night.

"All of you are invited to come in." Kane's voice drifts on the breeze to the ears of his confederates scattered up and down the street, lurking in the alley, hiding behind the building's spires and gables.

Kane's form dissipates. Mist seeps through the crack between the church's double doors. In the foyer, the mist swirls into a tall column. Kane, taking a hatchet from the sheath at his waist, steps toward the gloom of the chapel.

From behind him, Jay whispers sharply, "Wait for us."

Kane stops on the threshold of the chapel. Before him stretches the long aisle to the raised sanctuary; to each side of the center aisle are rows of pews, many splintered planks. Boldly stroked spray-painted graffiti scar the pious tableaux of the stained-glass windows.

With John and Jay beside him, Kane advances up the littered aisle to the sanctuary. The other men and women fan out along the side aisles. Sprawled on the ruins of the altar lies the skeletal remains of a large dog, the sacrifice that defiled the church. Dark stains of old blood riddle the floor. The toppled pulpit is blackened from fire. Although he cannot see it, Kane feels the presence of a crucifix concealed in the rubble.

Kane tenses, hefts his axe. He scans the balcony at the back of the chapel. A spear hurtles down; Kane leaps aside. The spear lodges into the sanctuary steps.

From the balcony's darkness, a dozen men leap over the railing to charge Kane's forces.

Kane rushes to the attack. Jay holds him back; his insistence that Kane is too weak for battle flashes in his eyes. Kane growls at the insubordination.

With the clank of axe to sword, the melee rages through the chapel. Infused with religious fanaticism, Guthridge's henchmen accurately wield their weapons. A sword slashes Jessica Miller's throat. A Guthridge man impales Tom Evans on a wooden plank, then heaves him through a stained-glass window. Bearing power-saws, two of the enemy carve Simon Johnston limb from torso.

Kane stuggles against Jay. He cannot stand here while his people are cut down.

"I'm not helpless!" he snaps.

"You're not expendable!" Jay returns.

With a growl of impatience, John rushes into the fight. Brandishing a sword, he hacks at their opponents. Following John, Kane's heartened men and women take up the battle. Yanking a man's head back, Deborah Neame drives her hatchet into the exposed throat. John, Makoto Saito, and Amy Reid transmute to bats and gouge at the enemies' faces. The tide turns. Overwhelmed, Maxwell's men fall to rot in the dust.

Behind Kane, a door slams against a wall. Hatchet readied, he wheels about. Carmen Kahlo-Abriz rushes through the chancel door. At the railing, she halts, surveys the scene.

"They doubled back on us." She lowers her machete. "But the rest of the main floor is definitely deserted. I have felt some nasty vibes coming from the basement." Her thin hand coils around the machete handle. "A dungeon ambush."

Vaulting over the railing, Kane joins Carmen. Jay and John, who carries a hard-won power-saw, join them. With a curt nod, Kane orders the detachment's six other survivors to follow.

"Maxwell and the woman?" Kane demands.

Carmen shrugs. "I wouldn't know the slime's scent. The woman — there's only a whiff of expensive perfume."

Allowing Carmen to lead them through the chancel door to a back hallway, Kane extends his perceptions. He senses the proximity of unfamiliar auras — and an essence that he will never forget. Maxwell is yet in the church. Fortune is on Kane's side.

Jay leads the way down the stairs. At the bottom, longtime ally Jean Claude Seigner greets them.

"We have them trapped in the sub-basement," Jean Claude says, matching his gait to Kane's. "More than twenty men."

"Carmen suspects an ambush," Kane says.

"They did give up this level without much of a fight," Jean Claude offers.

"Then perhaps Maxwell isn't as trapped as you think," Kane says. Sensations of Maxwell, waiting, confident, drift from below. "Don't underestimate him."

As they pass through the twisting basement hallway, sided by numerous doors, Kane asks, "Have you found the computer room?"

"We're still looking," Jean Claude says.

They round a junction of the hall. Kane's associates fill the corridor to the end. Kane, with John, Jay, Jean Claude, and Carmen, edges through the men and women. Kane glances into Maxwell's open office. The desk lamp casts its pale yellow light, heightening the room's shadows.

"Search this room." Kane says. "Collect all their records about Vampires Anonymous."

Jean Claude gestures two women toward the room.

Kane stops before the door to the sub-basement. Maxwell's scent wafts above the odor of earth, decay, and stale blood.

"We'll be picked off," Jay says, craning over Kane's shoulder to look down the narrow staircase. "Kane, wait here." Jay squeezes past him. "Carmen, Jean Claude, join me?"

Jean Claude follows Jay down the rough steps. Pausing at Kane's side, Carmen flicks her fingernail against the machete blade. "We'll call you when the fun starts." With a wink, she descends into the sub-basement.

"I feel like the troop mascot," Kane says.

John manages a flicker of his wry grin. "A thankless part."

"Feeling better?" Kane asks.

"Somewhat," John replies. "You are right. Andrew is resourceful. Whether or not I want to admit it."

Carmen emerges from the sub-basement. "Lovely lair," she says. "Jay has given his permission, however reluctantly, for you to descend, Kane."

At the bottom of the earthen stairs, Kane, John, and Carmen join Jay and Jean Claude in an antechamber to the catacombs.

"What have you discovered?" Kane asks.

"They're everywhere." Jay waves an impatient hand at the half-dozen tunnels. "Take your pick, you'll run into someone."

"Six groups of ten," Kane says. "Jean Claude, Carmen, Jay, Candice, Holly — you're leaders."

"I'm going with—"

"I'll keep John at my side, Jay," Kane says. "I need your leadership ability now, not your nanny instinct."

Jay straightens his shoulders. "The usual signal when we find Maxwell?"

"The usual signal," Kane confirms.

Disciplined, orderly, the men and women assemble into six units. The detachments file into the tunnels. Leading his group, Kane summons the childhood lullaby his mother sang to him to accompany him into battle.

Not far into the low tunnel, John whispers, "You've chosen the right path."

"I know," Kane replies. Maxwell, with Louis, waits close at hand. The lullaby, quavering in his mother's voice, repeats, stronger.

"Should I send for the others?" John asks. His face darkens when Kane looks at him. "You've planned this."

"He's spread his men thin," Kane says. "We can manage."

"What if..." With a tight grin, John shakes his head. "You're never wrong."

"On occasion." Kane places his fingers against John's lips.

The earthen tunnel opens into a long chamber. Set behind a table, a single brazier casts smoky light, creating secretive voids. Kane wipes the blade of his hatchet against his jeans. Tonight, Maxwell's hiding-in-the-shadows game will be futile. Kane scans the darkness quickly, for the Beast waits within.

There, in a shallow niche, he gloats. Louis lurks with him. The rest of his bodyguard has been well concealed.

"Kane *Davies*." Maxwell's voice rumbles through the room in deafening echoes. "Helmut's compassion has brought you to a horrible end."

John at his elbow, Kane enters the chamber. The memory of his mother's voice retreats. Terrors hold reign here; their specters breathe cold drafts of dread against Kane's face.

The ten men and women behind Kane project growing fear.

Even without direct contact, Maxwell lays his hypnotic traps. Foreboding penetrates Kane's brain and spreads. His people whimper, fidget on the verge of flight. Muttering a curse, John trembles against Kane's arm.

Noises scrape from the wall and floor. Figures rise from the shelves cut into the wall. The earthen floor fissures. Grimy hands squirm out of the ground. The dirt breaks, parting as the bodies rise.

"Horror-show tricks," John breathes with disgust.

Kane meets Maxwell's eyes — the violet eyes of the Beast.

I have you, I possess you, I consume you, gloats the Beast.

You escaped the craw of the Beast once, Kane commands himself. *You can escape again — victorious.*

A note sounds in Kane's mind, rises to a melody, then transforms into an intrepid theme.

Gripping his hatchet, Kane marches to one of the men climbing out of the floor. Kane drives the hatchet into the man's skull. The man's shriek resounds off the cratered ceiling. Kane tugs the hatchet free and lops off the man's head.

Maxwell growls.

"Horror-show tricks," Kane repeats, turning to his people. "There are no terrors here you cannot defeat." He wheels toward Maxwell. "You must dirty your own hands in this fight, Maxwell."

Fifteen men spring out of their graves and charge.

Side-by-side, Kane and John counter Maxwell's henchmen. Kane's hatchet and John's confiscated power-saw flash in ceaseless arcs. Limbs drop to the ground. Kane's people leap to the attack. Steel sings against steel, thuds into flesh. Growls and shrieks reverberate. Blood splatters and sprays.

Kane dodges a gory axe, chops down the assailant. Heat flashes past Kane. He stumbles back from an enemy wielding an acetylene torch. The white flame jets toward his face. Lashing out with the hatchet, Kane feints left, then lunges below the jet of flame to tackle the man. The torch rolls across the floor. Clubbing Kane's face, the man scrambles for his weapon.

Kane leaps over him, snatches up the torch. Twisting the gas valve, he sprays the man with fire. Engulfed, shrieking, the man stumbles into one of two coffins against the wall. Flames engulf the wooden casket, burst toward the low ceiling.

Gasping, Kane glances toward the niche. Maxwell, fury a stench around him, surveys the defeat of his bodyguard. His gaze on Maxwell, Kane fires the second coffin. The Beast snarls. Kane strides through the carnage. John joins him. At Maxwell's sides, Louis draws a scimitar.

"Our numbers are limitless," Maxwell said, staring at Kane. "We are stronger." He touches his temple. "Not perverted."

"Your values are perverted," Kane says. "You can't control our race, Maxwell."

"Stop me. If you are strong enough."

Kane swings up the acetylene torch. John brandishes the power-saw. Kane's people gather behind him.

Maxwell sweeps them with a contemptuous glare. *"Adieu."* The back wall of the niche swings open. Maxwell and Louis retreat into another tunnel.

Kane sprays the niche with acetylene flame. The secret door slams shut. Shoving the torch at John, Kane runs his hands along the door frame, but cannot locate the release handle.

John places his hand on Kane's shoulder. "There is still the cottage."

Shrugging free, Kane storms away. "Providing he doesn't have other hiding places." He paces the length of the room. He glares at the trenches in the floor, the decomposing corpses. Against the wall, the coffins smolder. "Torch this room. Don't leave him anything to come back to. John, come with me." He marches toward the tunnel.

In the catacomb antechamber, Kane and John are met by Jay and his detachment. Blood splotches Jay's white shirt; the sleeve is tattered, soaked.

"This place is riddled with secret doors," Jay snaps.

Kane senses stragglers fleeing the church. He berates himself for overlooking the possibility of hidden exits. He struggles against his frustration, compounded with grief for those of his own people destroyed this night — in vain, because Maxwell Guthridge escaped to continue his plots against Kane's kindred.

"What do we do now, Kane?" Jay asks.

Now he can only salvage what he can from a failed mission. Kane shoves Jay toward the stairs, gestures the rest after him. "We find that bloody computer, get whatever we can from its memory," Kane replies. "Then we destroy everything. I don't want Vampires Anonymous rising out of the ashes."

O

"Andrew didn't do as much damage as he thought," Carmen states. "If he deleted anything, it was probably a back-up file."

Kane glances at the terminal set up on a library table, the single printer, and a waist-high metal cabinet with a smoked-glass top. "What can you get me off of this?"

"Whatever your heart desires," Carmen says, her fingers tapping over the keys. "Whoever set this up didn't have a flair for passwords. A child could access this system."

"Andrew did," Jay says. He lifts defensive hands at John. "It was just an observation."

"They probably never expected anyone to find it," Kane says.

"So, what does your heart desire, Kane?" Carmen asks.

"Printouts?"

"That will take till dawn. A luxury we don't have," she adds wryly.

"We've already collected a great deal from Maxwell's office," Jean Claude interjects. "Nationwide offices. The foreign exchange — VA leaders' addresses from here to Paris."

"What's this?" Kane asks, walking to the metal cabinet.

"The disk drive," Carmen replies, joining him. She lifts the lid, revealing a stack of copper-toned platters. "And this is the disk pack where all the data is stored."

Kane studies the platters, then glances at John. "My friend, I need your new toy."

"Sure," John replies, a smile lighting his smooth face. He hands Kane the power-saw. "That's the switch you want."

The saw roars to life, vibrations course up Kane's arms. With a nod, he orders the others aside. Revving the motor, Kane drives the whining blade into the disk pack.

XI

RABID BATS

1

*I*n search of Ryan, I twist my way through the pack of tourists gorging Ocean Village. I'm still in shock about Kane's little trick. *I thought you wanted to avenge Pablo.* Kane is narrow-sighted not to realize that Pablo is gone and Ryan isn't. Although I want to see Maxwell tormented beyond the farthest terrors death can conjure, right now my obligations are to Ryan.

On the common, I catch a scent of my night urchin. I wade through the throng with my gaze focused low to the ground. I recognize that thatch of blond hair. And what's this he's pursuing with the purposeful gait of the undead? Another little boy, a couple inches shorter, dark-haired. I hurry toward the far side of the common, calling Ryan's name. He's enough to cope with. Maybe he can have a brother next century.

On his way to one of the intersecting sidewalks, Ryan pauses. He tosses a what-are-you-doing-here? glare at me, then resumes the hunt. Beyond him, the dark-haired child stands with a woman wearing a black, hooded cloak — unusual attire for a tourist. Picking up the boy, the woman carries him up the walk.

Ryan stiffens. He snaps his face toward me. His lips quiver back from his fangs. Abruptly, he turns and chases after the woman and child.

Apprehension worms through me. I know who this skirt is: his 'mother' — using the term loosely. Making a four-year-old a vampire was bad enough; deserting him in *this* city was obscene. Andrew has some words for this skirt. I step to after the kid.

Did a swarm of bees just soar past my ear? *Twang!* A wooden arrow strikes the building ahead of me. Whoa, bros, who thinks this is an archery range? I glance over my shoulder. I should have known.

At the end of a corridor walled by horrified humans, Steven-Old-Boy inserts another wooden arrow into your basic family survivalist crossbow. He draws a bead on me. From out of the crowd Eddie lunges at our favorite bonkers bartender. Without much effort, Steven-Old-Boy flings Eddie aside. Gracing me with a brilliant mad smile, Steven-Old-Boy takes aim.

With petrified fascination, the humans watch the flight of the arrow. I can hear their collective thought, *Wait until they hear about this in Ohio.* I turn tail and scram.

I dash a wild helixed path down the byway. From behind me, I hear the arrow whistling in pursuit. I unleash my full speed — too late.

I'm hit ... Fire pierces my back and lodges into my shoulder blade. I stumble, crash to my knees. Pain sears. Is this the agony my Pablo suffered before they cut off his head?

Squeezing my eyes shut against tears, I fumble over my shoulder. My fingers slide through the blood that soaks my jacket. I rear back, twisting my head to see the shaft jutting out of my back. I grasp the arrow. Pressure builds, explodes as I yank it out of my flesh.

The world spins at a cockeyed angle; I pitch forward into the bushes bordering the sidewalk. And I fall through a concealed hole in the fence. I tumble into a dark wood and down a hill until I crash into a tree. I stagger to my feet, a hand pressed against the already healing wound in my back.

Dizzy with pain, I force myself into the thick of the trees. Undergrowth tangles around my feet. I grope at the trees for support; rough bark bites into my palms. I push on. Steven-Old-Boy won't be long in picking up my trail.

Logic urges flight to escape Steven-Old-Boy and his nasty arrows without further delay. But I have to find Ryan before he catches up with that skirt. I have this haunting vision of her doing unspeakable mischief to the tyke.

I take a bearing. Behind me, at the crest of the steep hill, stands the wall of Ocean Village, an irregular black gap in its face. From my left comes the ceaseless thunder of the ocean. Ahead, mist seeps through the trees, carried into hollow and uphill by a salty breeze.

Andrew wants to get as far as possible from that wall before Steven-Old-Boy pops out of that hole. Slipping and sliding, I work my way down an incline. The mist thickens around me, stinging my eyes and nostrils, burning my throat like — smoke. Someone's set a fire and not invited me.

I reach level ground. Searching my way past hanging branches, I follow the crash of waves. The smoke grows heavier, choking me. I need a deep breath of ocean air to clear the nasal passages, or I'll never pick up Ryan's scent.

The trees open onto a wide promontory over the water. Leaving the smoke behind, I walk to the edge. I wipe my eyes, suck down a breath. The pain in my back is lessening; a tingling sensation courses through my muscles, replacing agony with numbing coolness.

To the north, I spot the origin of the smoke. A building set on an outcropping blazes against the night sky. Even I, Mister Not-Too-Swift, can identify it as the cottage where Helmut tried to destroy Kane. This is not the work of angry villagers cottage-storming. I have a strong hunch that Kane's battle against Maxwell Guthridge has moved location.

Instant verification of my suspicions wings into the sky.

Two bats — of extraordinary size and wingspan — burst out of the trees near the burning cottage. On their tails, a dozen more bats pursue. Bat fight! The first two head out to sea, then attempt to double back. Their adversaries attack. The two put up a good fight, clawing and chewing. The largest dives toward the ocean. It wings low over the water toward the woods.

The second one remains in the tangle. From every direction, the creature furiously assaults the attackers. Then he is overwhelmed. Fur flies. Blood showers. A dismembered wing drifts downward. The mauled bat plummets toward the waves, dragging a squealing opponent with him.

Andrew doesn't know whether to cheer or boo. At this distance, I cannot perceive which bat is who. For all I know, that bat disintegrating in the vast running waters of the ocean could be John Studnidka.

"Surprise."

Nasty words!

I turn from the dispersing bats. Steven-Old-Boy, toting his crossbow, emerges from the trees. In the thin starlight, his once handsome face is cadaverous; red scratches on the cheek and brow heighten the sallowness of his skin. His blue eyes are eerily bright. His thin lips twitch. His shirt hangs from narrow shoulders, his belt is cinched tight to hold up his jeans. On the whole, Steven-Old-Boy is not a healthy sight. I suspect he has spent too many sleepless nights pursuing bats.

"You're gonna hurt someone with that thing," I tell him, pointing at the cocked crossbow.

"Plan to." He flashes his mad smile.

Steven-Old-Boy and I have come full circle.

Two years ago, we stood on a cliff overlooking a college town, debating the pros and cons of vampirism and head snatching. I refrained from killing him then, even after he shot me with silver bullets. I would just as soon refrain from killing him now. After all, his present state can be attributed to only one person — me. He didn't lose his mind from serving drinks to spunky boys in a Village bar. He lost his mind from discovering what I am, and from trying, in his own peculiar way, to stop me.

But here's the clincher — since my transition to the undead eight years ago, I never feel more as if hot blood courses through my veins than whenever I know Steven-Old-Boy is closing in. Gives death a little bite, some excitement — that challenge everyone looks for in order to feel alive.

Of course, that sentiment does not allow me to stand here while he takes potshots at me with wooden arrows.

"Are you still collecting heads?" I inquire, hoping a discussion of his favorite hobby might delay his twitchy trigger finger.

He winks. "Only need one more."

This isn't going to be so easy, Andrew. Increased dementia has fed his determination.

I sense that someone is hiding in the trees behind Steven-Old-Boy. If it's Eddie, why doesn't he do something?

"Who's your friend?"

Steven-Old-Boy grins coyly. "Great vampire hunter."

The great vampire hunter is here? What an honor — I think. I stretch out my senses to our shy observer. A vile sensation snaps back at me. Steven-Old-Boy, you have been badly duped.

"I think we'd better have a chat about your great vampire hunter," I say, edging toward Steven-Old-Boy.

"Stay back," he orders, leveling the crossbow on me. "Get too close, I won't get clear shot."

"Steven, listen to me for a change," I say. "Your great vampire hunter is a lot deader than you think."

Cocking his head to the side, Steven-Old-Boy squints at me. Then he chuckles. "Andrew plays trick."

"It's not a trick. Your great vampire hunter is a vampire."

"Don't listen to him, Steven," a deep voice says from the trees. "He is a wily one. Destroy him. Now."

Steven-Old-Boy takes aim.

"Does your great vampire hunter live in a deserted church?" I ask. "Does your great vampire hunter have a friend named Louis? Does your great vampire hunter only come out at night?"

Under the roar of the surf, a snarl filters from the trees. Steven-Old-Boy doesn't seem to hear, nor does he sense Maxwell Guthridge creeping up behind him.

"I gave you what you wanted," Maxwell whispers close to Steven-Old-Boy's ear. Startled, he looks into Maxwell's violet eyes. "Andrew Lyall, vampire. On a platter. So to speak."

"Check out his teeth, Steven," I say.

Steven-Old-Boy tears his gaze from Maxwell to glare at me.

"Come on, Steven, this is Andrew. We've known each other for years. Who you gonna believe — me or that corpse?"

Uncertainty spreads across his face. I've struck some chord that Steven-Old-Boy cannot deny.

"Finish him, " Maxwell coaxes. "You've waited. So long."

"I've always been up front with you," I press. "I've never denied what I am. I've never tried to trick Steven-Old-Boy."

His confusion becomes pitiful. "A vampire?" Anger takes over. He turns on Maxwell. "Lied." He lifts the crossbow.

Maxwell's face contorts. With a swift movement, he closes his hand around the crossbow, bending the aluminum, breaking the arrow. He grasps Steven by the face. "Unruly lad."

Helmut's destruction flashes before me. "No!" I lunge toward Steven and Maxwell.

With a sneer, Maxwell snaps Steven's head to one side. The crackling of bone counterpoints Steven's whimper of pain. Maxwell hurls him against me; I fall. Pain from my wound jars my teeth. Steven's body sprawls on top of me.

Face mutated to the worst of hell's denizens, Maxwell towers over me. Clawed hands extended, he advances.

I see my death flash before my eyes.

Maxwell abruptly snaps his face skyward. Several bats fly over the promontory. Snarling, Maxwell flees into the woods.

I slip from beneath Steven. The silver bullet, lodged against my spine for two years, throbs agony more crippling than the pain of the arrow. I sit beside the body, its head at an odd angle, and meet the staring dead eyes.

I remember a young man from my college days, a good-looking, happy-go-lucky sort who used to tease me about my extensive wardrobe. He even had my junior yearbook photo captioned "Captain of the Shopping Club." I look at him now, lying in the dirt, his neck broken. I wish I had not been the one to drive him to madness and finally death.

My pain begins to fade, as if the silver bullet has shifted away from a nerve. I close Steven's eyes. Whatever suffering insanity caused him is over. Leaning close to him, I pull his shirtfront tight against the cold. When all is said and done, death is Steven's only way out.

O

Over the land's irregularities, through pockets of smoke, I pursue Maxwell's scent. The trail leads toward the cottage where the smoke is thickest and the scent difficult to trace. I pause, switchblade ready, and scour the air for that evil essence.

A familiar voice drifts through the woods. I listen carefully, pinpointing direction. A new instinct dictates that I follow a different trail, one that will lead me to Ryan.

I descend through a bank of smoke into a clear hollow. Ryan is up to his lost-child routine. I could swat his butt for choosing Eddie Cramer as his mark.

"Don't you lay one tooth on him, Ryan," I warn, hurrying down the incline.

Eddie, kneeling before the tyke, gives me an odd look. With a glance at Ryan, he springs to his feet.

Scowling, Ryan crosses his arms. "I'm still hungry."

"We have other problems, kiddo." I clamp a hand on top of his head. He cranes to look up at me. "No more running off. There are some truly bad corpses in these woods. I don't want you running afoul of them. Cut the pout. Got it?"

"Yessss." He slips his gaze toward Eddie. "Is he one of them? I'll finish him."

"No." I study Eddie, hands deep in his jacket pockets where I suspect his crucifix is on standby. "I don't think so."

"I tried to stop Steven," Eddie says, squirming under my gaze. "Did you get hurt?"

"I'll survive." I study him more closely. "You won't have to stop Steven any more."

"Jesus..." Eddie backs away from me. "Andrew—"

"His 'great vampire hunter' — the vampire — killed him."

That takes a moment to sink in. Eddie relaxes until a fidgety Ryan attracts his attention. "Who's he?" Eddie gives me an admonishing look. "Did you..."

"For the last bloody time, no." I pick up Ryan. "Come on. Maxwell's probably waiting to ambush us. Hopefully, my friends are nearby. Even a vampire knows there's safety in numbers."

"Don't say that word to me right now," Eddie says, climbing out of the hollow at my side.

"Reality getting a little too close for comfort, Eddie?"

He sighs. "The universe is topsy-turvy, Andrew."

We steal through the woods in silence. Eddie has become morose, probably in shock about Steven's death. They must have shared a bond; they spent a year together pursuing Pablo and me. In my arms, Ryan sniffs at the air for trouble. I calculate who's left to deal with: Maxwell, of course, possibly Louis. Anneliiese might haunt these woods. I shrug off an urge to tremble. I'm not up to a confrontation with vampire-she-wolves.

Growling, Ryan digs his hand into my shoulder. He's found us some trouble.

The three of us step out onto the outcropping where the ruins of the cottage smolder. The smoke is stirred by the ocean breeze. Waves of heat brush my face from the glowing timbers and flashes of fire.

"What's your problem?" I ask Ryan. "No one's—"

A tingling sensation probes the back of my brain. Setting down Ryan, I turn. Maxwell stands at the edge of the woods. Three ambushes in one night; my senses need sharpening.

"Replay," Maxwell says with a smirk. "With a difference."

The sensation in my head expands, spreading a black-red fire. Helplessness. Hopelessness. Torture. Destruction. All these and worse sear my consciousness. Maxwell's power — his spell — splinters confidence and defenses.

You're trapped, Lyall.

Behind me, a beam totters; sparks scatter, and a pillar of flame blazes into the sky.

Your cub can't fly.

Entranced, Ryan stares at Maxwell.

Neither can your human.

"Is this the great vampire hunter?" Eddie levels his revolver on Maxwell.

"Useless," I mutter.

"I can still make him bleed," Eddie says. "For Steven."

"You *boys*," Maxwell snarls, "always playing at melodrama." He turns those hypnotic eyes against Eddie. "Always reaching for high emotion to mask your shallowness."

Overpowered, Eddie lowers his revolver.

Visions of previous violence flash behind my eyes. Pablo — staked. Pablo — decapitated. Colin — dismembered. Hart — embalmed. The crackle of the fire resounds in my ears. New images rise — acts of violence yet to be committed. Against me. Against Ryan. Against Eddie...

Maybe we are doomed. I can't fight this — he's too strong...

Smirking in triumph, Maxwell advances.

I'll watch the fire devour your face, Lyall.

Yes ... I can see it...

I'll watch your cub roast.

I don't want to look...

Your human is for Anneliiese. Her toy.

Poor Eddie.

Lifting Ryan by the scruff of his neck, Maxwell carries him to the ruins. The flames shimmer, leap higher. Maxwell holds Ryan at arm's length over the smoldering beams. Ryan doesn't struggle. Mesmerized, he stares into the fire. The bottom of his shoes begin to smoke.

Watch your cub burn, Lyall.

I watch, paralyzed. My boy...

Beside me, Eddie shakes his head. With trembling hands, he forces up his revolver and squeezes off a shot.

The bullet splatters into the front of Maxwell's shirt. Blood oozes down the gray fabric. Maxwell drags a hand over the wound, stares at his bloodied palm.

Monstrous wrath twists Maxwell's features. The aberrant denizen of hell has returned. The violet eyes flame from beneath a ridged brow. The wide mouth yawns open, accentuating cadaverous cheeks, revealing saber-tooth fangs. Maxwell releases a deafening yowl of fury.

The malicious cocoon imprisoning my brain cracks. I struggle against submission. Fed by Maxwell's wrath, the evil strengthens. I fight back, unleashing my own hatred for all the violence, past and future, created by Maxwell. I see Ryan clearly, the beast that threatens him. I break free of Maxwell's spell.

Maxwell hurls Ryan into the flaming ruins. I lunge to catch him. Maxwell grabs my shoulder, jerks me up against him. I gape into his raging eyes. Taloned claws coil around my throat.

"Eddie!" I choke. "Help Ryan!"

Eddie races through the flashes of fire. Flapping his wings madly, Ryan rises from the flames. Eddie snatches Ryan out of the sky. Swinging the kid under an arm, Eddie leaps back onto the outcropping.

Gripping my throat, Maxwell forces me backward into the ruins. Charred wood explodes to flame under my feet. He pushes me down, bending my spine. My knees weaken; Maxwell shoves me to the ground. Flames gnaw at my slacks; embers burn into my skin. Heat scorches my back and shoulders. A sharp odor mingles with the smoke. I hear the hiss of singeing hair.

"Ryan, no!" Eddie cries.

Movement flashes above me. Arms and feet transformed, Ryan pounces on Maxwell's face. Blood sprays. Howling, Maxwell releases me. He swats at Ryan. The kid wings a few inches out of reach, attacks again. His talons gouge.

I scramble to my feet. I snag the back of Ryan's coat. Holding him tightly, I stumble away from Maxwell.

Hands over his face, Maxwell prances before the ruin's scattered flames. "Anneliiese!" Maxwell bellows, dropping his hands from his face. His forehead and cheeks are ravaged; Ryan has clawed out his eyes. Maxwell wheels from side to side. "Anneliiese!" His voice thunders with the surf.

Ryan strains to get at Maxwell; on my other side, Eddie lifts his revolver. I push them both back and give them an I'll-handle-this look. They obey.

Transmuting, I whip around Maxwell, bite his flailing hands, maul his scalp. I shove him back toward the ruins. He tries to escape; I dive into his face, ripping the torn flesh.

His hands wrap around my lower torso. He staggers backward through the hot ash. I claw at him. He won't let go. I hear boards cracking. I flap my wings harder, lift Maxwell off the ground. The ruins collapse into the waves. His fingernails tear at my flesh. My wings are exhausted; my shoulder hurts. I'm losing altitude fast. Ash and spray splatter us. My fur burns.

A ferocious shriek pierces my ears. Another bat loops around us. It butts Maxwell in the chest. A second bat clamps onto Maxwell's back. I don't need the extra weight. We're sinking like a stone toward the turbulent water. The first bat chews at Maxwell's wrist; the second slices at Maxwell's neck with its fangs. Maxwell's grip on me loosens. Twisting free, I dash skyward. The other two bats follow.

Maxwell plunges into the ash-strewn water. Agonized screams echo. The water foams red. Maxwell thrusts to the surface. His face is stripped of skin. The bloody muscles melt down to the skull. The scarlet waves engulf him.

Good riddance.

2

I drop to dry ground — in mostly human form. I shake my left claw; it seems content as it is. Wings flutter behind me. I face Kane Davies and John Studnidka.

"Thanks for the help," I say, hiding my claw behind my foot.

"I'm glad we got here in time," Kane replies.

I'll second that.

John nudges my shoulder. "Problem?" he inquires.

"No..." Picturing in my mind a perfect thin foot, I shake my claw again.

"Calm down," John suggests, massaging the back of my neck.

Shutting my eyes, I take a deep breath. The muscles and tendons at the end of my leg tingle. When I open my eyes, I have a human foot again.

"Look at my clothes!" I grope at the back of my head. "Look at my hair!"

"Look at your face. You got hit by water." John skims my cheek. "It might leave a scar."

I touch the tender patch of skin.

"It'll give your face some character," he adds.

Lifting a disdainful eyebrow, I survey his ensemble. "You look as if you work in a slaughterhouse."

"Part-time," John returns.

Smothering a smile, I follow Kane to Eddie and Ryan, with Jay, at the edge of the woods. I pick up Ryan; he fusses with the collar of my shirt. "What's new, you little hell-raiser?"

Ryan squishes up his face into a dazzling smile.

I say to Kane, "Nice of you to bring the party here so I could join in the fun. What happened at the desecrated church?"

"Maxwell escaped us," Kane replies, a trifle embarrassed. "We didn't know of any other hiding places." He wanders over to where the cottage had stood. "We destroyed this refuge—"

"And from there all hell broke loose," John interjects. He's standing awfully close. "With some prodding from you."

"I don't take credit for anything," I say. "I was just looking for the tyke." I ask Kane, "How do you know Vampires Anonymous won't continue without Maxwell?"

"We don't. But we destroyed his computer, confiscated his records," Kane replies. "Tomorrow we start retracing Maxwell's steps to eliminate any outposts still in operation." Hands in the pockets of his bomber jacket, he approaches me. "I didn't play fair earlier. I hope you can forgive that and join us."

Ryan watches me closely. I glance over my shoulder at Eddie, the lone human in this clutch of deadbats. I shake my head. "I've been on the run enough in the last year." I hoist Ryan tighter in my arms. "I need to settle down for a while."

Amusement sparkles in Kane's dark eyes. "I never expected you to take on this role, my friend." He tousles Ryan's hair.

Swatting at Kane's hand, Ryan narrows his eyes at us. "I don't want to be petted."

Kane takes my hand in his. "Andrew, we'll meet again."

Ryan abruptly pricks up his bat ears. Snarling, he squirms out of my arms and circles behind my legs. Half his face transfigured, he glares toward the woods. "Bad!" He gives me his you-just-thought-it-was-over look. "Bad!"

A mingled howl-wail reverberates from the trees. Branches thrash. A wild-faced Anneliiese bursts onto the outcropping.

"Bad!" Ryan cries, cowering behind my legs.

So the skirt who made Ryan a vampire is Maxwell's right-hand blouse. These corpses have been making the rounds.

"Maxwell!" Anneliiese cries, lurching into our midst.

"You're a bit late." I smile when she looks at me. "He's off on a world cruise with the fishies."

Anneliiese's hands snap out at her sides. Hair sprouts; talons grow. Raging, she contorts her body to a lupine torso. Shaking her mane of streaked hair, she stretches her face to a fang-rimmed snout.

The vampire-she-wolf springs at us. Eddie fires his revolver; bullets explode out of her back. She tumbles to the ground — but only for a moment. The she-wolf leaps to her paws. I flip out the switchblade. She bounds at us. The others scatter. Kane tries to drag me back; I shrug him off. When she's almost on me, I step aside, drive the knife to the hilt between her shoulder blades. She bucks away, then snaps back at me. I almost lose a hand yanking out my switchblade.

She isn't finished. She leaps toward Eddie. Stumbling against a tree, Eddie brandishes his crucifix. She's not feeling religious; she lunges onto Eddie, drives him to the ground. Eddie kicks wildly. Her claws tear at his heavy jacket. He shouts pain. Her jaws champ inches from his face.

Get off that boy, you flea-bitten hell hound! I charge. Kane grabs my arm and flings me back.

In the snap of frothing jaws, Kane metamorphoses into a huge black wolf. He springs onto Anneliiese, gashing, gnawing. She writhes beneath him, tries to shake him off. Kane drags a taloned paw from her shoulder to her hip, latches his fangs into her throat.

Eddie stabs the crucifix into the she-wolf's temple. Fur and skin flame. Wailing agony, she rears off him. She shakes herself free of Kane. With the crucifix protruding from her flesh, Anneliiese flees into the woods.

Kane isn't finished this time. He bounds after her. Jay transmutes into a bat and follows.

I gape after Kane. We hadn't finished our good-byes.

All my wounds flare pain. None of them are going to heal with the miraculous power of my race. They will remain open, seeping — if only inside — until I see Kane Davies again.

He said we would meet again, a rare, soothing voice whispers in my head.

But in what century? Kane will always be occupied in some worthwhile battle against some vile foe. He won't have time to look up someone like me, who's never involved with anything but himself.

Let's piss and moan our death away, Andrew.

I square my shoulders, grit my teeth against my pain. Kane may be the kind of vampire I could never aspire to be, but I'm grateful to the sunset that he lives his death with a purpose.

A howl resounds from within the woods. Ryan, face white with fear, leaps into my arms. I start to pat his head, then think better of it. Eddie sulks against a nearby tree. John loiters at my side.

"Could you give us a few moments?" I ask John. I nod toward Eddie. "Unfinished business."

John surveys Eddie. "I'll meet you at the house," he mutters to me. Pouty, he transmutes and wings up the coast.

I set Ryan down, instructing him to wait right where I plant him. He nods. His sudden obedience unnerves me.

I cross the outcropping toward Eddie. The ocean breeze tosses his long dark hair around his handsome face. His tight jeans have a seductive tear up the inside of one leg to his crotch. What's that peeking at me? I tug up my gaze. The shoulder of his police jacket hangs in shreds. I gently touch him. He doesn't flinch.

"Are you all right?" I ask.

"Bruised." He reaches into his jacket, withdraws a hand smeared with blood. "Maybe scratched. I'll live."

"You proved quite the cop-in-boy's-clothing tonight," I say. "Thanks for looking out for the kid."

"Cute kid," Eddie murmurs.

"Adopted, of course. No blonds in my family." Except my mother and brother ... Details!

I scuff my toe across the ground. How do I ask this man if he wants to expose his throat to my fangs? "I was curious about where we stand," I spit out. That's intelligent.

He stares at me sullenly.

"You don't have to make any momentous choice this minute." Lordie knows *I'm* not ready to make any momentous commitment this minute. "Just whether you want to keep seeing me." I take a deep breath. "We could court each other. It might be fun." Moon above, Andrew, you sound as if you're begging.

"It might be," he replies. His gray eyes are shuttered; he doesn't give a clue one way or the other.

"I don't expect you to answer on the spot," I say. "But I can't wait around for eternity either. I'll be at my apartment."

He stares at my muddied shoes.

"You still there?" I inquire.

Face blank, he looks at me. "Give me a couple of hours."

Nodding, I walk back toward Ryan. I sneak a peak at my watch: fifteen minutes after midnight.

O

Three in the morning. A brisk wind whips around the roof of my building. I pull my overcoat snug. I'm chilled to the bone. The wind has nothing to do with it.

From the eaves, I watch the street. In Andrew's book a couple of hours means two. Eddie is forty-five minutes late. To be fair — and aren't I always — the burden I dumped on him deserves more than a couple of hours' thought. But I have a death to lead, a bat-in-arms at the sitter's. And I can't cope with this kind of suspense. Patience, as so many have eagerly pointed out, is not one of my virtues.

Headlights cut through the dark street as a Jeep turns the far corner. The sound of the engine purrs on the wind. Even before the Jeep stops below, I know that Eddie is behind the wheel. No special feat; I can see that far.

He gets out of the Jeep and looks up at the building. I decide to spare him the climb upstairs. I drop to the street.

"You're full of tricks," he says.

"Some are better than others."

"Sorry I'm late," Eddie says. "I had to get Steven's things and call the police about his body." He levels those clear gray eyes on me. "Someone beat me to it. The police got an anonymous phone call about midnight telling them where to find Steven."

"Did they?" I couldn't leave the old boy out in the cold, could I?

"My universes are jumbled," Eddie blurts.

His 'universes'?

He drills me with those gray eyes. "You're asking a bit much. I don't know if I love you enough to die for you. I'm scared of death, Andrew. I'm only thirty."

"Men won't find you attractive once you pass thirty," I say. Shame on you, Andrew, especially considering the horror on his face. "A stereotype some hetero-hick likes to spread around. Don't worry, you'll have 'em breathing heavy when you're sixty."

"You're not making this any easier," Eddie admonishes me.

I know that. But why should I make it difficult? He's being honest with me. And I am asking a bit much. How many human boys want to date an undead guy?

Especially this human boy. He isn't ready to become a vampire. Deep down, I've known that. Yet, knowing that he loves me almost resurrects my soul. That pleasure is beyond anything I've felt — dead or alive. But I can't allow it to rule me. Eddie *is* a human boy. And some people are better off human.

"You don't have to give me any more explanations," I say. "Maybe just a quick but memorable embrace."

Rounding the Jeep, he moves right into my arms. How close he holds me. If only he could stay. If only to the end of time.

The temptation rises. My lips quiver against my teeth. I press my face at his throat. Breath held, he tightens his arms around me. Neither of us is willing to accept the way things have to be. But I must stop this now. Eddie doesn't have what it takes to survive this existence. He would become like Pablo; I could not endure watching Eddie suffer as Pablo suffered.

I gently push him away. "Good-bye, Eddie."

"I love you," he breathes.

"I love you, too, Eddie. Good-bye."

He nods, gasps a breath. "Good-bye, Andrew." He climbs into the Jeep. "Don't forget me," he says in a tremulous voice.

"Not for all eternity. Hit the road, kiddo."

Eddie Cramer, boy-in-cop's-clothing, drives into the night.

I guess the good things don't stand much of a chance when reality only comes around with dusk, and your universe hangs in a darkness rarely pierced by the faintest of moonbeams.

Drawing a calming breath, I study the stars in the hazy sky. I bet I could touch that one if I *really* tried.

A hand closes around mine — not Eddie's, much too small. I look at Ryan. His it's-so-sad-but-you-still-have-me expression lifts the spirits. I kneel in front of him. "Hungry?"

He nods vigorously.

"I thought you might be."

"Surf's up." A shyly grinning John Studnidka joins us.

"Eavesdropping, Stud?"

"We were on the roof until he left," John says. "We couldn't hear a thing, could we, baby bat?"

"Pretty liar, don't teach him bad habits."

"I was thinking—" John begins.

"Were you indeed?"

"No smart-ass comments until I've had my say, please." John steps up close to Ryan and me. "Since your gear is already at my cave, maybe you could hang out for — oh, a decade or two. You, me — and baby bat." He pats Ryan's head.

I wait for the tyke-who-doesn't-like-to-be-petted to take a chunk out of John's hand. He simply looks at John, then at me.

"The anti-nuclear family."

"Anything is worth a shot, Andrew," John says, more defensively than necessary.

I can't very well argue with that. Not to sound as if I'm settling — never! — but with Pablo at rest, Kane off to finish his holy vampire mission, and Eddie destined to grow old and hunched and bald and ugly and toothless and wrinkled, what else does Andrew have going for him?

I have my bat-in-arms — he's quite the responsibility. Who am I to say that the Stud won't make as good a guardian as I?

And who's to say that John won't prove a perfect bat on the wing for Andrew? He's devoted, he overflows with personality, he likes the tyke ... he's a hunk and a half. To the point, I personally think John is an exceptionally righteous carcass — I would, even if he weren't the Stud. Others may scoff, but, hey, my death ... my choice. At this point on the road to eternity, Andrew could use a few years of good laughter. What other vampire has a sense of humor warped enough to provide that?

"All right," I say, feigning painful resignation, "with one big condition — no more planting boys in the garden."

"That's it?" John asks.

"What do you want — a ring?"

"Sounds romantic—"

"That, I'm not."

He nudges my shoulder with his. "Pretty liar."

"Screw a lid on real tight, Stud," I suggest.

Laughing, Ryan transmutes face to a snout, arms to wings, feet to claws — the whole ball of fur. He soars skyward.

"Look at the little sucker go!"

"That's my—" I look at John, all crooked grin and bemused eyes. Swinging my arm around my Stud's shoulders, I point toward the baby bat looping-the-loop overhead. "That's our boy."

Other books of interest from

ALYSON PUBLICATIONS

SOMEWHERE IN THE NIGHT, by Jeffrey N. McMahan, $8.00. Here are eight eerie tales of suspense and the supernatural by a new-found talent. Jeffrey N. McMahan weaves horribly realistic stories that contain just the right mix of horror, humor, and eroticism: a gruesome Halloween party, a vampire whose conscience bothers him, and a suburbanite with a killer lawn.

FINALE, edited by Michael Nava, $9.00. Eight carefully crafted stories of mystery and suspense by both well-known authors and new-found talent: an anniversary party ends abruptly when a guest is found in the bathroom with his throat slashed; a frustrated writer plans the murder of a successful novelist; a young man's hauntingly familiar dreams lead him into a forgotten past.

CHROME, by George Nader, $8.00. It is death to love a robot. But in their desert training ground, Chrome and King Vortex are forming a forbidden bond, with neither one knowing which is man and which machine. The results could bring intergalactic warfare.

THE GAY BOOK OF LISTS, by Leigh Rutledge, $8.00. Rutledge has compiled a fascinating and informative collection of lists. His subject matter ranges from history (6 gay popes) to politics (9 perfectly disgusting reactions to AIDS) to entertainment (12 examples of gays on network television) to humor (9 Victorian "cures" for masturbation). Learning about gay culture and history has never been so much fun.

LAVENDER LISTS, by Lynne Y. Fletcher and Adrien Saks, $9.00. This all-new collection of lists captures many entertaining, informative, and little-known aspects of gay and lesbian lore: 5 planned gay communities that never happened; 10 lesbian nuns; 15 cases of censorship where no sex was involved; 10 out-of-the-closet law enforcement officers; and much more.

THE ALYSON ALMANAC, $9.00. Almanacs have been popular sources of information since "Poor Richard" first put his thoughts on paper and Yankee farmers started forecasting the weather. Here is an almanac for gay and lesbian readers that follows these traditions. You'll find the voting records of members of Congress on gay issues, practical tips on financial planning for same-sex couples, an outline of the five stages of a gay relationship, and much, much more.

WORLDS APART, edited by Camilla Decarnin, Eric Garber, Lyn Paleo, $8.00. The world of science fiction allows writers to freely explore alternative sexualities. These eleven stories take full advantage of that opportunity with characters ranging from a black lesbian vampire to a gay psychodroid. Here are adventure, romance, and excitement — and perhaps some genuine alternatives for our future.

THE WANDERGROUND, by Sally Miller Gearhart, $7.00. These absorbing, imaginative stories tell of a future women's culture, created in harmony with the natural world. The women depicted combine the control of mind and matter with a sensuous adherence to their own realities and history.

REFLECTIONS OF A ROCK LOBSTER, by Aaron Fricke, $7.00. Guess who's coming to the prom! In the spring of 1980, Aaron Fricke made national news by taking a male date to his high school prom. Yet for the first sixteen years of his life, Fricke had closely guarded the secret of his homosexuality. Here, told with insight and humor, is his story about growing up gay, about realizing that he was different, and about how he ultimately developed a positive gay identity in spite of the prejudice around him.

THE MEN WITH THE PINK TRIANGLE, by Heinz Heger, $8.00. For decades, history ignored the Nazi persecution of gay people. Only with the rise of the gay movement in the 1970s did historians finally recognize that gay people, like Jews and others deemed "undesirable," suffered enormously at the hands of the Nazi regime. Of the few who survived the concentration camps, only one ever came forward to tell his story. His true account of those nightmarish years provides an important introduction to a long-forgotten chapter of gay history.

EIGHT DAYS A WEEK, by Larry Duplechan, $7.00. Johnnie Ray Rousseau is a 22-year-old black gay pop singer whose day starts at 11 p.m. Keith Keller is a white banker with a 10 o'clock bedtime — and muscles to die for. This story of their love affair is one of the most engrossing — and funniest — you'll ever read.

CODY, by Keith Hale, $7.00. Steven Trottingham Taylor, "Trotsky" to his friends, is new in Little Rock. Washington Damon Cody has lived there all his life. Yet, when they meet, there's a familiarity, a sense that they've known each other before. Their friendship grows and develops a rare intensity, although one of them is gay and the other is straight.

Ask for these titles in your favorite bookstore. Or, to order by mail, use this coupon or a photocopy.

- -

Enclosed is $_____ for the following books. (Add $1.00 postage when ordering just one book. If you order two or more, we'll pay the postage.)

1. _____

2. _____

3. _____

name: _____

address: _____

city: _____ state: _____ zip: _____

ALYSON PUBLICATIONS
Dept. H-83, 40 Plympton St., Boston, MA 02118

After June 30, 1993, please write for current catalog.